Awakening

A Novel of Aliens and Consciousness

STEPHAN A. SCHWARTZ

D1451767

Greenwood Press
Langley, Washington

© copyright 2017 by Stephan A. Schwartz

Greenwood Press
P.O. Box 905
Langley, Washington 98260
www.greenwoodpress.net

All rights reserved. No part of this book may be reproduced or utilized in any form of by any means, electronic or mechanical, including photocopying, recording, or bay any information storage and retrieval system, without permission in writing from the publisher.

Cover art © copyright 2017 by James Francis Yax used by permission

L.C. Cat. No.: 1-5766434781

ISBN: 978-0-9768536-2-6

This book was typeset in Garamond.

Correspondence: To send correspondence to the author: saschwartz@schwartzreport.net

Other Books by Stephan A. Schwartz

The Secret Vaults of Time
The Alexandria Project
Mind Rover
Opening to the Infinite
The 8 Laws of Change

In Memory of
HLC and EA
Who helped me awaken

CHAPTER ONE

It was early May and there were cherry blossoms on the trees of Washington, D.C. as I drove down Constitution Avenue to the Federal Courthouse. I was picking up Maggie Pugh, then the major woman in my life. Even with my Senate parking pass, finding a place was still a hassle. I needn't have worried; when I got to the courtroom she was still arguing the government's position against a military contractor who had poured the wrong cement. I went in and sat down. It was a big technical litigation involving arcane federal regulations and lots of experts, and sitting there was like watching a play boringly acted and translated badly from another language. I've never had any interest in being a lawyer, and listening to the arguments about cement, particularly after hearing at least the government side develop like a script week after week as Maggie worked it out, didn't hold my attention. I fell asleep and my head fell forward so hard I bit my tongue; it hurt.

I looked up and saw Maggie watching me tenderly touching my protruding bleeding tongue. She gave me a look and turned back to the court, going into a detailed description about the tensile strength of some kind of rebar. I had had enough. It was going to go on for at least another hour, and could run as late as four, when the courts adjourned. But I wasn't going to listen to any more of it, so I went out and wandered down the hall.

Mostly empty of people, my footfalls echoed as I walked past the identical brown leather covered, brass nail studded doors. On the wall next to each courtroom entrance was an impressive small bronze plaque giving the judge's name and below, held up by sticky tape, a creased sheet of photocopied paper citing the case underway. It was a vignette of the contrast between judicial image and reality.

At random, I picked one of the courtrooms and went in; it was as empty of an audience as the one I had just left. I stood in the background for a while, but then felt conspicuous and sat down. It took me a few minutes listening to the back and forth of the lawyers and the court, to understand it was a Freedom of Information Act suit. The plaintiff's lawyer was asking the judge to release papers 1664/37-A through 14766/37-A. I was getting ready to get up and leave when the petitioning lawyer mentioned that the documents being sought concerned an event I knew about. Twelve years earlier a meteor had crashed in Glacier National Park near Kalispell, Montana, causing a lot of damage in the forest, like a bomb had gone off. It had knocked over trees like matchsticks. Why would information about something like that, I wondered, need to be obtained through a FOIA action? I sat back down.

After a pause the judge looked down over her glasses, pinning the attorneys with practiced gaze. When they were immobilized to her satisfaction, she said, "It is not in the best interests of the United States to release the information you seek, Mr. Hardwicke. After reading summaries of the documents, I have decided that to release them, including even the summaries, would not be in the best interests of national security and the stability of the country." The judge's gavel came down, and the court was recessed.

I couldn't believe what I had just heard; it made absolutely no sense to me. I was then Senior Analyst for the Senate Committee on Science, Commerce, and Transportation. A couple of years earlier, Senator Wilson, junior of Montana, had asked me to prepare a report covering all studies about the event. I had dug out and read the Department of Interior report of the incident as well as a dozen papers it was based on. There was nothing indicating the need for a FOIA.

The judge got up and left, and I watched as the lawyers packed their bankers boxes and loaded them onto luggage carriers. The two government attorneys went out first, and the attorney who had brought the suit was just passing me, when on impulse I stood up and put out my hand.

"Arthur Davies."

"Yes, Mr. Davies?" He was a middle-aged man and I could see he was immediately on guard. "Are you a reporter?"

"No. No. I'm the Senior Analyst on..." suddenly I felt I was putting myself into a compromised position. In the middle of my sentence I changed course, sounding awkward to my own ears and said, "I'm on the Hill."

"Of course you are, Mr. Davies," the man said, his cynical tone making both his disbelief and uninterest obvious. "What can I do for you?"

"Well, you could tell me what that was all about?"

"It's about a UFO, Mr. Davies. A UFO and one of the greatest cover-ups in government history." He fiddled with his airport luggage carrier, trying to get past me. I was kind of semi-deliberately blocking his way. I stepped aside, and once past me the man stopped and, looking back added almost parenthetically, "Everybody knows about it, but nobody knows the truth."

"Are you claiming that the meteor that landed in Glacier Park was a UFO?" I said, and I'll be honest my disbelief was obvious.

"That's my point," he said, and then began moving again. "You think you're smart and well-informed. You're 'on the Hill' as you say, so you know the official story, I'm sure. Every network in the world has been spewing it out for years now." He looked back over his shoulder and said with so much scorn I was taken aback. "Enjoy your willful ignorance, Mr. Davies. You don't know anything."

CHAPTER TWO

When I left the courtroom Maggie was waiting for me in the hall.

"I figured that's what you'd do."

"I had been to all the rehearsals," I responded.

"You fell asleep. I saw you."

"I bit my tongue," I said.

Maggie was a Deputy Assistant Attorney General and we went back to her office at the Justice Department where she left her baggage cart with all the trial paperwork. We took another cab to the Old Ebbitt Grill's bar which was filling up with older lobbyists and younger staffers. Maggie and I had to push our way through to the section set up with tables. We had a reservation and ate there frequently, so we got a table. We ordered a good Chardonnay, a Caesar salad to split, veal for Maggie, and a grilled sea bass for me. I couldn't pass it up; wild seafood is hard to get now.

"I've got them," she said, her intense golden-brown eyes crinkling at the corner with a kind of glee looking into mine.

"Got them?" I asked.

She brushed her sable hair, so fashionably cut, back from her face. Maggie is a good-looking woman, and more than one man has failed to see the steel behind those eyes.

"Typical males. They never thought I would get down into the details of the cement. That bridge failed because they shorted the..."

"You think you're going to win?"

"I do."

"May it be so," I said and smiled at her. We went back to eating for a moment, then I said, "Maggie, why would the government consider something about a meteor strike in Kalispell, Montana, to be a matter of national security?"

"What? What are you talking about?"

Breaking off a piece of bread and dipping it into the Cajun olive oil, I thought for a minute before answering. "Well... while you were going mano a mano with those guys about cement, one of us males almost fell asleep..."

"That's when you left?"

"Right. I have to be honest I don't really care about cement," I smiled and added, "but you did look very tasty walking up and down our bedroom practicing your argument, in that silk thing I brought you from Paris." Our eyes connected, and I went on. "So after checking my phone I decided to sort of walk around. I wandered into another courtroom. Some kind of FOIA suit was going on. It was about what I thought was that meteor that crashed into the forest out in Montana about 12 years ago … has that anchovy been abandoned?"

"You can have it. That's Gregson's loony suit. His penance for crossing Pickerson on that civil rights case. The plaintiffs claim it was a flying saucer. Totally mad," Maggie said, as the waiter brought our entrees and poured us each a final glass of wine from the bottle.

I wasn't exactly sure how to get into this so I took a moment to fiddle with the anchovy, putting it on a piece of bread and then biting into it. "The looneyness, I don't doubt. What I don't understand is why a federal judge would rule that releasing the papers on something I would have thought every tabloid television show in the country had milked 'til the udder bled would constitute a threat to national security and the country's stability."

"Maybe it had something to do with the way the information was gathered," she answered as we ate.

"I thought of that. But I was involved in the Committee's hearings on declassification about the Shamrock thing, and they voted to do that. How could an event that almost caused a war and involved the most sensitive intelligence gathering techniques of its time be released when data about a meteor crashing in the forest is held back?" I found myself looking at my sea bass, as if it might be able to provide an answer. "The judge wouldn't even release the summaries for God's sake. Maggie, we didn't do that when CNN sued to get CIA's papers on that Russia sub crash."

"I don't know. I'll ask Gregson. Why do you care anyway?"

"Because Senator Wernicke is building a case about nuclear pollution events that have been covered up by the government, and I think that might be what's going on here."

"A nuclear accident," Maggie said, taking the conversation seriously for the first time.

"Don't know, but it might be a Soviet era satellite crash; some of them had poorly shielded nuclear reactors for power."

I could see Maggie's career path computer click into place. From a year's relationship I knew she saw everything from its impact on either of our careers. She carefully cut and chewed a piece of her veal, a meat I never order, before saying, "Are you sure that subject is a vein worth working? If it was nuclear wouldn't it be awfully hard to conceal? And if it is just space junk falling in a forest, who cares. I thought that had been done to death years ago. Does Wernicke think the media are still interested?"

"There are other criteria than whether the media are interested," I said, knowing we were on to the thin ground of our relationship. "I realize that's something of a minority view now. But, just to show I'm as cynical as you are, I'll admit the administration beat Wernicke up badly over that sea rise bill he sponsored, and he's looking to get his back. Topher Kelly and I have been working on it all week."

"You didn't say anything to me."

"You were prepping your case, you wouldn't have heard me if I had. I'm sorry though, didn't mean to cut you out," I said, as I reached across and held her hand for a moment before we went back to eating.

"You're wrong about the media by the way," I said after a silence. "They're going to go crazy when they understand the health threat in Louisiana as New Orleans floods out and the cleanup costs. Maybe $300 billion. Serious money. And the migrations away from the coast are becoming important, and real estate value is plummeting," I said, and she looked up. "No one is talking about it." The administration doesn't want this on its watch. This could end up in your lap at DOJ."

"I'll bear that in mind... do you want the rest of your wine? This could put you in the spotlight Arthur."

"Maggie, I analyze."

"Well analyze this Mr. Davies. We've got 20 minutes to get to the Kennedy Center before the ballet starts."

I like ballet, and it is hard to get tickets. It's so antique that it has become modern and very popular, particularly with my generation in their 30s. They were dancing a new interpretation of Petipa's and Minkus' Don Quixote, a favorite. But I couldn't really focus on it that night. I just let the music give me the space to allow me to feel what I had just experienced, to really take it aboard. I kept going round and round with it, until I finally realized I was avoiding what the lawyer had said. UFOs.

CHAPTER THREE

The next morning I took an early lunch and caught a cab to the bookstore near the National Press Club building on 14th Street. It was one of the last ones in the city and prospered in its uniqueness. I felt a little silly asking the young woman at the counter where the UFO section was, but her response was so cheery and bored that my embarrassment faded. There were dozens of books; an entire niche market existed, I realized, of which I was vaguely aware but to which I had never paid any attention. Things which could not be quantified, could not really be analyzed to a conclusion, didn't really interest me much. UFOs, ESP, astrology, and religion all fell into that category. As I pulled the books from the shelves I realized that most them seemed to deal with abduction cases and featured covers with small gray hairless beings with big teardrop-shaped eyes and no ears. There were others on strange incidents, including two on the Roswell Incident. I took a selection, and it made a large enough pile it was hard to balance as I walked across the store to where the same young woman was still behind the counter. As she charged up the books, she noticed the titles.

"Yeah, like, my girlfriend's interested in all this stuff. She's like, missing this time... about an hour, maybe. She went to an astrologer who's also a hypnotist, and she'd like put her to sleep, and she remembered it all.... You know, like the probing they did." The woman gave a

little suggestive giggle and looked down her body. "Did that happen to you?" She asked with seriousness.

"Not that I know of."

"Well, it's happening every day to like, thousands of people. Like, look over there on the bulletin board," she said, with a movement of her head towards the doors.

Because I bought so many books she gave me a smart hemp bag that I liked, and with the books in it, I walked over to where she had gestured and found a corkboard filled with broadsides. In the middle of them was a yellow quick printed sheet, "An Abductees Seminar. Learn the Truth the Government is Denying." It gave a weekend date and a locale in the basement of an Episcopal church on 31st Street in Georgetown. On impulse I scribbled it all down on the back of the receipt.

When I got back to the office, I piled the books on a chair and logged in. There was email telling me about a meeting with the chairman and ranking member with whom I worked the most, a rude limerick from Don Jay at Health and Human Services, and a message slip to return Maggie's call. I clicked on her link and when his face appeared asked Bob, the man she had selected for her secretary, to pass me through.

"Where were you? I thought we might have lunch," she said when she clicked on.

"I went downtown to a book store to buy books on UFOs."

"You can't be serious." Her expression said much more.

"I got to thinking about it at the ballet, and during the hearing I thought: how can you form an opinion without the relevant data?"

"Arthur, the New Age is over. That was the 80s, you weren't even born yet. Trust you to be decades behind the social curve. What's next, channeling? Don't answer. Change of subject. You weren't answering my texts. We're due at Admiral Miller's at seven. Can you pick me up?"

"I might, but you'd have to leave your car at Justice and sleep over."

"A nasty bit of work, but I guess some girl's got to do it."

Until four o'clock I worked on the paper concerning the effect on naval port installation in the face of the sea rise. The issue had become very hot, because it involved hundreds of billions, or maybe just because the Jefferson Memorial was now an island. I got a call from Senator Camilia Singh, the first Sikh woman ever elected to the Senate. I liked her a lot, and she had sponsored a bill I had proposed to her on converting the higher ground of abandoned military bases into low income housing for the growing number of people migrating away from the coasts.

She could see the problem growing when it became impossible in her district to get insurance on housing a half a mile from the coast. A lot of the houses had been destroyed outright. Just as happened on the Outer Banks in North Carolina, where I come from. She wanted to know when the report supporting the bill would be ready. It was up to me to make sure the numbers made sense. But, as hard as I worked, a part of my mind was over at the pile of books I had just bought. I got a draft of the paper finished, got up and closed my door, and sat down in my armchair to read.

I was getting ready to leave at six when Topher Kelly stuck first his head and then his body through my door. Topher is in his late twenties. He worked for the senior senator from Massachusetts. Well groomed, dark haired and stout. Not a word you hear often, I know, but just right for him. He always reminded me of a young country squire from another age. Bespoke tweeds with a deep green vest. I liked and respected him. He was so smart that he had worked on the Hill while still going to Harvard Law. He would read all the case documents and the books about them, and his classmates would send him the exam schedule. He would catch the high-speed train to Cambridge, take the exams and come back. I think Harvard knew what he was doing, but since he led his class no one said anything. He was a wily collaborator who could be counted on when I needed to change a senator's mind with a critical piece of damning evidence.

"Got a minute?"

"Just. Push something onto the floor and have a seat," I said, sweeping my hand across my office crowded with boxes or files, piles of books, and hearing reports. "But I really gotta go or Maggie will kill me."

Topher lifted the bag of books from the bookstore off the brown leather chair, set it down, and it overturned, spilling its contents across the floor. He picked first one up, and then another, looking at the titles and back at me, then again at the book he was holding in his hand.

"Getting off into some uncharted waters are we?"

"I had to look," I told him, and explained what had happened, adding, "I don't think that's what this is. I think it may be a nuclear event, but I couldn't discard a hypothesis until I had the data."

"I'll believe you but thousands wouldn't," he said, smiling at his own cliché.

"Topher. I have been looking at everything."

"No argument from my side."

"Then why would a federal court, yesterday, on an FOIA case, rule that releasing old files about that meteor that fell near Glacier National Park 12 years ago would be against national security, and destabilize the country?"

"Is this a quiz?" Topher said. His tone was still bantering but I saw I had his attention.

"Yeah."

"Well, assuming such a ruling took place it would have to be something about how the data was gathered. Although that would only cover the national security slant. Destabilize the country... Did the judge really say that?"

"Exact words."

"Damned if I know. If the last administration didn't destabilize the country I wouldn't think it could be done."

"The judge wouldn't even release summaries of the documents," I said, getting the expected dog-on-point reaction I had hoped for from Topher.

"No summaries, not even expurgated ones?"

"Nada. Zip. But now you want to hear the really weird part?" And I told him of my exchange with the lawyer as he was leaving.

"A flying saucer crash? Are you serious?"

"Exactly my first reaction."

"And what was your second?"

"That it was some kind of contamination issue. At first I thought nuclear. I had in mind the 1961 Goldsboro, North Carolina, B-52 crash that involved four hydrogen bombs, as well as the plane, but now I'm not sure, and think it might be biological.... It's certainly something."

"That would suit Senator Wernicke's grand plan to make space debris an issue... making you the wizard who found the critical clue," Topher said, and I could hear admiration in his voice. "God, you never miss a trick, Art. You think this was all about contamination?"

"Read that stuff," I said, indicating the pile of books. "It's gotta be about something other than UFOs. Listen I gotta run."

As I was at the door, Topher held up his hand saying, "Hold on a minute. In 2016 the second stage of a Russian rocket, filled with thousands of gallons of Hydrazine, crashed into the Canadian arctic. It cost millions to clean it up."

"Can you put something together for me on that?" I asked, and was out the door.

I drove the Tesla 8 Maggie had talked me into buying the previous month up to Justice and waited. Just as a policewoman was coming towards me with her ticket book out, Maggie ran out of the building and climbed in. I pulled away and Maggie waved to the policewoman, who smiled and waved back.

"Know each other?" I asked.

"Yeah. She's going to law school; I'm her mentor."

We threaded our way through traffic, past the Lincoln Memorial and down onto Rock Creek Parkway. It was my favorite short cut because I love to drive through the woods; I grew up in Asheville and spent much of my life in the Smoky Mountains.

"Now listen, Arthur. This is very important. You've got two shots I think. General Sinclair will be there, and Representative O'Reilly."

"The guy who pats bottoms."

"The same. And he can pat my bottom if it will help you get this base closure thing moving," she said, leaning over to kiss my ear. Then, more seriously, "Arthur, if you get his committee's agreement on the low-income housing, the Washington Post will do a major piece... and you'll get credit."

"Where would I be without you, Mags."

"Two pay grades down, sweetheart."

"Did you talk to Gregson about that FOIA suit?"

"Arthur, what are you doing?" suddenly Maggie was hyper alert, and looked at me. "Why are you pursuing this?"

"It's not about UFOs, Maggie. I spent all afternoon going through books on flying saucers. As I told Topher, it's not the reports, it's the conclusions. I think most of these abduction cases are false memories or just made up. I mean the people are sincere probably, but it's a false memory invoked by bad interview techniques that are too suggestive. I'll bet if I read the complete transcripts... forget about body language, tone, all that... just the words... it's all so… I can't imagine how anybody takes it seriously."

"What do you mean false memory?" Maggie asked.

"Remember that sociologist I met in Chicago during the crime hearings? Remember the story I told you about how he interviewed a sheriff charged with molestation it became known he did not commit? The guy, the professor, interviewed the sheriff, made up a story on the spot and fed it to him, and the sheriff confessed to all of it, even signed a confession swearing he had done it. For God's sake man, make up your mind which lane you want. That's one case, there are others. I'm surprised you guys at Justice aren't aware of the peer reviewed literature on this."

"I didn't say we weren't aware," said Maggie with asperity.

"Something happened out there, Maggie."

"You're right. The court wouldn't rule without reason. But if it's not a UFO... what is it?"

"I told you yesterday. I think it's about contamination of some kind. Now I'm thinking either biological or chemical. Just as I was leaving to pick you up, Topher came into my office, and when he heard what I was doing reminded me of a toxic space debris event in Northern Canada in 2016."

"You really think there is something to this?" Maggie turned in her seat and gave me her appraising look. "You're onto something aren't you Arthur. I don't believe you don't care about your career." She turned in her seat, leaned over and said, "Maybe I could give you just the tiniest bit of head, since the traffic is moving ever so slowly."

CHAPTER FOUR

On Wednesday I went over to the Congressional Research Office at the Library of Congress and ran into Rachel Carter behind the counter. She was about 5' 8", slender and well proportioned. Part Black, part White, but other things I couldn't identify as well. Soft black hair, high cheekbones, a full mouth. Café au lait skin tone, but with reddish highlights as well. Pale green eyes that seemed to look into me. I found her exotic and sensual.

We had met at a Sierra Club hike in the Appalachians two weeks after I had begun seriously getting involved with Maggie. We had reconnected when I sent a query to the LC and she got it. Since then she had helped me several times with tough searches in technical databases. Strangely enough she was an electrical engineer who had found her way into computers, and then into very sophisticated data searches. Her technical competence and interest in the environment had brought us together as I spent more and more of my time working on the growing climate crisis. I had always felt an attraction to her, which I thought was returned, although the only result was we were always very very nice to one another.

"Hello, stranger," she said.

"Good to see you." There was an awkward beat.

"Listen, Rachel," I said, and she leaned forward slightly.

"I'm trying to find out everything I can about some kind of strange accident. It happened in Montana."

"You mean the meteor in the forest?"

"You're familiar with it?"

"Arthur, everybody knows about it."

"I'm just beginning to understand that"

"Do you think it's for real?"

"For real… what do you mean?" I asked.

"I mean, there are so many rumors about it. Flying saucers, that sort of stuff."

"I don't know. I just know the government feels very strongly about keeping what it knows to itself, even to the Congress as far as I can tell. Could you spend some time pulling together everything about it you can find?"

"Have you been through the stuff the Obama Administration dumped?"

"Not in fine detail."

"Okay. I'm tied up until the end of the day with the fisheries issue for Fitzgerald. Could you come by tomorrow? We could have lunch." We set it up and I turned to leave, then turned back. "Something definitely happened there Rachel. Something beyond what is in the obvious record, even classified as far as I can go."

"You know I thought at the time it was a flying saucer. When I got here and realized what I could do, it was one of the things I spent a little search time on. In the fire crew digitals, there were some odd first reports that I only heard once and never again. Do you think that might be possible?"

"Actually, I don't."

"What about all that stuff you just told me?" Rachel said, unconsciously sucking in and biting her lower lip, which I found very sexy.

"I don't know, Rachel. What I am sure about is that something significant happened."

"I don't get it."

"The other day a federal court ruled that even summaries of the reports on the incident could not be released without a threat to the safety and stability of the country. That's heavy mojo."

"Why wouldn't a UFO qualify?" she asked, and I realized that Rachel was open to an idea it had taken me days to even consider. "What could be more destabilizing to an already insecure America than to learn they might actually be the universe's small-town hicks. Makes sense to me," she said, and looked up at me with her mouth slightly parted. I found that sexy too.

"Okay, okay…. Maybe you can convince me."

"What constitutes evidence?"

"What?"

"I said, 'what constitutes evidence?' Let's define our terms, Mr. Rational, and then 'test the hypothesis' as you would say."

"Am I that pompous?"

"Yeah, sometimes," she said, but her warm smile took the edge off her comment.

"Okay. You could be right. I'm not sure what constitutes evidence. It's like a detective story. We just have to follow the leads. But are you willing to admit that it wasn't a saucer? Are you open-minded enough at that end?"

"Arthur, I'm just like you. I'm willing to go wherever it goes. Look, I'll find you an open carrel to work in. Come see me tomorrow morning, late," she said. I thanked her and left.

The next morning at about 11:30 I finished what I had been working on, got up and walked over to the Library.

Rachel met me at her office, and I followed her into the stacks of the library up the wonderful old cast iron staircases leading to the in-between floors, two in the space of a regular floor, that made up the stacks. We stopped at a door with a frosted glass pane. "We can use this one, it's not assigned," she said, opening the door to the small carrel office at the end of one of the rows of stacks. "I'll put your name on it."

After three hours of looking, interrupted by two long phone calls I had to take, we had a library cart full of printed material, and I had filled up a 2T flashdrive. We each began to go through a stack, Rachel making notes on a yellow legal pad, while I dictated notes as I scanned through the files.

We worked for a while not saying anything, searching the indices and web archives for contemporaneous coverage. Then Rachel said, "Most of this stuff is secondary or even tertiary material. It's all based on the initial site reports. It all seems to rehash the same handful of facts. What would you think about trying the University of Montana? They may have some proprietary databases."

"Good idea. There might be something that never made it to Washington or openly online."

An hour later, Rachel looked up. "Arthur, this thing is clearly in the courts. Are you still going with that woman lawyer from Justice?"

"Maggie. Yeah. I asked her about it."

"What did she say?"

"Funny thing is, she hasn't said anything. I'll check tonight." It made me feel awkward to talk about Maggie to Rachel.

"Do that. Listen. I've got to stop for now and get something out for the House Armed Services folk."

"Oh. I'm sorry. I didn't realize how long it has been. But can I count on you? Can we set this up for a while until I can get to what was really going on?"

Rachel looked at me before replying, then said, "Of course. I'll arrange it."

After she left I kept at it until almost six, then drove down to Justice to pick up Maggie as arranged. We were scheduled to have dinner with Wendy Vaughan, Maggie's former roommate who had married an attorney. I had briefly considered a short fling with Wendy, who had made it clear she was open to it one night in the pantry of another friend. She said her friendship with Maggie was in no way an impediment, but after considering what was offered, as attractive as it was, I decided the complications which were sure to flow from the deception required to carry off the act were not worth the hard-edged promise Wendy offered.

There had been a certain coolness between us ever since. I quite cheerfully loathed her husband, aspiring to a partnership in one of the city's major lobbying law firms, yet I was kind of fascinated with the man's absolute lack of character. What others seemed to interpret as bon homme, I saw as manipulation. I hadn't told any of this to Maggie; it seemed easier to let the deception pass than to get into an argument with her. She thought he was one of the hot ones. But more than anything I had begun to realize I was bored spending time with them. Wendy was

Maggie's oldest friend though, so I was resigned to many evenings to come.

We got through the conversation on which restaurant to go to, and by the time we got there the conversation had moved to the gossip that was the lingua franca of the Washington insider. Maggie and the others seemed to live on these topics, and how to maneuver them to their advantage. I found myself beginning to think about Rachel, and as Larry, Wendy's husband, launched off into a particularly byzantine anecdote in which his own manipulative skills seemed to be the main point, I took solace in composing a mathematical magic square in my mind, using the numerical equivalents of the letters in Rachel's name.

As soon as the car door closed, Maggie turned on me.

"Arthur, I need to share my feelings with you. You just weren't there most of the evening, in spite of everyone's attempt to include you."

"Maggie, I've told you. I can only do so much gossip."

"You better learn; this town runs on it. If you ever want to be anything but one of those backroom wonks, you better feel where the power is going. And it made me look bad."

"I'm sorry about that. I know it's important to you to do this social game stuff."

"Social game stuff...," Maggie said, her voice rising. "You really are amazing, Arthur. You seem to think that nothing matters but your facts and patterns. I have plans. I thought we had plans. Get with the program, Arthur. You only have a few years to make your mark. You're 34. By the time you're 35, you're categorized. That's it."

"Maggie. That's not how I work. My work is my passport. And it's done pretty well by me so far."

"That's because you're staff, you're not a principal," she said scathingly. "I'm not interested in being staff, Arthur. I told you that in the beginning. If we're going to be together, we have to be a team that has a plan."

We rode in silence, past the Chain Bridge out the C&O canal where I hold a lease from the U.S. Park Service. The white brick red-trimmed lock keeper's cottage is only 850 square feet, one bathroom, but it stands on the edge of a wood across the old tow path from the slow flowing canal. Just a few feet beyond lies the Potomac River. I could go across the plank canal trestle and just take a walk, or sit on the river bank, or hike or bike into the trail as it moved into the woods and go as far as Pittsburgh if I wanted to. I wouldn't trade my little cottage for the fanciest house in Georgetown.

I followed Maggie into my tiny living room. Gauging by the stiffness of her body we would not make love unless I spent at least an hour placating her mood. As I made two cups of tea in my galley kitchen, I realized I didn't care to undertake the penance sex would cost, but that I did very much want to know something only she could tell me.

After giving her a moment to drink her tea and prepare for what she was sure would be the beginning of my peacemaking, I asked her the question that had occupied me during the final quiet portion of our ride to my little house. "What did Gregson tell you about his case?"

"What?"

"What did Gregson tell you about that national security case?"

Maggie had been looking down at her tea composing herself for something very different, and she looked at me pointedly. "He told me he couldn't talk about it. And intimated it wasn't something I should pursue."

"Why would he do that?"

"What do you mean?"

"I can understand not talking about it, given the classification issues that seem to surround this... whatever. But why would he give you the sense that it shouldn't be pursued?"

"I don't know, Arthur. There's something very sensitive about this. At first Harry made a joke of the whole thing. But when I kept pushing, he asked me why I wanted to know."

"What did you tell him?"

"I said it seemed odd that national security issues could have arisen over something like the crash of a meteor, and I just wondered what it was all about." By now Maggie's irritation at not being cuddled and placated had been replaced by a kind of crafty evaluation. I could almost see the switch flip, and I knew that she was intrigued about why I was interested.

"What did he say then?" I asked, pouring Maggie some more of the Genmaicha tea I knew she loved.

"It wasn't so much what he said as the way he looked at me. Like he was measuring me as a problem. Anyway, I backed off. Not my case. Not my problem. Why do you care anyway, Arthur?" Maggie was now clearly engaged, and I realized that my answer and her response would determine where our relationship went.

"Because something that ought to be a silly season article in the paper seems to have a lot of high octane, and I want to know why."

"Who cares, Arthur?"

"The answer could be very useful."

As we climbed the narrow wooden stairs with their yellow painted wooden walls and white trim, I found myself once again thinking about Rachel, and I was very confused.

CHAPTER FIVE

"Arthur, we're not getting anywhere. Almost everything written about this is just a rehash of the same handful of first site report facts. I've never seen so much that says so little."

We were in the little carrel office, and Rachel was closing yet another site.

"You're right."

"Pam Weinstein, a Forester with University of Montana, says she couldn't find anything either. Not so much as a slip of paper. There is one thing I've noticed though."

"What's that?"

"I've been making lists of all the names. It's relatively small, and most of them are government, civilian or military. The ranking people are on record with statements, but you know how it is. After they take an initial statement nobody pays much attention to the enlisted guys or firemen."

"What are you suggesting?"

"We might be able to get a list of the firefighters. It was a horrible explosion, and blowing down trees for almost 100 square miles. There must be lots of them. And sheriffs and state police as well," Rachel said turning her head. She reminded me of a cat, and I found her very sexy. "Maybe we could track down those guys," she said. "Maybe they know something new. If you're right that something really happened out there, then if anyone could tell us something that isn't part of this record, it would probably be the guys who worked it."

"Rachel, you're right."

There was a knock on the door. We turned toward it, and Maggie stood at the threshold. I could see her take us in. For just a second her true feelings were evident, then her litigator's training clicked in.

"Arthur, your office said you were over here. I was at the court and thought I would come over to tempt you away from what you were doing, but you seem..."

"Maggie, this is Rachel Carter." I felt Maggie's jealousy and anger even though her face was a study in open affability. "Rachel this is Maggie... Margaret Pugh."

Rachel's glance did not retreat from Maggie's chilly stare, as they shook hands.

"Rachel has been helping me on my research."

"I'm sure she has," Maggie said, looking at her watch. "Oh gosh, I didn't realize how late it had gotten. Nice to meet you Rachel. Arthur, give me a call when you get home," Maggie said with a smile before leaving, closing the door softly behind her.

"A very tough lady there, Arthur."

"She is. It's what makes her a good fighter in the court room." I did not want to get into it. Truthfully, I wasn't sure exactly how I felt and that always made me feel vulnerable. I was very appreciative that Rachel seemed to sense this, and was willing to let the subject change when I said, "Where do we get such lists so we could contact them?"

"I'll make some phone calls. They're two hours ahead of us, we should just make it. 'Hello, is this the Federal Locator?'" she said into the telephone, then asked for the U.S. Forest Service at the Park.

"This is Rachel Carter at Congressional Research in D.C. I wonder if you could locate some files for me. You could. Great. I have a Congressional inquiry for the staffing records for firefighters on these dates. Thanks so much, here's my email..."

They talked on for a few more minutes, then Rachel hung up, looked at me, and smiled that cat smile.

"We'll have the email within the hour." Rachel had a kind of delight in her face.

"You like this." It was not a question.

"I do," Rachel answered with a smile. "I think I got out of engineering and into research because I learned I could put those analytical skills to work in another area. Also," and she looked down for a moment, then smiled, "because I love gossip but hate inaccuracy. It's like being a detective, and I love it when you can work it out."

"Yeah. I understand," I said, and realized that Rachel saw me, really saw me. "I particularly like teasing out patterns that matter but are often overlooked. It was something I learned I was good at when I was in high school. I just kind of fell into it." As I told her this I realized that I had been more honest in my answer than I had ever been with Maggie, and an intimacy between us had formed that I liked. "I don't think I've ever been that honest to myself about my real motives," I thought out loud.

Almost an hour to the minute later, the phone rang and Rachel picked it up. She listened without responding and then said, "Thank you," and hung up.

"The list is classified, she can't access it."

"Are you... is she... sure?"

"Quite. She looked the records up through several avenues. Nothing. What do you think it means?"

I didn't answer right away and she didn't press me; I just sat silently rolling a pencil between my fingers.

"The obvious answer is that the men saw something they have been ordered not to talk about. And they've made it difficult to even know which men were involved, although I am sure we could work that out over time, but would they talk to us?" We looked at each other and I think realized at the same time that if we pushed further we would draw a lot of attention to ourselves. I put the pencil down and covered Rachel's hand with my own. "There is something very strange here Rachel. This is not how the system works. Something else is going on. This has got a bad vibe."

I held up my hand and folded my fingers down, one by one, as I made my points. For me it now added up to a biological accident of some kind, and it hadn't been a meteor but some kind of large satellite.

"Arthur, doesn't someone keep track of all the satellites? I've seen graphics showing their orbits. There are thousands of them."

"NASA, the Pentagon, and I think NSA also keep various forms of databases. I might be able to get access to some of them but probably not all of them. I don't officially have a need to know."

"This isn't going anywhere, Arthur."

"You're right. How about dinner? It's early but neither of us had any lunch."

We left and walked over to a good fish restaurant, and I confess I felt a twinge of disloyalty.

We were almost through a swordfish dinner with citron sauce on a bed of spinach. Both of us chose the same entree, and I was thinking how easy it was to talk with Rachel, when she put down her fork and said, "I just had an idea, Arthur. I have... I don't know... something like a second cousin who lives out toward Frederick, Maryland. Somewhere in the woods."

"Okay, but what does that mean?"

"John is slightly autistic, Asperger's Syndrome, but he has an eidetic memory. If he sees it he never forgets it. Like a lot of ASD people, he doesn't do well having a lot of interaction, particularly in groups. But he can get by on his own, particularly online."

I didn't know where she was going with this, so I just nodded and smiled and listened.

"He inherited a little money and an old farm house on some acreage about 10 years ago, and spends all his time on the net. He can interact with things at his own pace, and he's better than most so he's in control, and he's really into the dark net. He gets hired in some way I don't understand to find stuff people don't want found. And he does it. I confess I don't understand much of it; it's a different kind of very technical programming. But I know he can get things I never could."

I could see where she was headed. "Could he search for us?"

"He likes me, maybe because I've never talked down to him. He's smarter than I am and he knows I know that, and we've always gotten along. I don't actually see him very often, but if you'd be willing to drive out there with me, and we thought the question through carefully, I think he would do some work for us."

We exchanged a look. "You game?" I asked, signaling, by writing in the air, for our check.

"What about Maggie?"

"Yes. Maggie, Thanks. I better call." I reached for the bill, but Rachel took it, and waved me to my phone as she took hers and paid the bill. As I was punching my iPhone Rachel said, "There's going to be a price for this outing Arthur; it's going to cause a problem, your call... maybe we can do it another way."

"I understand," I told her. "Thanks for thinking of that, but this needs to be done just as you laid it out."

Maggie answered the phone and when I told her what I was doing it was not a happy conversation, just as Rachel had predicted. To give me some privacy Rachel walked off and called her cousin.

"He is agreeable; let's go out now," she said when she hung up.

"It'll be late."

"Doesn't matter to John. I don't know when he sleeps, but late is not a problem."

We caught a cab back to the Hill and walked down into the Senate garage to my Tesla.

"Nice car," Rachel said as she buckled her seatbelt.

"Maggie wanted me to get it," I said as we pulled up the ramp. "I wanted to get a small truck, one of the new extended range EVs, so I could take my bike easily." I laughed. "But it wouldn't do pulling up at an embassy in a pickup. Where are we going?" I asked as I waved at the guard.

"Do you know where Frederick, Maryland is?"

"Yeah" I answered, then told the GPS, "The next voice will give the destination."

Rachel gave the address then turned to me. "Listen, Rachel, about Maggie. I need to tell you...

"You don't need to tell me anything, Arthur," Rachel replied speaking softly.

"Thanks."

The roads got narrower and narrower, and soon we were on a 'school bus road' unpaved and only maintained by the county to allow children to be reached by their rural school bus.

"It's amazing isn't it how quickly it becomes isolated and rural as soon as you get out of metropolitan D.C.?" I said to Rachel, making yet another turn onto a tiny lane.

Old locust posts and rails made a fence, probably from the 30s or even earlier, that lined its sides. They say a locust post will wear out three holes, and these looked committed to the task.

"Oh, quick... Arthur turn left at that mailbox."

We went down a dirt track across a field with grass in the middle and parallel strips of bare earth where tire treads had worn the vegetation away. An old-fashioned round-top garden wire fence with white posts marked the yard within the field. Inside this enclosure sat a small white clapboard two-story house in need of paint. There was a long shallow screened-in porch with a green painted floor across the front.

Lights were on in the front windows, and an old Chevy truck was parked in the carport built on one side of a small barn. We pulled up just outside a once-white arbored gate with roses prolifically growing over it. Even from where I was, with the window down I could smell their fragrance. When I turned the engine off, after a short silence the chorus of insects resumed its buzz. Rachel got out, stood next to the car and called "John," then "John" again. "It's Rachel."

A light went on in the ceiling of the porch, the front door opened and a tall skinny man in blue jeans with a flannel shirt hanging out and felt slippers on his feet walked across the porch, opened the porch's screen door and leaned out.

"Kinda late for a call, but it's always nice to see you Rachel." He had the gravelly voice of a man who has smoked too many cigarettes. "Who's that with you?"

"This is Arthur Davies, John. He works for the Senate."

"Well, come in or the mosquitoes will eat you alive," John said with a kind of laugh.

We walked into a typical modest late 19th century center hall Maryland farmhouse with a staircase coming down one wall of the hall. There were rooms on both sides, two rooms to a side. John steered us into what was obviously the main room he used. It had an old corduroy sofa and chair set, and a big curved screen that was playing. The remains of a dinner of what looked like chicken and greens was sitting on a TV table in front of the couch.

"Get you a drink, or a cup of coffee?" he asked with absent-minded civility.

"Nothing thanks, John. I was telling Arthur about you and your work, and he is doing some research that you might be able to help him with. I don't think it would take too much of your time and I would appreciate it."

"You know I'll do it for you Rachel." Then he looked at me and said, "The new series about the detective in medieval England is about to come on, and I would hate to miss one. What is it you need, that someone like you already in the government can't get?"

"Rachel says you're really good at searching things out." It sounded lame to my ears, but John nodded, turned, and led us across the hall through a door into what must once have been the dining room. Now it was lined with unpainted flat wooden doors on sawhorses on either side of what was originally the dining table. It formed a U around three sides of the room. On the table tops and also the walls were 37-inch 3-D displays. At the middle of the table was his main workstation, but there were keyboards spaced along the way. Boxes of cables and a box filled with SIM card size microdrives sat on the floor. Little scraps of post-it paper were tacked to the shelves or pasted to the monitors in what was obviously a personal filing system.

"Mind the dust," John said, brushing his hands on the shirttails of his flannel shirt. He picked up a clipboard with legal pad clamped to it and sat down in an old-fashioned wooden thatched seat wheelchair with rubber bicycle wheels on either side.

Pushing himself over to the dining table, he said, "okay, what is it you need?"

"John, about 12 years ago a meteor crashed in Glacier…"

"…National Park. I remember. It knocked down 36,642 trees."

"You know how many trees were knocked down?" I said incredulously, looking at Rachel; she just shrugged.

"Got int'rested in it. They estimate the meteor was about the size of one of those old Volkswagen beetles, 'cept I don't think it was."

"You don't think it was what?"

"A meteor of course."

"What do you think it was?" I couldn't resist asking.

"It was a UFO."

"A UFO, why do you think that…?"

"On the Dark Net there were people… backpackers, some bikers, went up there. They saw two Army trucks takin' stuff away. Took pictures."

John started typing with an astonishing rapidity, and images began to flash by, clearly pictures of the crash site.

"25 Gigs?" I asked.

"1T," John said without turning his head.

"Where did you get those, John? I have never seen any of those, and I looked at everything in the official file."

"You looked at what the government wants you to see unless you've got need-to-know clearance. On this one even if you are in the government, you don't see much more than what they let the media see," he said, turning back to the screens.

His hands slowed the rate of pictures flashing by. Finally he stopped and I was looking at the crash site. It was clear there were pieces of metal scattered about.

"I think it was a satellite, John," I told him. "Something that came down and polluted the site in some way, that's why they quarantined it."

"Think so? … then how do you explain this?"

The image on the screen, clearly taken with some kind of telephoto lens, was of a piece of equipment broken and warped, but with some kind of writing that didn't look like anything I had ever seen before.

"Can you make me a copy of that?"

"I 'spec so." John said almost to himself, then walked over to a wall with a shadeless, curtainless window and looked out.

He came back, reached into the box of microdrives and picked one up. "Untraceable, get them out of Hong Kong. Take a handful, you may need 'em," he said, gesturing at the box. I went over and did as he suggested. They were 300 Gig, top of the line.

He put the drive into a port, saved the picture, ejected the drive and handed it to me.

"Why didn't you just send me an encrypted email?" I asked. John looked at me as one might a slow child.

"Transmitted that way it would have been caught. The image would be matched somewhere and they would know each end. Don't do that."

"Could you give me a printout?"

"Can't give you that. They'd find me, know I had it."

"How would they know?" I asked, suddenly chilled by John's paranoia.

"You know you're going to get in trouble if anyone sees this. The government doesn't want anyone to know about this. If they got hold of a printout they could trace my printer. Now it's on you," John said, pointing to the drive in my hand. "The identity code on the disk is meaningless. They can't track back to me, even if they get the drive from you.

Rachel and I looked at each other without a word.

"Are we asking you to do something that could cause you problems? Is that a consideration, John?"

"Nah. I'm in the government's panties almost everyday… they'll never know about this little probe," he said, laughing as he took the notes he had written and put the pages through the same classified-level shredder I use in the office.

"Heavy duty gear; I didn't even know that was commercial."

"Isn't… but you can get them in the dark world."

"Okay John, I want you to assemble anything you can find. Just let me know."

"We'll come back out, John. No transmission."

John heard the theme from his show come up, and without another word went back into the living room and sat down.

"Then there's no question there's a cover up," Rachel said.

"I agree. Rachel, I don't know what is going on here. UFOs …
Really? Have I gone through the looking glass?

"Oh, yes. I think we both have," she said.

We walked out and John was taking his meal out of a small black
microwave I hadn't previously noticed set up next to his couch, where
he had reheated it. He raised his hand, turned his head and waved to us
just as the commercial ended and the show started. Rachel went over to
him, bent over and kissed him on the head and whispered something in
his ear. He turned again, smiling, looked at me and went back to his
show.

We drove back in silence for a long time while I navigated the dirt
school bus road, each of us cocooned in the soft glow of the Tesla's
dashboard instruments. As we reached a road with a paved surface,
Rachel broke the silence.

"Arthur, why would the government hide something like this unless
John is right? It doesn't make any sense to me."

"It isn't 'the government,' like it was some kind of monolithic whole.
You know that, Rachel. But somebody who is, or was, part of the
government at a level where they could do it, is definitely trying to make
this all go away."

"You still think it was some kind of nuclear or biological accident?"

"I can't get to UFOs yet, I admit it. You don't have to leave earth to
find an explanation for government cover-ups. Look at Hanford, or
Savannah River."

"Yeah. Okay," Rachel said reluctantly.

"Look at the facts," I said, turning to her.

"How 'bout looking at the road," she responded.

"Sorry," I said, and swerved to avoid two rabbits standing frozen,
stunned by our lights and the onrushing car, turning just enough to miss
them and looking into the rearview mirror to make sure. "But think
about it," I added after a pause that extended as we both thought about
what was happening.

As we drew closer to the city Rachel suddenly said, "This is kind of scary. I feel like I'm in a movie."

"Do you want to quit?"

"No, but I want to acknowledge to myself that I'm about to cross some kind of line I don't even see, but I feel sure is there."

"Rachel. You don't get paid to do this sort of thing. Neither do I for that matter. But, at least, I have a reason. I can take you home, and we can forget about this. Where do you live?"

"Turn right and then left. Don't get noble on me Arthur. This is a lot more exciting than answering Congressional inquiries on hog production in Nebraska. You know what I think?"

"What? Did you see that?" I shouted as we were almost driven off the road. "Just because you've got immunity...." I shouted at the retreating taillights of a Mercedes with diplomatic plates.

"I think you should try and get some of those papers that the court didn't want to release. Stop in front of that red brick house."

"I think you're right," I said as I maneuvered my way to a space in front of a fire hydrant. "I can't ask Maggie," then, after a pause, "After tonight I probably can't ask Maggie anything." I said it with a laugh for effect, and without a beat Rachel responded in the same light tone.

"I'd like to say I was sorry, Arthur, but I'm not. I enjoyed our first date." She leaned over and kissed me on the cheek, then quickly moved out of the car. At the top of her wrought iron steps she called back, "Call me tomorrow."

I thought about what that meant as I drove home, alternatively thinking about Maggie, Rachel, and whether I could believe in UFOs.

CHAPTER SIX

When I got back to my cottage the light on my answering machine was blinking. It was the usual assortment of calls, except notably nothing from Maggie, until a man's voice came on.

"Hello. Dr. Davies. This is Peter Sturmont. My name will probably mean nothing to you. I'm a physicist at the Princeton Center for Advanced Studies. You contacted someone about a matter which he referred to me. Perhaps you'd give me a call at your convenience." It was followed by a number. Maybe because of what had just transpired, the call unnerved me. It was so deliberately ambiguous. As I looked in the long mirror on my closet door, I said out loud to myself, "Rachel and I have somehow disturbed a network." Staring at my reflected self I added, "My God, I'm getting paranoid." As I undressed, I thought about the idea that our search was more widely known than we had realized, and I didn't feel good about that.

The following morning, when things seemed far less conspiratorial, before going to the office I returned the call. Peter Sturmont, Professor Peter Sturmont, was professorial and vague. We arranged a meeting at the Union Terminal just down from the Russell Senate Office Building. After hanging up and replaying the call in my mind, I realized that Sturmont hadn't really told me what the meeting was about, even though I had ad him twice. I laughed at myself, then sobered and wondered: No one is that ambiguous except deliberately. The only thing I could think of that would prompt Sturmont's call was the research Rachel and I were doing. But I could not figure out how he could be involved.

As soon as I got into my office I called Rachel. As I let it ring I realized I was not just calling because I felt she was my research partner and entitled to know what was happening.

"A mysterious phone call from a Princeton physicist," she said with a laugh. "My goodness this is getting intriguing. Do you want me to come to the meeting?" It was a question with several levels of meaning.

"I do."

I walked over to the library in the warm morning air, finding Rachel waiting for me in front of the main building's wonderful green bronze fountain statutes of horses and nymphs spewing water. We were shy together, and we walked down to the terminal, at least I did, feeling the attraction that neither of us was quite ready to talk about.

"Nice day."

"Yes it is, isn't it."

"I always like the birds singing here."

"So do I."

"Do you think we could be more inane?" I asked.

"Not without cue cards," she responded with a laugh.

The Union Terminal that was our destination came into view as we walked down the hill. It had been designed to impress; its marble facade surmounted with statues of anonymous but symbolic women in togas met the early 20th century's public minds' expectation as to what the formal rail gateway to the nation's capital should look like. For years there hadn't been much rail travel, and I'm told it had become a forlorn symbol of another age. But with the new Japanese and Chinese high speed trains running up the East Coast, train riding is once again a part of many people's lives, and the terminal has become a sort of trendy mall. In cavernous marble rooms once lined with wooden pews, there are now shops and restaurants. When I got there it was crowded with travelers and Hill people stopping for lunch.

Sturmont had come down on the 8 o'clock train. At 250 miles per hour the 180-mile trip only took about 45 minutes, and he was punctual to the minute. A serious person, obviously a highly intelligent academic who impressed me, but in person as vague and reticent as he had been in our correspondence. Sturmont and I played a game of "who do you know," listing people in government and academe whose acquaintance or friendship we shared, as Rachel sat quietly watching the conversation going nowhere.

It seemed very peculiar to me that a man like Sturmont would come all the way from Princeton and then have nothing really to say. But at the end of an hour brunch of croissant sandwiches, just as I had had enough and was about to say we had to get back to the office, the professor pulled out some money, put it on the table, and stood up, announcing that he had to catch the train back. He shook our hands and walked away, leaving us looking at each other with the memory of his cool platitudes. We were completely mystified.

The next day Sturmont called, and without referring to our meeting the day before, asked Rachel and me to visit him over the weekend. The call, and the request coming on top of the earlier strange meeting, I think normally would have made me decide to decline. But I could not get past my feelings that a man like Sturmont would not be doing this unless it was serious. So I accepted.

As soon as I hung up Maggie called.

"The Wallingfords have invited us out to their place in Leesburg. I know you don't care much about riding, but it should be great fun. Congressman Delgato will be there. It's your chance to make your point about that education legislation. I could leave late on Friday or early Saturday."

"I can't go, Maggie. I have to go to Princeton." I said it quickly so that there would be no meaning in my tone for Maggie to pick up. Maggie caught the nuance anyway. There was silence for a beat.

"I see."

"I'm doing some research and there is a professor up there I have to see."

"When did this come up?" Casual interest was the intended message. I was not fooled and dreaded what was coming.

"I just hung up with him. I just accepted. I'm really sorry Maggie. If I'd known..."

"Are you going alone?"

I thought seriously about lying. Almost started to, why get into the hassle, but decided it would ultimately just make things worse. "Rachel Carter from Congressional Research may come with me."

"May?"

"I haven't asked her yet. But she's been helping me on this..."

"This isn't more of that ' is it?"

"It has nothing to do with UFOs, Maggie, I told you that, and for God's sake don't go jealous on me."

"Do I have something to be jealous about Arthur?"

"No. You do not. But I need help here. I've seen enough now to know that some kind of cover up went on, and I want to find out what it is." As I spoke, in my mind I saw the picture John had shown us.

"Well, I hope you have a nice trip up to Princeton. It should be lovely this time of year. I'll tell the Wallingfords you're tied up." Maggie's tone was bright and easy. I knew it was her negotiating voice, and that she had chosen not to engage.

"Please do. Tell everyone I was really sorry not to be able to make it."

Two days later Rachel and I were on the highspeed train headed for Princeton. The cars were crowded and I was glad I had made reservations so we could ride sitting together, and in thinking that realized that I had made them, instead of asking my secretary Karen to do it, and wondered what that meant. Once again, I found myself conflicted. Talk with Rachel flowed in a way it did not with Maggie. I tried to identify what it was, and decided that the difference was that Rachel did not have an angle on everything.

Maggie was special ops. Every statement was a soldier sent out into the night on patrol. Yet I felt that Rachel was the smarter of the two. I was acutely aware of her thigh pressed against mine, and wondered if she was also aware of the contact. At one point she leaned over as I reached across and my hand brushed against her breast. I found the contact very erotic, and the silence that followed only heightened the impression, because it gave me time to think about it.

"I was wrong the other day," Rachel said, breaking the quiet in which we sat.

"Wrong?"

"Yeah, wrong. How long have you and Maggie been going together?"

"About a year, I guess," I said after a moment. "We met when the Attorney General told her to call me," I volunteered.

"But you don't live together." It was not a question.

"No. I wanted to, but Maggie said there was no real point, and it would look... well with the current mood on the Right, she didn't think it was... I feel kind of disloyal talking about this, Rachel. Maggie's a good lady."

"I'm sure she is. That's what I meant when I said I was wrong. I'm not usually predatory, Arthur."

The exchange was unsatisfactory for us both, and we lapsed back into silence, but this time not a comfortable one. At noon the train arrived at the Princeton station, and as we stepped down from it an attractive middle-aged woman came toward us, saying "Dr. Davies? Dr. Carter?"

Her name was Pamela Sturmont, and she drove us back through the elegant old town of Princeton to the neighborhoods where senior academics live. The Sturmonts' house was everything one expected in the Ivy League. Brick with ivy growing up its walls; its central hall was dim and cooler than the outside. Pamela Sturmont led us back along its length to Sturmont's study, a kind of many windowed sunroom at the back of the house. As he heard our footsteps, Sturmont, who was standing, turned with his hand extended. Pamela excused herself saying, "Let me put a few things together. Peter will make the drinks."

Seated in the book-lined room with plaid fabric on the walls, was another man whom I recognized instantly.

"My God, Moshe... Rachel, this is Moshe Greenberg one of the country's major astrophysicists."

"Moshe said he knew you from testifying before a committee where you were staffing," Sturmont said to no one in particular as he walked over to an art deco marble-topped washstand now doing duty as a bar.

"Moshe, this is Rachel Carter from Congressional Research."

"Nice to meet you Dr. Carter."

"I can offer you a cold Pinot Grigio with some pretensions, or anything hard you like," Sturmont said, turning to face us.

"Just some wine for me," said Rachel.

"The same for me." As Sturmont poured, Greenberg and I looked at each other.

"I would never have expected to see you here, Moshe," I finally said, indicating by my tone that I hoped for an explanation.

"I never expected to see an ambitious Hill staffer like you, if you'll excuse my candor, Arthur, here either," Greenberg responded.

At first the meeting started off with the same genteel measured pace of the previous brunch. After about 10 minutes I was becoming antsy, and I am sure it was obvious. Pamela came back in with watercress and grilled chicken sandwiches and some crudités with a dip, and sat down next to her husband on the couch. He got up to pour her some wine and, in the silence her entrance created, Greenberg turned in his chair to face Sturmont.

"Peter we've got to tell them. This is silly." Sturmont looked at his friend for a moment, and then his wife. She nodded her agreement.

"Moshe and I and a small group of other scientists, mostly physicists, but with some physicians, neuroscientists, and psychologists, have been carrying out a search similar to yours. It has been entirely discrete because we can not risk our reputations or," and here both scientists laughed, "our funding."

"How did you find me?"

"What do you know about the net, Arthur?"

"Until a couple of weeks ago, I thought I knew a lot. I saw the web as being in two parts, public and classified. Beyond knowing it exists I didn't know anything about the Deep Net, the sites that search engines don't find, or the deliberately hidden Dark Net that is some subset of it."

"We found you through someone you either know or hired."

Rachel and I turned and looked at each other.

"We don't know his name, just that he has been searching on your behalf."

"How could you know that?"

"Someone we work with cross-correlated the video in the courtroom where the FOIA case was heard with the LC records Rachel made, the linkage between the two of you," Greenburg answered. "We don't know anything about how the linkage occurred, but we could detect that certain dormant files were being visited."

"I went down to meet you because we felt we had to make a human assessment."

"My God, it's like a private intelligence network," I blurted out.

Peter shook his head. "No. Not really. Intelligence networks are surveying masses of data. You have to command enormous resources to do that. But if you're clever and have a certain level of access and resources like university computers, you can monitor one small thing. And that is all we care about."

"Was it a satellite? Nuclear? Biological?" I interrupted, leaning forward.

"Neither," both men spoke at once.

Sturmont started to speak again, then stopped. He and Greenberg exchanged another look, and the silence drew out. Finally Greenberg looked at me and said, "Arthur, there was no nuclear accident. Nor was it biological, at least in the sense you mean. We have come to believe that the meteor was really what the conspiracy people believe it to have been. Isn't that ironic?" Moshe stopped. No one else spoke and in the silence I could hear the high pure voices of young boys calling to one another, then the sound of them tearing across the yard in some intense activity.

"This is, well, I know it isn't easy to take aboard, Arthur, and I suppose we could mislead you and Rachel. But I know how tenacious you are, and eventually you'd find your way back to us, I'm sure, and you'd be unhappy to boot. Peter, give Arthur a refill. Here's what we know."

Greenberg went on to tell Rachel and me that an actual space craft did crash in the National Forest but that beyond that, much of the popular information was just the repeated recitation of the few facts that had leaked. "They've become canonized through repetition into an urban myth. But, at its core, there is truth. What's being hidden is not so much the physical material of the craft, although this does exist. The real secret is that one of the aliens survived the crash, was captured, and taken away. It has been kept for almost 12 years now at a special installation built exclusively for that purpose."

As Greenberg spoke Rachel reached out and held my hand. I, myself, was beset by conflicting emotions. I thought, I know Moshe Greenberg. He's a man of impeccable character. His position as a scientist is unquestioned. He's been nominated for a Nobel, and I think he is going to win. I had to take what he was saying seriously. At the same time, I found the whole story somehow embarrassing. It made me uncomfortable.

"Moshe, I would never doubt your word. I'm sure you believe what you are saying. But, well. Is there any proof? Anything at all that you as a scientist feel is real?"

Sturmont got up and walked over to his desk. Beside it was his briefcase. He opened it and extracted a file. "Strangely enough sometimes the most secure way is the old-fashioned way: paper," he said as he handed it to me.

Rachel and I leaned together so that both of us could see the contents.

There was the same picture John had found us, that in fact I had at the moment on microdrive in my pocket. Then there were construction orders for a very strange building, although I didn't really understand all of it.

"With all respect Moshe, Professor Sturmont, I've seen this picture. It is definitely weird, but none of this rises to the level of proof." I felt an enormous sense of disappointment in Greenberg, and the older man sensed it. Sturmont got up again and went over to his desk. He took out a key and opened the lower drawer, taking out a small flat round plastic container which he handed to Greenberg, who handed it to me.

"Open it," he said.

I unscrewed the lid. Inside was black plastic foam used to pack delicate objects for safety. An indentation had been cut in the middle of the foam, and inside, somewhat smaller, nestled an irregularly shaped piece of silver metal about the size of the palm of my hand. On part of it Rachel and I could see some kind of hieroglyphs, only a portion was there. It was embossed in pink, outlined with a thin purple line that had a faint glow.

As I looked up at the two men, Sturmont said, "We think this is part of the interior of the craft. The marking is obviously some kind of writing."

"We have tested it in every way we can. Pick it up."

I did. It felt like thick aluminum foil, but was duller in color and didn't crinkle as foil does. I handed it to Rachel. "Squeeze it," Greenberg indicated with his own hand the motion, and she did. The metal bent and when she released pressure it resumed its flat shape, without any line or sign of the bend.

"It is a titanium alloy, of a nature and purity impossible on earth, treated in some way we can only imagine, so it can do that," Sturmont said handing me the container. I put the small piece of metal back into its foam pocket, handed it back to him, and he set it on the coffee table in front on Rachel and myself.

"You're sure about this?" I asked.

"Very. The tests have been done independently at four different laboratories."

"I don't know what to say," I admitted.

"How did you get it, Professor?" Rachel asked.

"It was found by a local cowboy, drawn by stories of crashed spacecraft, who arrived on the scene long after the Army had swept the site. The debris was scattered over miles of burnt forest, some of it deep in the ashes. He just got lucky and hid it in his boot. A few years later he told his son about it. He was a graduate student in a class taught by one of our group. They became friends and the son told him. A year later it came to us."

"So you think an alien from the craft survived and is being held at a completely off the books facility?" Rachel asked.

"We do," Sturmont replied. "We've been banking on the courts releasing the old information, but with the ruling the other day, we don't think that will ever happen."

"What we need, Arthur, Rachel, is someone in the government who might be able to find out what those papers contain. None of us can do it," Greenberg said in answer to my startled look. "We don't have the operational clearances."

I picked up the piece of metal in its case and looked at it. "Do you know what you are asking, Moshe?" I asked softly.

"Yes. I worked on the Red Duck Project. I know about secrecy."

"Why not use this piece of metal? If it's what you say it is..."

"Because it cannot be said absolutely that it is the product of the technology of another planet," Sturmont replied.

"It's not the secrecy, Dr. Greenberg," Rachel said, speaking for both of us after looking at me. "It's a question of loyalty. You're asking us to jeopardize our careers over what, you'll excuse me, is still mostly a rumor or a myth. In any case a very weird subject. This isn't like going to bat to uncover an accident which has poisoned the lives of hundreds, or even thousands, of people with radiation."

"If this UFO event was as real as we..."

"If. Are you willing to risk your tenure on this Professor Sturmont?" I got up as Rachel spoke and walked over to the window, where I looked out at the boys who had organized themselves into a game of "kill the man with the ball." Their cries carried their energy into the room.

"I take your point entirely," Sturmont answered, and for a moment no one had anything to say. There was a general sense in the room that there was nowhere to take the conversation. In recognition of that, after Sturmont and Greenberg had looked at each other, Greenberg said, "Arthur, think about what you feel comfortable doing. Obviously, you have concerns that we must respect. Think about it and get back to us."

As if on cue, everyone rose, then I looked at my watch. "We need to get back to the station if we want to make the 3 o'clock train."

As we got to the station Greenberg was subdued. We got out of the car and Greenburg came over to Rachel and me. He looked at us for a beat and warned us to be careful. "No one takes this stuff too seriously until someone like you decides to take it seriously."

CHAPTER SEVEN

The next day I was tied up all morning at the Department of the Interior, and did not get to my office until almost 11. When I did I found an email from Senator John Pardoe, the chairman of my committee and one of the Senate's most senior members, asking me to call, also a call slip from Maggie. I called the Senator first, and when I did so Jan, the senator's appointments secretary, asked me to meet the senator at his hideaway office in the Capitol at 11:30.

There was no time to call Maggie. I locked my office and went down to the first floor. I stuck my head out but it was still raining, so I went down into the basement of the Russell Office building, named as all Congressional building are for former members, this one Senator Richard B. Russell of Georgia, an old school Southern Democratic racist. I walked quickly down the hall, dodging the stacks of boxes, furniture and computer cartons which seemed to perpetually fill the basement corridors of all buildings on the Hill, until I got to the little stainless steel underground train that takes you across to the capitol. It was nearly full, and about to leave. I just made it and was sitting down as the train began to move, when the operator saw Senator Phelps, stopped, and waited until he was aboard and seated next to me in the only space remaining.

"Well, Arthur. Just the man I was looking for."

"Good morning, Senator. How are you?"

"Much better since you sent me that paper on base closures, Arthur. Very adroitly done. Things like that make a difference as election time draws nigh. You saved me a lot of trouble, Arthur, I won't forget that.

"Thank you, Senator," I said truthfully. I appreciated the praise and knew that the Senator knew I did and that he meant it. I'd been given a chip. But it was unsaid. So much of the Hill is like that. I also knew that Senator Phelps appreciated the fact that, even within the confines of the Senate, I did not press to get even semi-public credit for what I had done. What mattered to me is what the Hill knew. That and the forested hills and mountains were my world.

We rode in silence for a moment. As the train was pulling up, Phelps said to me, "I passed your memo along to Susan, and she's turning it into a speech for next week." Then, with a look, "You still smoke those Davidoffs, Arthur?"

"It's been known to happen after special dinners, Senator," I told him with a smile, and understanding what was transpiring, didn't mention I rarely smoked anymore because Maggie hated the smell.

The little train eased gently into its docking bay, and we all quickly disembarked. The Senator patted me on the shoulder and went on without another word.

I don't think I have ever entered the Capitol without feeling I was in a very special place. There is no other building like The Capitol in the United States. It surprised me when I arrived in Washington how small the great power buildings of America are, how scaled to the people. The surprisingly small Supreme Court chamber with its austere intimacy, and the Oval Office more living room than office and also surprisingly small; in size a fraction of modern CEO offices to be found across the country. The Capitol, the people's house, had the kind of wonderfully ebullient over-decoration that I also associated with St Peter's in the Vatican but on a smaller scale. I love walking through this building, the genius of Constantine Bermudi, an Italian-American who had died in poverty, but who covered every wall with faux marble and painted scenes. There are still brass spittoons in corners, and unnoticed by most, secret Masonic symbols carved at metaphysically significant points throughout the building.

I worked my way along the corridors pausing only to knock on the cream yellow outer shutter door of a room identified with a little black rectangle and a white hand painted number. Every member of congress gets a hideaway office; they're tucked throughout the Capitol. Some are like large walk-in closets. But senior committee chairmen get something special: a comfortable residential study that they decorate in a much more personal way.

Senator Pardoe, who had come to power with the change of control of the Senate, had taken over from his Democratic predecessor. In a world based on power, changes here are clearly remembered and often painful. It had been like pulling badgers out of their holes to move the senior chairmen out of their private spaces to lesser places with the changeover.

"Come in Arthur," a voice came from the other side, and I opened the door and went in. When Senator Proft from Maine had been chairman, a man whose family had a long association with the sea and the Navy, the walls of the room had been lined with 18th and 19th Century seascapes and ship paintings passed down to him through his family. Senator Pardoe was from Oklahoma, and now the room was filled with cowboy memorabilia and pictures of oil wells and men standing with the senator in front of oil wells or pipelines. I doubted they looked as good today; it's an industry going through a painful downsizing.

The senator himself, now in his later sixties, was standing in front of a small bachelor kitchenette which was new I realized. It was hard to imagine the patrician Senator Proft doing anything in a kitchen. Senator Pardoe was stirring something in a pot.

"Assume you haven't had lunch yet, Arthur."

"No, senator."

"Thought we might have a quiet bowl of chili," Pardoe said. He was one of those stringy muscled men that you think of coming off the range in the West. He hennaed his sparse hair now to maintain its color, which was a deep auburn. His colleagues called him "Red."

"You've had my chili before, Arthur?"

"Once. I remember it with great fondness, Senator."

"Learned it from my grandmother," he said, as he spooned out the chili into two bowls. "She was part Cherokee... walked on the Trail of Tears."

"I didn't know," I said, accepting the bowl he proffered.

"Like a beer?" Pardoe said, reaching into a small ice box under the stove top and pulling out two bottles before I had time to respond.

"That would be fine."

"Here are some onions and cheese, get it flown in. You've got to have the right cheese, just like you've got to have the right spices," the senator said, as he settled the condiments onto the large table that ran down one side of the room. Then he went back and got a box of oyster crackers. "Can't forget these, right? Have a seat."

We ate in silence for a while, and he was right; it was good chili. Unlike a lot of the senior staffers, I always allow the senators to pace the meeting.

"I hear nothing but good things about you, Arthur."

"Thank you, Senator."

"How are we coming on the hearings?"

"I'll have my analysis and some suggested questions over to your office within a few days. If you like I will schedule some time at your convenience to go over them."

"Good. Good. My grandmother used to use possum," the senator said with his mouth full. "I suspect it was fine, but it's hard to get possum these days... eh." He laughed so hard at his own wit that his wiry frame shook.

"Arthur, how old are you?"

"Thirty-four, Sir."

"What's your next move?"

"I don't know yet, Senator," I replied with honesty.

"It's getting time for you to move up, Arthur," Pardoe said, crumbling more oyster crackers into his remaining chili.

"Perhaps you're right, Senator," I said, wondering where this was leading.

"How would you like to be Deputy Assistant Secretary of Defense, Arthur?" Like most politicians, Senator Pardoe had the knack of surprising you, and using your name frequently in conversation. It implied intimacy and a familiarity with a person's concerns. I rather liked being the focus of the technique, as I was supposed to, but I had no illusions about what it really meant. However, I also knew this was a serious offer.

"What would the White House say?"

"The President, God bless the poor sonavabitch, will be amenable."

"I hadn't thought about Defense, Senator. Thank you for considering me. It's a wonderful promotion opportunity but it would also change the focus of my life. If I may I'd like to think about the track that would put me on."

"The country needs people with your ability to think things through. You could finish out the term there and then, when the White House changes hands, as I'm sure it will." The Senator gave a mordant chuckle at the thought. "You could go over to the Woodrow Wilson Center as a Fellow and write a book. After that… well, why don't we wait and see."

"I had no idea you had thought about any of this. I'm very touched, Senator," I said, and I meant it.

"You've made friends here and we like to bring promising young people like you along, Arthur. Oh, one thing."

"Sir."

"The position would require confirmation."

"Yes."

"Is there anything that could make that difficult?"

This was a very serious question, and I took it that way. I mentally reviewed my life, and Senator Pardoe, to give me time, picked up the dishes and put them in the sink.

"I don't think there is anything to be concerned about there."

"What about this UFO business? It would look gawdalmighty odd to have an Deputy Assistant Secretary of Defense involved with those UFO nut cases. I know Congressman Blanchard talks about 'em and I wouldn't say he was wrong. But in a public hearing…"

I was completely unprepared for it. The trapdoor had opened beneath my feet without a hint of warning, and I knew that only absolute candor was safe.

"I didn't think it had anything to do with UFOs," I said, with no preamble, letting him know I knew he had been briefed by someone. "I thought…" and here I realized, even as I was saying it, that I was not going past a certain point. "I thought and still think, that the meteor incident was some kind of nuclear or biological accident. You obviously know I've been doing research on whistleblowers and cover-ups in governments programs, as part of S46. You're the one who raised the issue."

"Arthur, you don't have any partisan association. Hell I don't even know your political affiliation," the Senator got up and walked over to a dish of mints, several of which he popped into his mouth, then handed the dish to me. Almost as an afterthought, "You do vote don't you, Arthur?"

"I take it very seriously, Senator, I've never missed an election," I responded, declining the hidden question that was the principal point.

"Well, it doesn't matter all that much at the Deputy Assistant Secretary level, but I can tell you, you'll have to show your colors after that," the Senator said, sitting down on one of the Senate's signature black leather couches forcing me to turn to see him.

"I see."

The Senator looked very hard at me. "Anyway, even if you found something, I know it would take until after the election to bring it out. That would not be on our watch, although begun under this one," he said, and I could see him weighing tactics. "Assuming the White House changes over, it could embarrass the hell out of the party and the senior senator from New Mexico, who would not appreciate that at all… not at all… I can tell you."

"You'd prefer that I drop…"

"I can't tell you what to do, Arthur, not if a Democratic senator is asking you to look into something. I can just share my own thinking."

There was a buzz on the telephone and the Senator picked it up. When he put it down, it was clear that the meeting was over.

"Thanks for coming over, Arthur," the Senator said, as if I had done him a favor. Politicians all have that knack too.

"Thank you, Senator. The chili was great. Let me think this over... all right?"

"Of course, take the time you need. It's an important decision," the Senator said with a meaningful look. "Oh would you close both doors when you go out, Arthur? Thanks."

Just as I was closing both the mahogany solid door and the outer shutter door, I heard the Senator pick up the telephone again.

CHAPTER EIGHT

All the way back to my office, I replayed the conversation with Pardoe, turning it this way and that, trying work out what I knew were the multiple levels of meaning in the meeting. Before I had gotten back to the Russell Office Building I had decided to call Maggie. This would be a peace-making move, and the sort of thing she was good at. She would see the undercurrents and appreciate being asked, and I wanted to see if her assessment matched mine.

She was out for lunch so I tried, without much success, to go back to work. At two I tried again, and she was in. As soon as I began to launch into the story I knew it would never work on the telephone.

"I'll pick you up at six. How about dinner at The Riggsby?" It was Maggie's favorite restaurant.

"My you do have an announcement." Her tone was warm. Maggie always responded positively when I turned to her for help. I often wondered whether it was because she was supportive, or felt stronger in this area and appreciated my acknowledgement of that fact.

The maître' d' at The Riggsby knew us both, and saw that we got a quiet table in what was arguably one of the most discrete restaurants in the city; discrete and subtle but very elegant.

Maggie ordered a rack of lamb, and I the salmon. I chose a 2006 Trinitas Cab for which I knew she had a particular fondness, although the price was ungodly, knowing she would see it as an offering.

We ate in silence for a while, and then I began to debrief, watching Maggie turning over in her mind what I was telling her.

"Deputy Assistant Secretary. Very nice. It's really a very nice touch, Arthur. You have been doing all that sea rise base closure and other stuff. Very nice. Defense is not what it used to be, of course, but it's better than Energy or Commerce for sure, and you're not qualified for State." I had to admit she was really good at this. "Pardoe is planting a time bomb. If the Democrats take over the White House and you find something, it will blow up after the change, if it happens. He clearly thinks it will. If there is no change, it will get quickly tucked away. Really quite brilliant."

Maggie ticked off her points with small movements of the fork in her left hand, then stopped to eat her arugula salad. "You must see," she said looking at me pointedly, "that he's paying for this. True, it's marginally in your area, and if you do well it will certainly give him a chance to earn credits that he can cash in later. But what intrigues me is why you, why now, and what is he paying? Pardoe's right about the timing by the way," she added almost as an aside.

That was exactly my question. I thought I knew the answer, but I wanted to tempt Maggie to go further.

"Why does Pardoe have to have an agenda about me? I've done a lot of good work for him, and he's right. I've been thinking about it. It is time for me to move."

"Arthur, you're the smartest analyst on the Senate side, probably the smartest analyst on the Hill, everyone knows that. Except when it comes to yourself and your own career, you can see patterns nobody else sees. Everybody knows that too. You're also militantly non-partisan, which makes you acceptable to the White House and Johnson, the SecDef. But, I assure you, Pardoe is not doing this out of the goodness of his heart. It may be though... Arthur you really must try this cheese," Maggie said, offering me a slice on a piece of apple. "It may be that you are partly right."

"Part."

"Yes. Maybe I'm wrong about the time bomb. Look at it this way. Pardoe may not have an immediate objective. He may be banking you. If the Administration wins you'll stay. If the White House changes hands you are low enough down and known to be absolutely non-partisan, so will probably stay. Either way, you're there, his seat is safe, he's there, and you owe Pardoe for getting you the job. Think about it. The job is within his gift because of some other arrangement he has, and he's relying on your earnest honesty... I think we deserve some Chateau d'Yeim don't you? They have it here," Maggie said rhetorically as she caught the eye of the sommelier, who hurried over.

After she finished the order she picked up her thought without missing a word. "Don't protest, Arthur, it would be absurd. Everyone who works with you knows that your strategy is to do your meticulous special magic without taking sides. Your tent has been pitched on the moral high ground for so long it has ivy growing up its sides."

I felt strangely exposed by her words, as I often did when Maggie was following her plot lines, particularly when it came to me and my career.

"Should I take it?"

"Of course you should take it, Arthur. You'll do fabulously and, four years from now, after you write a book… oh yes, you are going to write a book… they'll make you an Undersecretary, or maybe give you an agency. Now take me home and let me give you my body."

The next day, as Topher Kelly and I were outlining questions for a hearing, Rachel stopped by. I could see she was excited about something, and I tried to bring the meeting to a close. Topher was mercifully sensitive, and excused himself as soon as he decently could. As soon as he was gone Rachel pulled some paper out of a brown government envelope and sat down.

"I've tracked down a Forest Ranger who was the first person to see this thing."

"Where is he?" I asked, and even to my own ear my tone sounded flat compared to Rachel's enthusiasm. She did not seem to notice though, carrying on under her own momentum.

"He's retired. His name is Frank Adams, and he's living with his son in Idaho."

"Wait a minute, Rachel," I said. She really looked at me for the first time, and her energy checked its momentum. "Adams made an initial statement; I've read it, and he's never varied from it over the years. According to him we're talking meteor." It was an attack and I realized it, even as the words were coming out. I found I could not make eye contact with Rachel, and moved some books and sat down in a chair in front of my leather couch.

"What's going on Arthur?" she said, her face flushing, accentuating its red tone. "Okay, maybe there's nothing here... but I don't think that's true. I think there is something, and when I called him on the telephone..."

"You called him?" I got up from my seat and closed the door that was still slightly ajar.

"You mean did I use your name or mention your committee?"

"Well I think..."

The telephone intruded and I walked back to my desk. "Hello. Arthur here... yes, no, that's fine Jan, I'll be there." I made a note on a yellow postit, then looked up at Rachel, who was examining me as if I were a specimen. I tried to make my voice neutral. "What did you say?"

"I used my own name, and I told him... what does it matter what I told him," Rachel was becoming angrier with each word, and she got up to leave.

"Sit down, sit down. Please, Rachel," I said, putting out my hand palm up. "I'm sorry, things have gotten very complicated for me suddenly."

Rachel went back to her seat and sat on its edge, waiting.

"I've been offered a job, Rachel. It's a significant appointment. It requires Senate confirmation."

Rachel's face immediately lit up. "Congratulations, Arthur."

"There's a catch. Well, not a catch actually, but... well, having UFOs surface in my life during my confirmation would not be a good move or appreciated by my sponsors." Instead of feeling good as I told Rachel this, I felt miserable. It sounded like such an obvious sell-out it did not even merit mentioning.

"Then drop it, Arthur," Rachel said with a genuineness that surprised me. I knew she was absolutely sincere.

"Look, Rachel." I was up again moving around my office, threading my way through piles of Congressional Records and stacks of brown and green bound proceedings of hearings. "If the people I work for don't give a damn about a nuclear or biological cover-up that happened 12 years ago, why should I?"

"You don't believe that, Arthur. But, even if you did, let me ask you another question: what if it isn't a nuclear or biological accident? What if Sturmont and Greenberg are correct?" Rachel cocked her head looking directly at me. It was the question I had been wrestling with since that afternoon in the courtroom. I really did not want to face it but I had to go where the data went. It has been my fundamental principle since I was 11 and reached down to pick poison ivy, only at the last minute really looking at it, and seeing the three-pointed leaves. Below even that, I realized, was my attraction to Rachel compounded by my confusion about my feelings for Maggie. That had started the night before when in the middle of making love I found myself looking down at Maggie's slightly opened mouth and passion relaxed face and wondering what Rachel would look like in this situation.

"I don't know... I don't know, Rachel." I must have looked as confused and miserable as I felt, because Rachel got up and walked across to where I stood by the window, standing close to me and looking up into my face. She put her hand on my arm and I was intensely aware of her touch. "Don't you think you should find out? I mean, is there a bigger story?"

"They'd hate it, but I could take some leave; God knows I have enough accumulated. We need to get past these hearings first, though."

I walked back and forth looking at her, "It would be a very serious job change and I need to think things through. I think taking time off after the hearings is the right move," I said as much to myself as Rachel, and realized I had reached a decision. Even as I said it, I felt better. At least it was an action I could take to give myself some time.

"I could take some leave too," Rachel said, coming close but turning her face away slightly not to have eye contact if I rejected her. "Do you want me to come?" she said.

I looked down at her and kissed her. Her body moved against me and she responded immediately. "Yes. But you need to know I'm in a strange space, a very strange place in my own mind. Suddenly everything is in flux."

"I know, I can see it in you. Arthur, we can keep this strictly professional. I don't want you to feel any pressure from me. You know where I am now, but I'm not in a relationship and you are. You need to do what your heart tells you to do."

"Thank you. That's one of the things I... that I am attracted to about you. Your patience and tolerance."

I walked across to my telephone and dialed the number of Jack Kazanjian, the Chief of Staff, all the while looking at Rachel. "Jack. Hi... This is Arthur, have you got a few minutes? At four. Okay. Four it is."

After I hung up Rachel said, "Your hearings are next week, Arthur. After they're over let's go to Idaho."

At 4 o'clock I walked into Kazanjian's office. We had once been close friends; Kazajian had brought me over from a staff job on the House side. But Kazajian, about four years older than me, was partisan and ambitious. Although he tried to hide it, even as he exploited my skills, he found my neutrality intensely irritating.

"How's Maggie?" Kazajian asked as I walked into his office. Much neater than my own, with Redskins memorabilia and federal traditional style, the way upper level government offices are supposed to look. Filled with culturally accepted totems.

"She's fine."

"What's up? Could you give us a moment, Topher?" this to Kelly who had stuck his head around the door, but who, after looking at me, quickly withdrew.

"Have you spoken to Senator Pardoe?" As soon as I said it a look passed across Kazajian's face that let me know he knew and realized what this conversation was going to be about. It ended with my asking for and Jack agreeing to my taking a month's leave as soon as I finished the hearings, maybe another week.

I was due the vacation anyway, so it wasn't a big ask; but just to make sure I didn't get too secure Jack made it clear with his tone that by taking time off now, he saw it as sliding "off the team" before leaving. I expected that but not what came next.

"We've gotten some inquiries about you from the NSA. Why would they be asking about you and your level of security clearance?" I told him I didn't know, but I was beginning to see a pattern. I was being watched.

CHAPTER NINE

I went down to the Senate cafeteria the next day and was reading the *Post* when Topher walked by me and said, "When you're done why don't you visit the Folger. Such a nice day." And then he walked on. It was very weird.

Two swallows and my coffee was finished. I got up, logged my tab, went out through the doors under the massive Capitol steps, and started towards the Library of Congress. As I turned up East Capitol I could see Topher ahead. He stopped at the Folger Library, perhaps the greatest Shakespeare collection in the world, and went in without looking behind to see if I were following. I thought 'My God I'm in a spy movie.' At the entrance I noticed they had an exhibit up on Shakespeare in America. There weren't many people; the Folger is beautiful but a bit off the beaten path. I could see Topher further down the exhibit hall and staying slightly behind him, we walked down the great hall looking at Theater broadsides from the 18th and 19th centuries, as well as other memorabilia about American theater and Shakespeare.

We both stopped in front of a display of 18th century theater costumes, and Topher very softly said, "What in the hell are you into Arthur? Yesterday I was helping Pardoe with that material he wanted, and he asked me to go the L'Enfant Club with him so he didn't have to wrestle with it. Have you ever been there? Of course you have. I must say I thought I was jaded, but walking into that room filled with the most powerful men in the West, if not the world, was a hit, for sure."

We moved further down the hall, seemingly without any connection between us, then stopped at an exhibit on John Wilkes Booth, where three nuns in traditional habits were looking at Booth's costumes. When the nuns moved on, Topher began again.

"Senator Pardoe and a thin older man had lunch," he continued while looking at a brochure in his hands, and up at the costumes. "You should have seen them in that clubby atmosphere, with those political paintings on the cream-colored walls," Toper said, then laughed. "As soon as Pardoe sat down they were hunched over like two medieval cardinals discussing what to do with Galileo. Everybody registered that they were there, but nobody paid any attention. There were half a dozen equally powerful meetings taking place, and it was only the first seating for lunch."

"It is a trip, isn't it?" I said. "What was the other man like?"

"Dressed in the uniform blue pinstripe wool of the senior Washington establishment. Very patrician. You could see his rank in the slight shabbiness of his custom shirt cuffs, and the shine on his bespoke trouser knees. He had an almost birdlike quality, the same supreme assurance and cool appraisal one sees in the grander hawks," Topher said very softly.

"Anyway, Pardoe called me over and told me to sit down. He began asking me for stuff from the briefcase I was carrying, and talking about it. They got into an argument and I heard part of the conversation before they thought about me. I just knew it had something to do with you."

"What did they say?" I asked as Topher began to move again. I waited until he settled before I moved. When I got near him he resumed his narrative.

"'There have been hundreds of these kinds of inquiries, George,' Pardoe says."

"'But not from the inside,' George says."

"'Inside, outside, what difference does it make?' Pardoe asked. Then he realized I was there."

"So that's all you heard?"

Topher continued as if I hadn't asked. "Then Pardoe called the waiter over and asked him to give me the table across the room."

"He told me, 'Topher you don't mind eating at another table, do you?'"

"I pulled out my phone and ear tabs and told him, 'Not at all Senator. I've got a book and music, I welcome the quiet. I appreciate you letting me eat here.'"

"'Not at all', he told me. 'Order anything you like; the filet is fine.'"

"I don't get it."

"You don't think I was listening to music, do you?"

"Ahh, yeah."

"Don't be an idiot, Arthur," Topher said in a harsh whisper. "I've got that hypersensitive listener app."

"I should have known. So what did you hear?"

"As soon as I was seated and apparently safely tucked away, the thin guy said, 'Don't be an idiot, John. This staffer of yours has security clearances. He has contacts. This isn't some tabloid reporter, or overheated zealot.'"

"You're right Topher, I am sure that's me they're talking about."

Topher laughed, then said, "I can tell you Pardoe, who's used to complete deference from everyone but the President, was stung by that man's tone as well as his words; but unless you knew him you wouldn't have seen a hint of it. Pardoe said, 'In any case he seems to be going down that well-worn conspiracy groove to Dayton and Wright-Patterson.'"

"'How do you know?'"

"'My Chief of staff. He's applied for a month's leave. And several people saw a pile of books in his office about Roswell and abductions.'"

"'What?'"

"'Now George, it will work to our advantage. No one will question when we move him over to Defense. I'm sure he'll take the job. Take the long view, George.'"

"The man still seemed agitated, so he said 'Listen to me George. I'm the senior member of the committee, I have kept this secret for 12 years, and it will not be broken on my watch. Am I clear?'"

"He got the point, and said, 'No one has ever challenged your clarity, John, least of all myself.' Then Pardoe walked over to my table touched me on the shoulder and I took my buds out. 'Let's go' he said. 'What are you listening to?' I handed him a bud and he got a shot of Jens Gad's *Glass Palace*. He could see the novel's pages on my screen." Topher gave me a serious look and said, "You want to tell me what's going on?"

"Topher," I told him, "I don't want to bring you into this. I'm not sure it is going to end well and if it blows up it will be messy for anyone in the loop. Just trust me for now, and help if I ask."

"Of course. We're going to need to set up a comm link."

"When did you go to spy school?" I asked because I realized there was a whole dimension to Topher I did not get at all. I knew he liked horse races. One of the reasons he had come down to Washington was because every day but one, I couldn't remember which, an operating track was within 50 miles. He made a tidy income betting, and I had heard he did some bookmaking for some members and staff. Topher's affect was prep school to Ivy League, but there was something else.

As if anticipating my thought, as we walked on into the next hall, he said, "My family lost their money in the savings & loan crisis. It killed my father, and we never recovered. I worked for the Lloyd B. Pelt Polygraph and Security Agency all through college and grad school before I came to the Hill and went to law school. That's how I paid for it. Go to the bathroom, I'm leaving. Wait a bit, leave from the other side. Let's meet tomorrow in the conference room behind the hearing chamber. I have files in there. Nobody will pay any attention to us and it's normal for you to be there, " he said and left.

I went into the head and took a leak, took my time washing my hands, and drying them in the air blaster, all the while processing what Topher had told me, and who he was. I think it was at that moment I knew this was not about a meteor or a satellite, and that I really had gone through some kind of looking glass.

CHAPTER TEN

That night Maggie and I were scheduled to have dinner with Representative David Kagan and his wife Cynthia. Dave looked like the lumber jack he had been during summers at college, now in a suit and custom shirts. Almost everyone who appears on television has extra high collars, which means custom shirts. Clothes make the man they say, and to look at Dave I think that's true. He looks like a Congressman, like a guy you would see being interviewed on *Meet the Press*. Looking at him you would never know he is a post-Sanders social progressive who represents Oregon's 5th District.

We met coming back from Iraq. Both newly-minted captains, second tours and getting out. Not brothers as I was with my guys. That bond is created only amongst people who have been in situations where your life is at deadly risk, and your only protection is each other. But he had his version of it, and I knew it as he knew it of me. Doing something primal but controlled not once but over and over, losing a few along the way. That experience simply has to be lived, it cannot be really comprehended from the outside.

So if Dave wasn't exactly a brother he was certainly family. And when he came to the House two years ago, he found out I was on the other side and we reconnected. He was younger than me, 33, one of the youngest members. He had been his Democratic law firm's social action guy, and they made him a partner when he ran. He had to resign to come into office, but they would welcome him back anytime, and he knew it. We were now in different hierarchies and he outranked me, but that didn't matter. It wasn't our work that connected us anyway, although we did have some interaction. It was Iraq and the fact that Dave and Cynthia were hikers and backpackers like me, and Maggie sort of. The four of us had walked several parts of the Appalachian Trail together.

We met at a new Sushi bar on Wisconsin, and although everything started out okay it got a little rocky. In spite of what Pardoe was offering, Maggie still urged Dave to try to convince me to consider running. This was the decision moment and she knew it; I was going to make a move, the question was where. I realized that to Maggie running for the House was the better move.

Normally Dave fell in with Maggie's schemes, but not this time. It had been a bad day for him, and Dave complained about money instead. He had to spend up to four hours a day at the Democratic call center; members of congress are not allowed to call for money from government buildings so each party has a call center set up for that purpose.

"Dialing for dollars, $15,000 a day, that's what I have to raise. 'Hello Bill,'" he said acting out a call, 'thank you for putting together that $80,000 check, I really appreciate it and yes, of course, I haven't forgotten. I am working up a rider that should help with the water treatment plant your company wants to build...' It's whoring Arthur, whoring. Legal corruption. If I had known that up to half of my day would be tied up with raising money… I don't know…"

"You can go back to the law firm, honey. I've told you I would support you in that. They'll make you a senior partner now, and they'll call you Congressman. It would be a lot more money, and we could go home," Cynthia said. It was clear she too was having second thoughts about Washington.

But the real turd in the punchbowl showed up on the way home when as we were just coming into Georgetown. Maggie turned and said to me, "I think you better take me to my place Arthur."

I turned on Q Street rather than continuing down to M and pulled up in front the building where Maggie's flat was on the second floor. For once I found a parking space and was about to get out, when Maggie put her arm on mine, saying, "Let's talk a minute." Not a good sign.

"What's going on Maggie?"

"That's what I'd like to ask you. You have said hardly anything about what you are planning to do when you take this time off to think about what Pardoe is offering. In spite of what Dave said tonight I still think you should think about Congress. Dave just had a bad day." Then, and I saw it coming, "What are you planning to do?"

"I don't know exactly," I lied, "but I think it's time for a backpack. I thought I would drive over to West Virginia and hike into some trout streams."

"Alone? No delete that. Arthur, I really care for you," Maggie said as we sat there in the car in the dark, not touching. "But these past few months I just sense we aren't moving in synch. Your obvious attraction to Rachel Carter, I know, is part of it, but not the main part. I could work with a Rachel phase," Maggie said, and put her hand on my knee, "but this fascination you have developed for a subject that can do you no earthly good and could inflict considerable harm, I do not understand. And cannot work with."

She turned to face me and went on, "I think we should take a hiatus. A timeout. You go off and do whatever it is you think you have to do, with whomever you feel you have to do it... don't bother to comment... and figure out what it is you want to do with your life. Then I can decide whether I want to sign up. You understand?" Maggie leaned over and gave me a kiss, opened the door and was out before I had fully taken aboard what she had said. There it was, though, and I realized I was at a crossroads with her.

I went home, got out the bug gadget that puts out nitrogen and eats mosquitos, got a folding teak boat chair, and went down to the canal and over the bridge to sit in the dark on the bank of the Potomac. I set up the chair, turned on the mosquito eating gadget, and just settled into nature's quiet, which isn't really quiet. I love the night music of woods and water. The bass line of the frogs, the thrum of cicada, night bird calls, and the sound of flowing water moving around rocks and fallen trees. And just a bit further out the burbling sound of the river's rapids rushing over the rocks that gave the canal its reason for being.

There was a change in the sound of the water, so I got up and walked to the edge of the trees overlooking the river. A group of fish were leaping in the rapids. It was nearly a full moon and its brightness left the trees on the distant bank in sharp silhouette, and splashed a line of light across the rock-filled water. After a moment I went back and sat in the darkness entirely alone. I had no concern about being interrupted; camping along the canal's entire 184-mile length is only permitted in designated campsites and the nearest was four miles either way. To be this private in nature, this close to a city, was one of the great things about my cottage.

I thought about Pardoe, Maggie, Topher. My reason for coming to Washington. Whether I had any responsibility to act on the information I was now convinced suggested something the government obviously wanted very much to keep secret. The more I thought about it, the more I thought that if the evidence was just bits of debris, that would be manageable. There had to be something else. What could it be but an extra-terrestrial being? That was fascinating, but was it my business? I considered just leaking the information to my friend Stan Issacs at the Post, but in the end decided that would just end up in a muddle. Finally about one a.m., still not certain what to do, I got up, took things back and went to bed.

That night I had the first dream, although I didn't recognize it at the time. In the dream I was meditating on my cottage terrace, and as I sat there, as I do almost every nice day, I had the feeling someone I didn't know was trying to contact me. It never quite jelled, but it left me with a strong sense of urgency.

Topher and I met the next afternoon in the conference room. We were pretty sure it was not being audited because this was where the committee met. I couldn't believe I was suddenly thinking about things like that. But I was, although I wasn't quite sure why.

We did business on the hearing, then without breaking the rhythm of his speech Topher said, "I have pretty good idea of what you're doing Arthur," and then laid it out quite accurately.

"How do you know this?"

"Peter Sturmont taught my honors physics course. He recruited me."

"Why do I suddenly feel this is dangerous, Topher?"

"Because it is. This is probably the biggest secret there is, if you think about it. What would it do to the psyche of humanity if there was suddenly clear and incontrovertible living evidence that there was other life in the universe, and it was more advanced than we were, so advanced we could hardly imagine it? How would religion, any religion handle that? If you went looking for this being and found him, and made him known, it would destabilize the whole world more than a nuclear bomb. A picture of Arthur and whosit walking down the street past a Bank of America. Think that video clip would go viral?"

We were interrupted as a page shot through the room on some Senator's errand. When he had crossed into the committee room, Topher began again, "Maybe Rachel Maddow could interview your friend. You see the point. People are not going to let that happen. That's why they tried to buy you off; surely you've thought of that. Promote him, he's due anyway, and he'll go away. Greed and ambition are pretty sure bets in our world," Topher said with a laugh.

"How did you work it out?" I asked Topher. Was I that transparent? I just didn't know what to do with that, and put it away for the moment. "Topher," I told him," I don't know what, or when, or even if, I need your help, if I do…"

"You'll have it. Now let's talk about communications. It is known that we know each other so I am going to assume I will be watched. You know I like horses."

"So I hear," I said.

"Lovely animals. The whole ritual is so mannered, and yet underneath it's as raw as a crap game on a ghetto corner. I love it."

"I'm not sure I follow."

"I go out to the track with a guy named Drugstore Carl. He's an Uber driver. I walk down to Union Terminal and along the way he picks me up. Anyway here's his number," he said, handing me a piece of paper. "Memorize it then destroy it. If you need me, call and say you want to reserve a pickup in the name of Dr. Williams and leave a number. You're going to have to use pre-paids, change them every week, and even then keep their batteries out when you're not using them. I assume you are going to try to find this being. I urge you to maintain appearances. You have leave; don't say anything else to anybody. The group will try to help you when we can." He put out his hand, and I shook it, then we hugged. "What are you telling people?" he asked.

As Topher straightened up the papers I explained my backpacking story to consider the job offer and to take a break before beginning the next chapter. "That's good," he said, and I left.

I went back to my office and looked around. Picked some things up and put them away. Put some special things in my backpack, then took them out, and put them back. Would I ever be back; I was no longer sure. That night I had the strange dream again of someone trying to contact me. But once again I couldn't make sense of it. It woke me at 3 in the morning and left me feeling very frustrated.

The next morning I called Rachel and told her about the dream and my conversation with Topher, and told her I didn't have any right to ask but was asking anyway: did she want to come with me?

"Of course," was all she said. When I hung up I wondered if my line was tapped. It's very weird trying to live like that.

CHAPTER ELEVEN

Two days after the hearings ended, Rachel and I caught a plane and flew with two stops to Kalispell, Montana. We rented a car and drove a little ways down the street, then I pulled over and took out the fuse that controlled the GPS.

"Take the battery card out of your phone," I told Rachel, as I removed it from my own. "I'm sure there is probably another way to track us, but we won't make it easy." I reached in my kit bag and brought out paper maps. "Some days the old ways are the best. Can you navigate?"

"Of course, you bozo," Rachel said, taking the maps from my hands.

Our first stop was the Airbnb we had reserved and checked in. It was on the outskirts of town, down in the flats between mountains. Then we got on highway 35 and headed out towards the mountains, turning on Swann Highway, State 83.

"That's Swan Lake," Rachel told me from the passenger seat. I had never been to Montana before and had no idea there were large bodies of water in this country I associated with cowboys. "Swan Lake," I said, and we both laughed.

"Go another two miles and we should be there," she said, looking up from the map. She was adorable.

Our destination turned out to be a tan-colored double-wide manufactured home with white trim on the lake's edge. There was a small dock sticking out into the lake alongside of which was moored a runabout covered with canvas. There were two Ford pickups in the yard. I pulled in off to one side so as not to block them.

"This is the firefighter who was first on the scene?" I asked.

"Yes."

As we got out of the car a young man in brown twill pants, a green-brown wool bush shirt, and what were obviously working cowboy boots, came out from the house. He looked suspicious but civil.

"I'm Pat Adams, Frank's son. You're the people from Washington, right?"

I introduced myself and Rachel, and he gestured for us to go inside, opening the white aluminum screen door.

We went directly into the living room as Pat told us, "Dad has a terminal lung condition. He's doing pretty well this morning so we better do this while he's able to." Frank Adams, the man we had arranged to meet, sat leaning back in a puffy tan leather Barcalounger with an oxygen clip in his nose, and tubing snaking down to the tank next to his chair. He must once have been enormous, but was now a shrunken hulk obviously too short of breath to get up. Pat pointed to the matching couch and we sat there for a moment without anyone speaking. Frank just looked at us for a disquietingly long time. At first he told us in halting sentences that he had said everything he knew years earlier. But as he said this he exchanged a look with his son, then was suddenly wracked by a fit of coughing.

"You're gonna hafta leave," Pat said getting up. "He just can't do it. His lungs were damaged in the fire and something he breathed, although no one will admit that, and we had to go to court to get full disability." You could tell it still rankled. There really wasn't any choice so I gave him the number where we were staying, told him our mobiles weren't working well, said goodbye, and we drove off feeling the whole trip had been a failure.

We went to Hops Grill, which Trip Advisor said was the best restaurant around, to cheer ourselves up, then went back to the little guest suite. About 10:30 we got a call. It was Pat. His father asked us to return the next morning. He had something he wanted to say.

We got up early and had a very credible breakfast at a kind of early 20th century diner. I didn't know they served grits in Montana. Then drove out as we had the day before. This time we found Frank in bed in an oxygen tent. His breathing was easier, but it was obvious he was dying. God what an awful way to go, I thought, slowly suffocating. As soon as I had the video recorder set up, without preamble Frank began. As he talked I could see relief flooding through him. It was a story long suppressed, and as he continued his body relaxed and his breathing got easier.

"It was smaller than I would have thought. A frame of a metal I couldn't recognize, covered by a silvery kind of thick foil. There was a funny kind of writing glowing pink and lavender on some of it. It was incredibly strong."

Rachel and I exchanged a look, and remembered Peter Sturmont.

"You couldn't tear it or punch through it. Hit it with an axe... nothing."

Frank paused and asked for a drink. Pat passed a thermal glass with a straw to his father, who took a drink before handing it back.

"The craft apparently had lost control in the air for some reason, and ploughed into the ground. The impact split it open, and there were three bodies on the ground. How they piloted the thing in the first place, I never could figure out. There were no instruments of any kind that I could tell. Nothing but the bodies and a few grey cubes, like hematite, scattered on the ground. When we got there a group of graduate students in archaeology working on an Indian site were riding up. It was a time when security was high because of fires. I had a crew of four guys. It was just chance that we were on the road when we saw it hit. We got there just in time to see a fourth one of them staggering away from the wreckage.

"They were all small, like a young boy, say 10...11 years old; about as big as my youngest son was then. Whatever it was, it was stunned. There was something in the air, that's what's wrong with me now. We caught him, although I can't really say it was a him. Anyway, I threw my jacket over its head. We handcuffed it and put it in the back of the truck." I could see Frank was reliving the experience and for a moment just watched as he was silent.

"Protocol... we had to do it," he said, then shifted his body a bit and went on. "That same night they sent us back, didn't want many people to be involved, and we picked up the debris. In the carpentry shop we built three child-sized coffins from marine grade one-inch plywood. By then there were several teams going over everything. Just as dawn was breaking, the wreckage, the bodies, those cubes, and the fourth one were flown out by C-130."

Frank looked up at me. "I have decided to tell this to you because I'm going to die. I know that. I accept it. It's not going to be very long. You can see it," he said running his hand down his body. "Didn't think it was right to take it to my grave. I prayed about it last night and decided to tell you."

By then Frank was clearly running out of energy, and his breathing was getting bad again. Pat suggested we leave, and we said goodbye and went down the hall following Pat into the kitchen.

"Lemme make you some coffee," he said, making it clear that he had something he wanted to say, now that his father had opened up. As we drank his coffee he told us about the security people coming to the house and taking away a few scraps of the craft which his father had kept, then assembling everyone in the living room and making them swear that they would never tell anyone about what they had seen and done, or they would be arrested for endangering national security. "'It is an urgent matter of national security,' that's exactly what they said and what can I say, we're Forest Rangers. My grandfather was a ranger in this forest. I'm a vet, my dad's a vet, we're government people, who take oaths. What could we say, of course we all agreed."

"I understand," I admitted. "I would have done the same," and I meant it. Topher's comment came back into my mind. We sat in silence for long moment. By now it was late afternoon. I was stunned by what I had heard and I could tell Rachel was as well. She caught my eye; it was time to go. I looked at my watch, said as much. As if on cue, we all stood up. We thanked Pat, asked to stick our heads in with Frank to say goodbye again, but when we went back down the hall he was asleep.

Standing on the porch of his home, Pat told us, "My father is an honest patriotic man. I guess he just came to feel this secret was wrong." He handed me an old dog-eared small address book. "They kept in touch, not often, but enough. They shared that experience, and there was no one else to talk to. Here are the numbers. I don't know whether they will talk though, or even if they are alive. I know everyone in Dad's crew, beginning about six years after the event, came down with some kind of lung disease. Nobody can figure it out; we've been to all kinds of doctors. They're all dying from it," he told us, his face flinching with anger.

Inside the little book were the names and addresses of the men we had tried to find earlier, the ranger crew no one could identify. Most names were crossed off, apparently dead, but three remained. That night in the Airbnb, I had the dream again. This time I could almost make out the words, only they weren't really like words, more like thoughts.

For the next week Rachel and I tracked down those people, one by one. One wouldn't speak, still bound by his oath. Two, Roger Owens, now living with his daughter's family in Pine Island Florida, and Jim Hammeroff, living in a Baptist eldercare facility in the Montana state capital, Helena, upon being told that Frank had talked to us, agreed to meet. Both seemed to have been almost waiting for someone like me, someone not a flake, a person who understood the government and who would listen. And Rachel in her special way, and because she explained she was both an engineer and an archivist, gave them a kind of nurturing support that made them feel comfortable about what they were doing. Like Frank Adams they had come to the decision that they could not die without passing on the story of their experience. We saw Roger first and he described for Rachel and me the packing of the bodies, and gave more details about the one alien who still lived. Jim confirmed all of this, and we now had a pretty good sense of what had taken place 12 years earlier.

Perhaps the most important thing we learned from all this came in that last interview. Jim had the name of one of the physicians who went with the alien. He had driven up as they were packing out, and needed help getting from the staging area to where the alien was. When they asked him why there seemed to be so few people, he told them that a decision had been made to keep personnel to a minimum. "We were told by the doctor, 'If there is a problem, whether it is information or bacteria, it will be contained.' In talking about it later, we figured fewer of us they would have to shoot to keep the secret," Jim said with a sardonic laugh.

And that was how we came to Carlos Menendez, who had officially been with NIH though seconded to an Army lab to develop techniques for manipulating DNA. He had a medical degree from Johns Hopkins and board certification in internal medicine, as well as a PhD in Neurophysiology with a specialty in DNA. A very accomplished guy. When I saw him, Rachel didn't go with me. He was in a special unit ward in the NIH hospital in Bethesda, Maryland, dying from a virus that had started two years earlier as nothing much but now didn't respond to anything.

To get into the room I had to suit up and use a respirator. I only got in because I had them tell him the names of the men we had talked to. Then he requested that I come in. He was about 60, and once must have been a handsome guy. Because his situation was different I didn't know whether his problem had anything to do with Montana. He didn't either, and told me he wasn't at the crash site anywhere near as long as the Rangers. I suppose we will never know. But I was struck by the fact that every one of those original guys we could track down seemed to have major health problems. I was surprised no one had picked this pattern up, or perhaps they had. These men now lived scattered all over the country, and had been for years. You wouldn't normally think to put them together. And if the goal was to keep it all secret, you'd see that no one drew attention to the thing they had in common.

Our interview was only about 20 minutes; that was all he could do before the nurses signaled his monitors were going off and I had to leave. But I had tried to be smart, so at the beginning I told him I knew the story at the crash site and he didn't have to tell me that. I sketched in a few highpoints to convince him, and told him what I wanted to know was where they took the alien. Like the others he was very clear that he was only talking because he had decided it was better to do so than die with the information.

Carlos had worked on the research team from that first contact, although he had never seen the alien again. He had been taken first to a holding site and, as soon as it could be built, a permanent venue. He worked on readouts of tissue and body fluid samples first from the alien corpses, which he did work on, and then the sensor feeds from the alien who was still alive. Then two years ago, he said, "I began to physically deteriorate, and three months later had to leave the project. I don't know what happened after that, but I am sure Blue Room still exists." That was the core of the core of the secret, he said. As I thanked him and looked down at his wasted body, I knew I would never see him again, and was lucky to have gotten to him before he died.

He told me the original research facility to which the alien was taken was Area 51 in Nevada. As he said it I thought, wow it's really true; this was a secret hiding in plain sight but so discredited as to be a cult belief. He told me the new facility was code-named "Blue Room," and when it was moved it was transferred over to the control of the Department of the Interior as a detached special unit, ostensibly under the control of the National Institutes of Health. "But it will show up nowhere in any paperwork," Carlos said. He also told me as I was leaving, "Knowing this is dangerous." I turned back to him, and he added, "This secret is not a gift, but you asked."

"Yeah, I get that," I said as I left his room.

I drove back from that interview with Carlos severely conflicted. What do I do, I thought, knowing that an obviously highly evolved alien being was alive on earth and being held in what must surely seem to it some kind of prison? I didn't really know how to process that at so many levels. Did I have an ethical responsibility to act in some way, was the next thought to assail me. I mean, what could I do? What could Rachel do?

She was waiting as I pulled up in front of her apartment and picked her up. She was coming out for the weekend, and we began debriefing each other as were driving up River Road, when out of a side road a UPS van almost smashed dead into us. It was such a close call we were sweating when it was over. The whole alien business disappeared for moment.

That night we realized we were going to be life partners, and that required complete honesty.

After making love, we sat naked on the bed. I was looking at her beautiful breasts, lost in a kind of erotic haze, when Rachel asked me, "Have you ever taken out a Black woman before, Arthur?"

"No. I have Black buddies from the Army I see as brothers, but I have never taken out a Black woman."

"We're challenging."

"I get that, but you are mixed race. Your beauty is a distillation of a lot of things."

"Yes. Native American, Asian, African, and Scottish. But to Whites that just translates to Black."

"How do you know all that?" I asked.

"DNA. Until recently if you were Black, things like your family's past used to be closed to you. You could only go back so far. They deliberately mixed the African tribal groups up when they brought us to America. They didn't want too many from the same group to be together. They might rebel. But now with the DNA... I did the mouth swab thing, and learned where my people had come from in Africa, and all the rest of it. That got me interested, and I had the Library of Congress available to me," Rachel said, looking at me.

"I started with my granny's stories, and about three years ago I dug in." She slid down and rested her head on my thigh and looked up at me. "My Scottish great great grandfather raped my great great grandmother, whom he owned. She was herself mixed race, a house servant living on his plantation along the James River in Virginia. She must have been pretty because he raped her repeatedly we know from his diary. He didn't see it as rape of course. She had a son. When he was in his teens not long before the civil war his father got into some kind of financial trouble and sold him and others to a tobacco plantation in LaPlata, Maryland. He ran away during the war, and because he was literate he could join the Union Army. After the war he went out West and was a Buffalo soldier, part of the Black cavalry. He took an Apache woman as his partner. Their first child was a girl; she was born on a buffalo robe on a Tipi floor, and she was my grandmother."

Rachel's mother was a teacher, and a single mother. They were very close, she told me. "There were just the two of us, and she was only 22 when I was born. School was the key; we understood that. I went to Colorado State, then MIT for engineering, and finally Harvard for my PhD. I have been working in the library for three years and I love it. What about you?"

So I told her about myself, going to a boy's school, then Chapel Hill, Georgetown and Yale. The war. How that got me interested in the environment, how I got to Congress. I told her the truth. I told her my fears, things I had never told Maggie. I told her why I worked as I did. I told her about Maggie. I was completely candid, and as we wound down, and lay back in each other's arms, I was very glad we had done this.

Early the next morning about 3:30 Rachel and I were awakened by my mobile. It was Moshe Greenberg calling from Zurich. He had just been called and told that Sturmont's house had been burglarized in the night, and he had been killed in what was being described as a robbery gone wrong. All very ordinary in a tragic age, even down to his missing briefcase and the floor vault which was blown. Except that Greenberg was having none of it and was alarmed. "When I was a young man I survived the Stasi by trusting my gut. It is very unscientific, but I am alive. There has been a kind of truce. We looked, they lied, we did not push too hard. The weirdness of the idea was its best protection. You are different. I think the truce has been broken. I had a pre-arranged exit door, and I have taken it. I think I would go someplace quietly, Michael, and I would do it quickly. I am telling you this, even though I know it is almost certainly being recorded." And with that he hung up.

It gave me a thrill of alarm. Everything was suddenly the same, but different. I knew he was right. Rachel and I had to leave Washington immediately. The decision was instinctive and easy. The question of how to do that, and where to go was not. What do you do in a surveillance age when you feel you must both run and hide?

I explained the situation to Rachel, who had heard only my side of the conversation. She agreed.

"Our lives just changed forever, Arthur. You realize that?"

"Yes. And I am not sure where our new lives are going."

CHAPTER TWELVE

After a minute of just lying in the dark with that realization we sat up and began to plan. "We must assume that all electronic transactions will be monitored. We have to get cash immediately. I have about $50 with me. You can get only so much out of an ATM, and you leave a trail," Rachel said, as she thought through what we were facing.

"Maybe I can solve that. Maybe."

We agreed that we had to assume that the powers of the government would be used against us. Flying would be too great a risk. Bus stations are small and easily patrolled. Trains seemed out of the question. There are cameras everywhere. I was sure our pictures were now in the system.

There we sat nude in the bed, with the covers around us as the first light of dawn eased the darkness. It never occurred to either of us to turn on a light.

"What about cars?" Rachel asked me. "We can't take your car."

"No. I'll drive it to the nearest long-term storage lot and catch an Uber back."

"The only way to do it would be to get an anonymous car. But again there are just too many cameras, I think," she told me.

"Yeah, I can see that," I responded.

"In any case, how could we get a car, one that could not be traced to us through rental or ownership? We're not going to steal a car."

"No."

"Okay. Cars are out," Rachel said. "But then what?"

I had been thinking about that. "Bikes. We'll bike up the canal. Who pays attention to backpackers and bikers on a canal path that is a national historical park? Who would even think of it?"

We dressed quickly. I drove the Tesla to the long-term lot, parked and waited for an Uber driver in a Prius who, as he told me, was a contract pharmacist when he wasn't driving.

By this time Rachel was laying out breakfast. There was no point starting on an empty stomach. She quickly toasted two bagels and put cream cheese, chopped onion, tomato, and capers on each half, and sprinkled it with dill. We didn't even sit down, just kept moving restlessly around the room pulling out things to pack as we ate.

"Do you have two bikes?" she asked, and I told her I did. When we finished, it only took a few minutes to clean up, and we went back upstairs. I realized that once you start down a path like this, like everything else the secret to success is in the prep, and we began working out how we were going to do it.

Rachel only had a little bag of clothes for the weekend, but there were things of mine she could wear. Luckily she had brought her hiking boots because we had planned to walk the canal. Her training shoes would work fine for biking.

I went into my closet and pulled out my daypack and two interior frame Balto backpacks. As I held them in my hands I was flooded with memories of what was ending, had to stop for a moment to let what we were doing sink in. At that point it seemed mostly negative. I got to thinking about our near crash. Could that have been anything beyond what it seemed? It was very hard to really comprehend that people might be trying to kill Rachel and me. But once again, in my mind I heard the urgency in Moshe's voice.

I looked over at Rachel and realized she was dealing with the same thing, then thought the best way to handle this was just to get on with the tasks in front of me. I went out to the big hall closet and brought out a poly cargo box where I had all my backpacking gear. There was some good news in this because most of the women I had dated did not have such gear, so I had two Therm-a-rest self-inflating sleeping pads and a second mummy bag. I pulled them out as well as my ultralight two-person tent. Rachel sat on the bed and watched me. Buried beneath the camping stuff was another cargo box with my Iraqi gear from my last tour and some old uniforms. Then I reached my hand underneath the shelf on which my boots and wellies sat. I moved a floorboard and reached in, taking out a green light canvas bag gathered at the neck.

"This is not a solution without its own problems, but I think I can see how to make this work," I told Rachel as I went back into the bedroom and handed her the bag.

"Oh, that's heavier than I thought it would be. What's in it, feels like thick playing cards."

"Open it."

Rachel looked in and pulled out what she saw was a black card in a bubble pak with "The Perth Mint" written in gold, and in the center a very elegant small gold ingot, with the mint's swan logo in gold and black, and the words "99.99% Pure Gold 1 Ounce."

"My savings plan to buy a cruising sailboat," I explained. "It may not make sense but it's the only way I have ever been able to save money. If it was cash or invested somewhere I know I'd be tempted to spend it or do something else with it. But gold is a whole scene in itself. It takes an effort to sell gold, and there are things you have to know... and I think I know where I can sell some," I said to her with a smile, and got a small one back.

We packed the bags, took them into the small carport next to the house, and strapped them on the panniers of the bikes. Side bags we loaded with the dried food I had left over from a week-long Appalachian Trail backpacking trip that never happened, as well as what was in the icebox. At the last minute, as I was locking up the house and closing the shutters as if I were on vacation, I went back in opened the back of my Mac desktop and took out the 1T hard drive, took my backup 3T drive, and got my Mac air. I think it was at that moment that I decided to keep the field log that has turned into this manuscript.

Once I understood that I was going to keep a record I knew I probably should take my small battery travel printer and our mobiles with the batteries out. This was all annoyingly bulky, but I planned to hide the drives where they would be safe and not be found. The Air and the microdrives I had gotten from John had everything. I was leaving nothing that would help find us. It felt very weird. As we mounted and pushed off, I looked back at the favorite place I had ever lived, with its picket fence and arbor of roses with the great wooden canal lock just beyond, and listened for a moment to the gentle murmur of water and wondered if I would ever see any of this again.

CHAPTER THIRTEEN

As Rachel and I pedaled up the towpath toward Harper's Ferry, I could see in my mind's eye what I conceived of as a van of a professional cleaning service arriving at my gatekeeper's cottage. I saw men dressed in mustard yellow jumpers and loaded down with equipment as they moved into my house. A variety of electronic and special lighting gear would show up. Finger print samples would be taken, placed on cards and filed. Closets would be tossed, air vents examined. Very calmly and methodically, the team would take my house apart. It took my breath away, and I realized once again my life was now going down a completely different path. I looked over at the canal, and the image of Maggie standing on the bank came into my mind, and I felt like we were pulling away in a boat leaving her. It was not distance but culture that now separated us. My career with Congress was over. I was not going to be a Deputy Assistant Secretary of Defense.

Rachel's voice brought me back, "Are you all right, Arthur?" and I realized I had fallen behind quite a distance. I caught up and we went at a steady but not attention gathering pace. At first there were a number of people on the towpath where the old mules and horses had trod pulling the canal boats; parts of the path are particularly popular. But by Marble Quarry there were only a few people. It was all very relaxed. People waved as we went by; we smiled and waved back. A day like any warm day along the C&O canal.

We stopped at Bald Eagle Island, and there was no one around. It was only about 4:30, but they only allow two tents per campsite, first come first served. So even though it was a little early I wanted to stop and think, fill up our water bottles at the old hand pump, and cook a meal down at the wooden picnic table that sat by the river. I've had the same little Optimus Svea stove since I was a Boy Scout; they're amazing little stoves, incredibly simple and sturdy. Checked its white gas, pumped it up and set it going.

I do not like discomfort, and women who aren't used to going into the woods don't either. I promise them they can wash their hair in hot water in the morning, and they do. It's easy with solar-heated water. I went over to the pump, filled the nylon bag with the larger thin plastic bag inside, and the stainless steel sauce pot. I laid the solar bag down where the sun would strike it in the morning, assuring us hot water by about 7:30. I put the pot on to boil and tore open a freeze-dried chicken entree. Rachel had made a salad in the other pot from stuff in the refrigerator, and we had a perfectly decent dinner.

After cleaning up we sat on the river bank and just looked at the Potomac for while, talked a bit and went to bed, both of us exhausted emotionally with what had happened.

It was mid-morning the next day by the time we got to Williamsport. I got out the small bag with the gold.

"Down that street and to the left is a guy who buys and sells gold. I got some of this from him. Nobody knows about this. He does it mostly online, but he has a cash trade too, mostly survivalists who don't want any records. People he doesn't know make him nervous, so go get a coffee and wait for me," I told her, adding, "There is nothing to draw attention in any of this."

I walked down through the old village, turned towards the big barn warehouse with Cushwa's Coal and Brick painted in white letters in a big black box. Just before I got to it I saw Daryl's gun shop. Daryl Meadows is a biker and a fanatical Second Amendment guy. I went into the small shop and Daryl was there reading the latest issue of *Guns and Ammo*. He had a biker leather vest, open over a T-shirt covered large gut, and an Afghan Vet baseball cap on. The reason Daryl would deal with me is because we had both been in Fallujah on my first tour. He was probably about 45 now, and there was grey in his bushy beard. He'd been an E-6.

"Hey, Daryl," I said as I walked in.

"Well, Lieutenant, what brings you here?"

I pulled out my bag and began to take out the Perth Mint ingots.

"You don't want to cash more than seven. Anything over $10,000 I have to report, and six ounces would be best," Daryl said. "I'm assuming you don't want any paperwork.

"You assume correctly, Daryl."

He offered me a washcloth and a bottle of alcohol.

"Wipe them down before you hand them to me. That way the only fingerprints will be mine."

"Do I look suspicious, Daryl?

"Lieutenant, you work at a job that pays you serious money. You wear suits. You have more than one bank account. People like you don't come into little gun shops in little Maryland villages early in the morning, dressed in what I take to be trekking gear, trying to sell gold for cash. Ya know what I mean."

I had to laugh, and he did too. I took the cloth, dampened it thoroughly with alcohol, wiped six of the little packets, and handed them to him.

"The going rate is $1,329.06 per ounce for Perth Mint ounces. I normally charge 15 percent for transactions like this, but for you 10 percent. I never saw you, and will have the video tape to prove you never came into the store."

"Blessings upon you, Daryl."

"So that's $7,974.36 minus 10 percent comes to $7176.92; I'm going to round it to $7177," he said, adding, "I'll be back in a minute," then went into the shop's back room. A few minutes later he came back with a brick of $20s, and reached into the cash register to finish it out.

"Hundreds draw too much attention," he said as he counted them out. "Nobody pays attention to $20s."

We broke the money into 18 little stacks, and Daryl put thick rubber bands around each one.

"That shouldn't be too bulky," he said. "Put one in your pocket, and the rest in your pack."

"It's a long story, Daryl…" I said.

"It always is," he said, finishing my sentence.

CHAPTER FOURTEEN

Two days later, when a couple coming the other way stopped, we fell into conversation, as you do. "We're coming down from Pittsburgh, and we just had the weirdest experience," the man told us. "There was a check point at Taylor's Landing. Have you ever heard of such a thing? I sure haven't."

"What was it about?" I asked, keeping my voice very level.

"They told us a trekker was somewhere on the trail and hadn't brought his phone, so they had set up a checkpoint. There was some kind of family emergency they said."

"Really serious," the blonde woman with him added. "You're not him are you?" I reached back into the side pocket of my pack and pulled out my phone, seeming to check just in case.

"Nope, nothing."

They finished filling their water bottles, and waving to us, were off.

As soon as they were gone we said at the same time, "We have to get off the towpath."

I looked at Rachel with what I hoped was a reassuring face and said, "I know somebody, about 50 miles from here."

We got off the towpath at Shepherdstown, West Virginia, and set out along the old highway, moving to smaller and smaller roads as we traveled into the West Virginia countryside. At a stoplight in a small town, I turned to see a television silently playing in a store window. It was a picture of my cottage with fire engines around it. A reporter in the foreground was doing a stand up, interviewing a man dressed in a mustard yellow jumper. I felt as if I had been stabbed in the chest; it was a physical pain that lasted several seconds. My mind was flooded with images of the cottage as I rolled past feeling suddenly vulnerable. One of the most special places in my life was gone. Then I realized and said aloud, "So is that life."

Rachel heard me, turned and saw the image.

"I'm so sorry, Arthur." We went on a little further then pulled over and got off our bikes and Rachel hugged me close, and we stood there in silence. But this was not the time, and we got back on our bikes starting off again.

By nightfall we were on Cacapon Road overlooking the valley where Berkeley Springs, a hot springs that was already famous in the time of George Washington, was located. In fact you can still see his tub. We pulled over into a heavily wooded area, private land, but well back from the road in a forest dense with pine trees. It had been a wonderful day in some ways and hellish in others. The good part carried us through setting up our tent, building a screen that hid everything from view. But, as we sat in the snug dark world of our nylon igloo, what we were doing began to overpower us again. Rachel shivered uncontrollably. Nowhere, in either of our plans, was there ever a scenario that saw us running away from our entire lives. Vacationing from them for a month perhaps, but not a wrenching permanent severance with everything familiar. I was overcome with guilt. I had gotten Rachel into this.

"No, Arthur, the choice was equally mine," she said. "What I don't understand is why anyone wants to kill us. Arrest us, sure, I can see that. Do you really think they killed Peter?"

"I don't know, but we should take Moshe very seriously. As to why, I have been thinking about that. Imagine this scenario: a senior analyst for the Senate Science Committee and a Senior Researcher from the Library of Congress hold a press conference and present the dying statements of Forest Rangers who were first on the site, as well as a fragment from the craft itself, analyzed by a prestigious independent lab, making the assertion that there is a secret facility where a living alien is being kept. What do you think the effect of that would have as it echoed out across the world?"

"Enormous. You're right. But Arthur, this is almost comical. Okay, what are our assets? You know about combat in urban and rural situations. We both know about camping. We're both in good physical shape. We're smart. And we might even get a few friends to help us. But what is that compared to the effort being made on the other side? I mean, I assume this is official, sanctioned."

"I don't know… I need to think," I said as we sat in the darkness. We had used no lighting once the sun was down.

"Okay, but you realize this could go on for years. I don't think I can do that," Rachel said.

"Neither could I. There is only one way out as far as I can see. I think we find the alien, then free it if that is possible," I said. After a pause, I added an idea that had just come to me. "We're in a kind of whistle blower situation."

After thinking about it for a minute, Rachel said, "You're right. Once we have the alien we could take him to any television station and we would be safe." Rachel gave me a smile and said, "Let's sleep on it and see how it feels in the morning."

We lay down next to each other; it was deeply silent, and so were we. As we were falling asleep, even though we were considerably back in the woods, we could hear a car go by. We were both awake in an instant. It seemed to stop and then back-up. Suddenly our tent seemed like a snare. We were trapped. But then we dimly heard voices and it drove on.

Early morning and we were on the road, dressed in the tight clothes of biking trekkers. Heads down. Not missing a beat, even as a Highway Patrol car went past us down the road. By mid-morning we came into Berkeley Springs.

For some reason I can't really explain, just something you learn in combat, I felt safe in the town. I tied a bandana around my head. I had a four-day beard, and sunglasses. Rachel also had a red and white bandana over which she wore a tan foldable canvas sun hat she had found in her pack. She had sunglasses as well. We looked like what we were, bike-trekkers. So common a sight in the small town as to be invisible. Even so we didn't stop there but kept going up the other side of the valley.

About two-thirds of the way up we came to a small roadhouse cantilevered out from the mountain cliff; a leftover from the 1930s, white with green shutters. We stopped for lunch and were served on an open balcony hanging out over the valley, we were the only table at that moment. A dish of the house Welsh Rarebit over homemade bread, "based on Mr. Jefferson's own recipe," the owner assured us, a glass of modest wine, and a salad of local greens with shredded chicken and almonds. It made a wonderful meal. We talked about ourselves, what we had gotten into, and what it could mean. By the time the meal was over we had a purpose. We would stop running and only reacting. Although we had talked about it earlier, it was at that lunch I think that we really committed to finding and releasing the being from the spacecraft. The bizarreness of the whole idea made Rachel giggle, and I, infected by her gaiety, began to laugh as well. The owner looked over and just saw two people in love, which was true. Once we got outside I took the map from my vest pocket, and we knelt and laid it out on the ground.

"We must get further away faster, and I think I know how we can do that."

Another five miles of hard pedaling and we pulled off the road and wound down a dirt fire road, up and down and around the mountain. We cycled past a shed with a pickup and a jeep, then into the yard of the home of Quinton Reynolds, an uncle of an earlier girlfriend, and Paul Liu, his partner. The house was part stonework from the colonial period, and part modern structure of stone and wood, elegant architecture, but almost monastic. We hadn't seen each other in several years because Quinton's niece and I had broken up shortly after the last time we had visited him. He and Paul were not survivalists or old hippies, they just lived the way they chose to live.

Twenty-five years earlier Quinton had been a very successful banker in New York at a boutique bank. He was the bank's number two, but he was a homosexual and not hidden about it, and they told him he would never be number one. So he took his considerable money and left. We had liked each other from the moment we met, and I just had a feeling Quinton and Paul could and would help. As we pulled up Quinton came out. It was amazing; except for grayer hair, which he still wore close-cropped, he looked unchanged: handsome, tanned, with a runner's lean muscles, austere, and sardonic. He wore khaki shorts and what was obviously once a custom-made white dress shirt rolled to the elbows. As I saw him standing there, I knew I was going to tell him the whole story.

"Arthur, to what do we owe this honor?"

I introduced Rachel, and he waved us in. It was as if we had talked last week. We went into a house almost academic in its attention to off-the-grid technology, and were met by Paul. He was Chinese, born in Hong Kong if I remembered correctly, in his late 50s, and about 10 years younger than Quinton. He had been some kind of floor trader at the bank, I think. He had on an apron.

We exchanged a hug and he said, "We've been picking berries," his gentle face breaking into a smile. "Now I'm making jam. Quinton has really done well with the strawberries, and the currants are splendid."

I introduced him to Rachel, and I could see them connect.

"Give me a minute to shift gears," Paul said, "and I'll put a lunch together. We'll eat out on the deck."

We went through the house. Not a single rug, lots of books, some very fine paintings and paper art, exquisite displayed silver, and antique Biedermeier and 19th century Swedish birch furniture. Quinton led us into the living room, a mix of modern leather sofa and matching chairs with the antiques. Through the windows lay their gardens, both flower and produce. I was struck once again by the sense of harmony they had achieved. Nothing was flashy, everything fit elegantly together, and the result was welcoming and relaxing.

Quinton made us gin and tonics, and I remembered they grew two trees in their green house, one lime, one lemon.

With drinks in hand we went out onto the terrace, where we sat down looking out across their small lake. I remembered it meant more than visual beauty. As such things were in the 14th century, the lake was also a fish stock pond. The Appalachian forest lay beyond. To the right I could see the raised, double-dug biodynamic organic mixed vegetable and flower beds of the garden, the orchard beyond on that side, and next to it chickens bobbed and weaved. Ducks swam on the pond and had a little house out on an island that kept them safe from predators. On the other side was the burbling of a lively stream where they had put a low-head hydrodynamic generator. There was a wind generator and solar panels on stalks standing in the field beyond the gardens, like sculptures. They opened like flowers following the sun, I remembered.

All of it allowed them to live entirely off the grid yet fully supplied with the latest technology. Paul had freezers of produce, home baked goods, and meat. They lived entirely on their own terms in the middle of 300 acres of personal forest, surrounded by a national forest.

After a few minutes of small talk, Quinton looked at me, and said, "What's going on? At first I thought you were just on one of your treks, with the lovely Rachel, but I can see that's not it."

Paul had come out of the kitchen by then, holding a tray with a big artichoke salad, some cold smoked trout from the pond, and a chilled bottle of Chenin Blanc.

After just sitting for a moment, thinking about where to start, I let out a puff of breath and began at the beginning, talking all through lunch with Rachel occasionally adding things. Both Quinton and Paul paid close attention to all of it.

When I finally ran down, Quinton said, "Stay here a few days. Things will calm down. You can reassess. I agree with you; the best course of action is to get this alien being, whatever, whoever it is. But have you considered that it might require some special environment?"

Rachel and I looked at each other. "We have not," I admitted.

Leaning towards us, Quinton said, "Well you've got the digital record of the people you interviewed; watch it again. Pay particular attention to what they say about the ET, particularly the doctor. You need to consider that aspect. How are you going to keep this being alive once you free him?" Rachel and I looked at each other and knew he was right.

We ended up staying there for five days. Using the circuitous route Rachel's cousin had given us, I made contact with him and Topher, requesting any refinement they could make to the directions given to me by Dr. Menendez.

When they got back to us, I felt we had as much as we were likely to get and it was time to move on.

I went to see Quinton in his library lined with books on economics, antique silver, 19th century furniture, poetry, biographies, and gardening. When I sat down he began without preamble, anticipating everything I was going to ask.

"You should take the old jeep. We rarely use it, it's innocuous," he said, handing me the keys. "It's licensed in West Virginia to a corporation I use for such things, that is linked to another corporation, and that to one in Turks & Cacaos. Even if anybody tried, and I doubt they would, it wouldn't be easy to trace. It can carry your bikes, has four-wheel drive and a short wheelbase."

"You might never get it back."

"Not a big deal. Your wellbeing is important to me and more than worth it." Quinton picked up an exquisite burgundy enamel and gold box, opened it, took out a vaporizer, drew in a hit and handed it to me. I did the same. We shared it a couple of more times, then he emptied it, putting it back in the box. When he turned back to me he said, "Arthur, I've made a shitload of money. I'm sure you probably guessed that when you were taking out Cynthia and used to come here, or she told you. But I assure you, you have no idea how much; I keep investing, and it just keeps growing. Paul does the same; he has his own wealth. You're going to get some of mine by the way. I decided that night before last, and Paul agrees. I wasn't going to tell you, but now I feel I should."

"I'm stunned. I had no expectation of that, Quinton."

"I know, that's the fun part about it," he said with a grin.

"Do you need money?" he asked. I got up took out my wallet and pulled out one of the little gold ingots in its card, handed it to him and sat back down. "I cashed $7,000 worth with a guy I knew from the service."

Quinton got up and walked over to a beautiful chestnut highboy and pulled open a drawer. He stood with his back to me then turned, walked over and handed me stacks of bills all neatly bound together with blue paper strips. "Here's seven more. It's all in used 20s, nobody notices 20s."

"That's what the guy I cashed the gold with told me. I get it," and as I took the stack of bills, realized $14K was not as bulky as I thought, just

700 bills. "I don't know what to say, Quinton. I mean, thank you, but it seems so inadequate."

He gestured with his hand, then pointed a finger at me. "I want you to leave me some way I can get in touch with you. It won't be often, it might be never, but I want the link, and I also want you to contact me through that link if you need anything."

He put his hand on my shoulder. "Take me seriously about this, Arthur." We both stood up and shook hands, then hugged. Just as we let go, Rachel and Paul came in, and after a beat Quinton continued our earlier conversation. "I think, and Paul agrees with me," he said looking up at Paul who nodded to me, "that you and Rachel are doing the right thing. Our civilization stands at a crossroads. It seems melodramatic to say that. But it's true. All my money was made being accurate about predicting things. And climate change is going to compel a fundamental alteration in the way we structure our societies. It's gonna be messy, and I am afraid very possibly extremely violent in some places. Fundamental changes always are. Why do you think Paul and I live as we do? Climate change? Financial bubbles? Love of solitude, two old Confucian warrior monks who are lovers. Probably a bit of all of that, who knows. But one thing is clear to me. We're on the precipice of massive change, and we need a shift of perspective. This business with the alien might do it. Suppose you could get this guy on television? Imagine what it would be like to watch a visitor from outer space speak to humanity. Do you think that might go viral… have an effect?"

We had a final dinner. It was quiet; nobody had much to say, and we went to bed. That night I had the dream again. Like the others I felt I was being called. I almost got some words, some thoughts, but not quite, and in the dream I was incredibly frustrated; a feeling that remained when I awoke.

We got up at dawn, were ready to go 20 minutes later, having packed the night before, and found Paul already up with eggs benedict coming off the stove.

With the bikes and gear loaded into the jeep, we all hugged. Paul said, "I think you two make an unusual but attractive couple, and it is going to take both of you working together to pull this off."

"Thank you, Paul, I think we know that," Rachel said, looking at me.

"We do," I agreed.

I got behind the wheel. Rachel pulled up our research on the computer, and we wound our way back into the world, with Quinton and Paul framed in the mirrors, arms around each other's shoulders watching us until we went around a bend and vanished from view.

CHAPTER FIFTEEN

We stopped at the end of the unpaved lane before going onto the narrow, paved county road.

"Which way did you work out?" I asked Rachel. She had been compiling everything we knew.

"Adding in what John and Topher found, I think the most likely place for the Blue Room would be a small government installation. It would almost have to be a freestanding kind of Camp David thing because if it were placed on a larger facility there would be a lot of people involved. In the course of time something this strange would be bound to leak out," she said, and I agreed with her.

"Whoa. I just found something; get us to a pay phone," Rachel said excitedly. So when I saw a small county park with an old-fashioned phone booth I pulled up in such a way that the jeep blocked anyone seeing into the booth. Rachel got out and opened the handset. Using alligator clips that I had gotten from Quinton's workshop, she unscrewed the handset and used the clips to link the computer to the telephone system. Watching her do it I could see Rachel was a much more skillful hacker than me.

Through a complex set of cut-outs John had taught her that made it very difficult to trace, she logged on to one of the computer networks. A highway patrol cruised through while we were doing this, then swung back around, making us violently nervous but unable to show it. I got out of the jeep and closed the door, hiding Rachel at her computer from view I thought, but wasn't sure. The trooper came back 20 minutes later headed the other way, and noticed we were still sitting there. I had the map spread out on the hood as he pulled over.

"Can I help you?" he said.

I told him we were supposed to rendezvous with another couple who were going to drive the jeep back while we took the bikes, and that our GPS went out. We were waiting for them, I said, and working out our route. He seemed satisfied, saw the bicycles, and drove off. This is a very weird way to live, I thought, and realized I was moving into the same mindset I had in Iraq and Afghanistan, a kind of hyper alertness.

Rachel finally surfaced from her search and told me that the largest concentration of possible government holdings that fit our profile were in the Sierras and the Ozark Mountains. For a number of reasons she leaned towards the Ozarks, near the town of Eureka, Arkansas. It was a little over 1,000 miles away.

What could have been done in 16 hours took us five days, staying entirely on the blue highways and sometimes fire roads, where the jeep really showed how right Quinton was that it would be an asset. As we drove through the countryside, helped by Topher and John, with whom we were twice in contact, we gradually worked out the most likely target: a research station carried on the government rolls as being run by the Department of the Interior, just as Carlos Menendez had told me. There was only one highway, only one way in or out, except by air. It was very isolated, yet a major military airport was within helicopter distance. We felt we were only going to get one shot at this. It had to be a single focus, and the one near Eureka was the one we decided on.

As we went along we also worked out what we thought we were up against: a kind of hybrid public-private hidden world. It operated using public money and facilities and personnel, almost all of whom we suspected had no idea what they were really involved in. The program, as we had come to call it, was so secret that in effect it was a committee-state within the larger federal state.

The helicopter access was one of the things that decided us on this location. If Senator Pardoe and his luncheon guest were amongst the small group running this, its high-ranking members could only afford small amounts of time away from their open schedule. We didn't think they would try to move the being to them because it raised the possibility of unwanted discovery to an unacceptable degree.

We assumed that whoever was pursuing us might figure out we had worked out where they were keeping the alien, and would try to stop us from getting there. We decided travelling by road in the jeep was too risky. We stopped in Little Rock and left it at a storage lot. We also purchased additional freeze-dried food, a compass, another set of binoculars, several camo rain ponchos, and a packet of 1:10,000 topographic maps. We didn't feel we could use GPS. It was camping as my father had done it before the digital world existed. A small bus line gave us a lift and took us, our bikes and gear to Eureka.

Using the topos we started out pedaling south down Arkansas Route 23 out of town and followed it for three hours of hard cycling up and down mountain switchbacks through a forest made up mostly of oak and hickory with a smaller percentage of conifers. Then following the map we turned into the woods at a trail head and cycled back into the forest for perhaps 10 more miles. We walked maybe an eighth of a mile off trail, dismantled the bikes and hid them between two camouflage rain ponchos, curled up the edges to keep them dry, then covered that with earth, branches and rocks. To fix our position we noted two large boulders next to a particularly ancient and grand oak tree, and I made a blaze mark on one of the root knees that would be unnoticeable unless you knew where to look. We put on our packs, lashing the bike panniers to them. It was heavy going as we walked off trail by compass.

At a clearing we could look into the valley and saw the buildings that were our goal. It looked like an old WPA camp, government green and brown wooden buildings. And it seemed absolutely peaceful. Parked in a gravel lot were two sedans and an SUV, all in the shades of green the government favors in the forests. It looked completely unexceptional. From backpacking and biking I knew that there were hundreds of places just like this scattered through the national forests. They were part of the government's belated climate remediation effort.

We set up our camp on a hillside overlooking the valley hidden behind a clump of oak and hickory trees, to which we added a screen of evergreen boughs and fallen oak and hickory branches We sat down with binoculars and looked across to observe at closer range what was going on, which wasn't much. Nothing in any way unusual; nothing that day or the next day, or the day after that. We became grubbier, and passed through the emotions of intense focus, boredom, crankiness, and settling in. Each day there was some slight activity, but very slight and very regular. We took turns working on the computer which we recharged with our little folding solar panel.

At 9 each morning the SUV with one or two men went down the road, presumably to town. At noon or a little after it returned, bringing mail and supplies, as we learned by watching what they took from the trunk. As we observed these mundane actions, it occurred to us both that viewed in another way, what we were doing was crazy.

At night we had no fire, just the little stove which I had put on a stone in a hole so there was no light. With my poncho I built a kind of hood for the laptop so I could do this log each night. But otherwise we sat in the dark with shafts of moonlight our only illumination, and on the fourth night we talked openly about our doubt.

"The truth is there is no evidence, and nothing but scattered accounts from obscure government reports and old men to support the idea that this is a base where an extra-terrestrial has been kept for more than a decade."

"That's true," Rachel responded. "What do you want to do?"

"Let's give it another two days. Then I don't know. Reassess… I guess."

The next morning, we decided to look at the buildings in another way, so we carefully moved through the forest up the valley until the buildings were long out of sight, then crossed over the valley and came back on the other side. I don't know, maybe it was the different angle of the light. When I looked through the glasses this time I "saw" the road, after looking at it for days.

With eyes now sensitized by hard miles up and down hills on a bicycle, I saw that the grade of the road was much too smooth, and thus too costly compared to the buildings, to be appropriate. It was also far too wide. Wide enough for an eighteen-wheel tractor-trailer. Using trees to block us from detection if they had cameras looking into the woods, we slowly worked our way back into the forest then made a long arc and came down near the road as far as possible from the camp. Through the binoculars we could now see that on the edges the tracks were there, eroded away, but even after almost 12 years the deep gouges of the heavy truck tires driving on not quite cured asphalt were softly visible. It made me much more confident that all of this was real and we were at the right place.

At the same time, I had begun to worry that knowing we were trying to find this place, whoever controlled it would have significantly increased security. That led to the first of several conversations Rachel and I had over how much longer we could stay here. We felt pretty comfortable that it would take serious searching to find us, unless they brought out dogs. But every hour here increased the risk of exposure.

Two days later, as Rachel was watching through her binoculars and I was searching something on the computer, a Department of Agriculture helicopter descended into the compound. I got my glasses and joined Rachel in time to recognize the face of the passenger, Senator John Pardoe. Only a few hours later he came out and the helicopter left. That was it. Our thinking focused now entirely on how to get into the compound and into the building.

That night I had another of the dreams. I was searching for a door and something in my head kept speaking to me, and this time I could almost understand it.

As we ate breakfast the next morning, we rehashed everything we had learned.

"Arthur, I think there are only a dozen or 15 people, I haven't seen all their faces clearly, ever present at this site, and at night there are considerably less," Rachel said. "The number seems surprisingly small to me if this is a working laboratory and a prison for a single being."

I had been thinking about that and responded, "Whatever could be learned from bodies or wreckage debris would have been completed by now, and would have been done elsewhere anyway, I would think. Maybe that was the tiny seed of truth that started the Area 51 meme," I said. As I did so I saw in my mind's eye Pardoe's face, and suddenly this whole compound stood in a different light.

"You know what I think this is, Rachel?" I asked her. "It's a kind of embassy in which the ambassador is also in prison. It reminds me of medieval London and the Tower. Kings were held there in the same way; remember James of Scotland? Elizabeth put Raleigh in the Tower. He wrote his *The Histories of the World* while he was there."

"And all they need is a small out-of-the-way environment that meets their prisoner-ambassador's needs," Rachel said. "A place a few people can come to very quietly."

"Exactly. But to do what? Consult? Suppose, Rachel they found a way to talk to this being, and they've made some kind of deal?"

"Yes, in which case the alien may not want to leave, and they certainly wouldn't want anyone to know about it," Rachel said.

We had worked out the routine. Aside from the car going into town and back each morning, there were only occasional visitors and deliveries. We settled on 13 people who seemed to be involved in maintaining the installation, with three living on site, but only five seem authorized to enter one of the buildings. That one, we felt, was the most likely place for the Blue Room. Through all this I was fretting that although the place seemed tranquil and unhurried, there almost certainly were elaborate surveillance and security arrangements in place. I was not at all sure we had the specialized knowledge to break into such a place. And once again, doubt emerged and my spirits sank.

For Rachel, though, this challenge allowed her to engage at a different level; it was a puzzle within her competence. The trees and mountains blocked microwave. And we saw only a television satellite dish. They were afraid to broadcast. To Rachel that suggested dedicated fiber optics. I knew government installations once set up tended to freeze in time, particularly highly secret ones. I had been appalled when I was doing research for a report and visited a ballistic missile site in Kansas where I discovered their computers were still using the original 8-inch floppies and drives installed in the early 1970s. I had never actually seen one before, only pictures. I explained this to Rachel and she said, "Then any communications is probably still in my area of expertise. Before I moved to the LC." We crept down along the road and she found what she was looking for: a small green metal stanchion that was a fiber optics node.

"I think I can do this," she said. "Everything is standardized. You're right by the way."

"About what?"

"The infrastructure being out-of-date. It hasn't been changed much since they installed it, and that's good, because this is a simple technology I know well. The new Nano and DNA stuff, I'd be out of my depth." As she spoke she continued to examine whatever was inside the stanchion.

"You'll have to go into town. I'll make up a list of things you need to get," she told me as we walked back up the hill into the forest. When we got back to camp she made up a list to which I added my own items, then printed it out on the PocketJet battery printer.

The next morning I got up at dawn and hiked back out, recovered and reassembled my bike, and rode back down Rt. 23 into Eureka Springs to get things.

I had my bandana on my head, ESS sunglasses, also a fairly significant beard and moustache, which Rachel loathed with real passion. "It's like kissing a brush," she said several times, but when I offered to shave it she said, "No, we have to be very rigorous about water, also it changes the way you look. I gotta believe they have pictures and facial profile data out on us. Please take great care," she said looking at me, holding my head in her hands, and then kissing me.

Even with my cleanest gear on I still looked like an old serious trekker who'd been on the road quite a while. It made me feel safe.

Eureka Springs, like Berkeley Springs in West Virginia, or Ashland in Oregon, is a 19th century town whose beauty and character have been preserved because of its hot springs. Each had the good fortune to have enough money to build at a time of good architecture, and the brick buildings of Eureka Springs were faced with heavily carved granite. Some had covered walkways and prominent balconies. The whole thing was built on a mountainside, so the streets twisted back and forth. There was also a residential section with gingerbread Victorian houses. It gave the town, which only had about 2,000 people, a magical frozen-in-time quality.

I went to the only electronics store in town and was the only customer. With the help of the clerk who took me around the store, I bought earphones, a voltmeter, a pair of cable pliers, a spool of cable, a pre-paid phone, a fiber lock assembly and a visual fault locator. To answer his curiosity I constructed a story of myself as a radio ham with an RV.

At an outdoors and hunting store I bought an entrenching tool, camouflage face paint, two ski masks. On impulse, as I was going by it, I ducked into the big architecturally out of place chain drugstore and bought some bleach and hair dye "for my wife," and on impulse another pre-paid phone.

Walking past the Local Flavor Café I realized how hungry I was, went in and ordered first the crab cakes, then the fish tacos which I had seen on someone else's plate as I walked in. They looked wonderful, and they were. So were the crab cakes. I felt guilty that Rachel didn't get to have any of this, but could think of no way to get them back in any condition to eat. And actually the food we were eating was okay. Years of backpacking and canoeing had taught me how to make decent meals with freeze dried ingredients. It can be amazingly good. And it was augmented by wild salad greens I found and some fresh trout taken from the stream over the hill. We were doing okay. But still....

On the way out of town I went past a high school with a lot of cars in the lot. As I got closer I saw a man coming out holding a bolt action rifle with a scope. Then I saw the sign; it was a gun show. I stopped and put my foot down on the curb. Did we need guns? I considered what had happened so far, and found myself cycling into the lot. There was a kid about 16 taking money for the Lions Club to park, and I asked him if he would watch my stuff and left my loaded bike near where he had set up his card table with his cash box.

Folding tables completely lined the gym except for the door, with more rows of tables inside that rectangle. Lots of people. Guys in camo. Kids with their dads. Boys in scout uniforms. A much smaller number of women, but more than I would have guessed. It was noisy, and as soon as I got into the room I was aware of all the weapons. At first I didn't want to touch them. When I came home from Afghanistan the last time,

I took my boyhood .22 bull rifle for competitive shooting, my skeet gun, and my match .45 out in a boat and threw them into the sea. I had never hunted; I had no interest in killing as a boy, but I had loved guns, match shooting, and the smell of Hoppe's No. 9. I had loved them at least until I started killing people.

But the part of me that knew the importance of prep was in operation and it overruled my emotions. I ended up buying an FN Herstal 17 shot, a Glock 17 Gen 4, and two boxes of ammunition. I paid in cash, no questions asked. Arkansas was no-license open carry.

I left the gym, went over to the kid with one side of his head shaved, gave him $20, unlocked my bike and pushed down the lot toward the exit to a clump of trees. When I was alone I took the guns out of my jacket and tucked them into my backpack. As I looked down at them I had a flashback so powerful I had to sit down on the ground under the trees. In my mind I could see a 14-year-old boy I had shot in the face as he was about to fire a rocket at a copter loading our wounded.

When the firefight was over, and whomever we were fighting had retreated, I had walked over and seen his body lying there with his jaw blown off. The image woke me again and again for months; it still comes up occasionally. I never thought I would pick up a weapon again, nor that I might even have to kill someone. It made me physically ill, and I pushed my bike further down the street to a 1950s era drugstore and bought a box of Zantac 75, asked the old-fashioned soda jerk for a glass of water, then a refill.

Further on was a hardware store where I purchased rubber gloves, polyester rope, pliers, a small power screw driver, some other small tools, a length of PVC tubing, a can of rubber spray, tape, and a spool of light wire. At a feed store on the edge of town I bought a small bag of fertilizer. When I got it outdoors I realized it was too heavy to carry on my bike, so I went back, bought a small nylon bag, poured in five pounds and threw the rest away in their dumpster.

By then it was 4 o'clock and I started back. The trip was awkward. I felt I looked strange and overloaded even for a trekker, and every time a car passed me I was very conscious of how I appeared; it made me even more uneasy. Happily there weren't many cars.

As I went along I thought there had to be some other way to deal with the staff at the facility. I didn't think I could shoot another person. A couple of miles out of town I passed a veterinarian's office. Not quite thinking it through, just gut feeling, I pulled off the highway and went behind the building. I stood there looking at the ground, then leaned my bike against the red brick wall. They were closed, but didn't seem to have any particular security. I pulled on the rubber gloves, and using my Swiss Army knife got the back door open doing as little damage as possible and went down the hall.

The animals could sense me and I could hear them begin to move around, but no one barked. I got to the surgery which was on the right and went in. There was still plenty of summer evening light coming through the windows, and I quickly went through the cabinets until I found a can of ether. I took that and nothing else, then left the building and began to bike again. When I came to a bridge over a stream I stopped, got both guns out and broke them down. After wiping them down I threw the barrels into the river below. Further along the slides, further still magazines, and springs, and finally, further yet the grips. When the last piece left my hand I thought that buying the guns had cost me money we couldn't really afford, but that throwing them away had been worth it.

A mile or so further along there was a convenience store, and I went in and bought a box of disposable diapers and a *New York Times*, which I read outside. There was nothing about Rachel or myself, and I threw it away.

It was about 7 o'clock by the time I got to the place where we had left the fire road. As I soon as I was off-trail I took the bullets out and threw them one by one into the forest. By 8 when I got to the place where we had left the bikes, I stopped, disassembled the bike, re-hid it and got everything I had bought arranged so I could carry it back to camp. By then I had just enough light to find my way down the trail, and when I arrived back at our camp it was dark. I found Rachel in the tent working on the computer. She told me that the batteries were low because the solar panel wasn't getting enough light.

"I think we should move. I've found a spot where a large hickory tree has fallen; we could go behind it and also mount the panel where it would get enough light yet not be noticed," she told me. The first thing the next morning she led me to the place she had in mind. Although the angle on the road wasn't as good, it was enough, and we knew the routine well now. In every other way it was a much better site.

We moved that night, after which I did the log. By the time I was through it was very dark. There was not much of a moon so using our night goggles we painfully and slowly worked our way down the hill and across to the roadway. Then about midnight we made our way over to the green cable stanchion Rachel had located earlier. On the way, as we moved through the hickory and oak trees interspersed with pine and cedar, she caught her foot in a root and painfully twisted her ankle. I went back to our packs, got an ace bandage and some arnica cream, went back to her, and wrapped her ankle. "Never let an injury go untreated," I told her, and after a moment, Rachel was ready to go back to camp.

The next morning after talking it over, Rachel bleached her hair and so did I, including my beard, which I trimmed. The bleach had turned my brown hair a kind of dirty blond. In the little hand mirror I saw looking back at me a face I hardly recognized. It was deeply sun tanned and much thinner. With all the physical activity and the diet we were eating I realized I had lost 20 pounds, maybe more, and was now about 185. The planes of my face had changed; it was the face of an aging Southern California surfer. Rachel was similarly transformed. I would have guessed she was about 135 when we left Washington, now she was about 118. She had restyled her hair and changed the color to auburn brown. She looked like one of those dream women in a tiny bikini you always hope to run into on a beach somewhere in Spain or Brazil or the island of Ibiza. It was as if we had become different people. When I told Rachel about my reaction, she said, "We are, we have to be."

It had one immediate positive effect on our spirits because we agreed it made us safer. We had always been leery of video cameras, and assumed that if we got captured it would probably be by facial recognition. For that reason we frequented small local businesses that weren't hooked into security networks. We figured the first firewall we had was just knowing where we were going and how. As I looked at my face I thought of the chain pharmacy, and wondered if someone had looked and if I had been identified. It just ratcheted everything up another notch. Rachel, who knew more about it than I did, thought that with bandana and sunglasses on I probably wasn't picked up.

That evening as soon as it was dark we made our way back to the cable stanchion and as quietly as possible dug down to the cable, each crunch of the entrenching tool seemingly as loud as a bell. We cut away insulation and tapped into the line. A little tentatively in the beginning but with increasing confidence and speed, Rachel checked the cable, did the splice, and checked it with the laser of the visual fault locator. We were good to go. She made it waterproof with the rubber spray.

"A bit crude but effective," she said as she backed out. Next to it was the cable that brought power into the facility. We had decided to monitor the optic cable which would carry internet and telephone. I re-insulated the cables with the tin foil from the dried food we had been eating and encased everything in liquid rubber spray until it was weather proof. We buried everything again, spread leaves and grass to hide our work, and slowly played the spool of cable into the valley's hillside trees, burying it just below the surface or covering it with pine needles and ground debris. Doing all this gave me another flashback.

Rachel noticed when sweat from my face fell on her hands.

"You all right, Arthur?"

"I was back in Afghanistan," I responded, and then told her about my experience buying the guns. She stopped and looked at me, our faces so close we could see one another in the night. She leaned in and kissed me.

"Thank you. You know, Arthur, I was thinking today that I trust you completely but I don't really know anything about you prior to our meeting at the Blue Ridge Sierra Club. Until you told me I had no idea you had been a Ranger in Iraq and Afghanistan. My grandfather was Special Forces in Vietnam. He had the same thing happen to him."

"I wasn't bothered much by these memories in Washington, probably because it was so radically different, and so intense," I explained to her as we sat there in the dark in the woods. "Doing this... with you... has evoked so many of the same skills and it's thrown me back into my past more than once." I reached out to touch her and when I did I said, "When we were planning this I was unprepared for the effect it would have on me. And the effect you've had on me as well," and there in the dark we kissed again, and I realized I loved Rachel.

"I love you."

"I love you too," she said smiling, "and you really know how to show a girl a good time."

We unspooled the cable until we were far back into the woods, and I linked the computer into the facility's traffic. We assessed the situation and agreed we weren't doing anything to reveal where we were.

"If we had had to connect through Bluetooth, Linkup, or one of the others," Rachel said, "I think we would have been detected. But cable and wires are for electropunks, who use transistors, incandescents, and hardwire."

I listened with the earphones while Rachel let the computer charge. We took turns sleeping, and in the early morning I heard the tones that signal a computer is logging into a network. I shook Rachel awake and she activated our link. After it was over she called the information up and attempted to make sense of the rows of figures. As we pored over the data, the morning car went by very slowly. Although we were well-hidden, had they expected us to be there and used infrared heat detectors, I realized, they would have detected us. That's the thing about combat; you have to keep going even though you don't know or have everything. Your life depends upon not freezing or going into fight or flight because then rational thought becomes impossible.

Finally, with a tiny huffed "Yes," which she quickly stifled, Rachel turned and smiled.

"I think we are looking at the psycho-physiological data of a living system," Rachel said, and pointed at one of the running charts. I studied it for a moment and agreed.

"The heart beats differently than a human's, and the temperature is higher," I said, pointing to one of the moving charts. "I'm not sure about this, but I think this graph is some kind of blood chemistry, but it's so different that I can't figure it out. I think they have completely immersive monitors sending out this being's data to some select list."

Rachel agreed with me and I went back to listening, and was rewarded with a brief call telling someone at the facility that a call would be incoming on the secure line. Then, almost as an afterthought, the voice said, "Nothing has turned up yet." I don't know how I knew but I had no doubt that the voice was talking about Rachel and me.

"I have to go to the bathroom," Rachel said, reaching into her pack for some tissues. As she was scrambling up the hill an unexpected car went by. From my perspective, she was caught for an instant in open space between two clumps of trees. I couldn't tell what they had actually seen and waited for a reaction, but there was none.

CHAPTER SIXTEEN

Later in the afternoon another burst of computer data came down the line, this one including a list of amino acids, neuro-chemicals, and other substances basic to life. That night we talked about what had happened and decided that we had to either attempt to get into the facility or leave. It was only a matter of time until we were seen and caught.

That night I left Rachel in the clump of trees and went down into the valley. As I drew closer I was fearful of tripping some kind of security system, and moved very slowly. But just as I came to the edge of the trees, about to go onto the grass of the campus itself, a siren went off and lights came on. A door slammed, and just at that moment an antlered buck, completely unseen by me until that moment, bolted from the trees. The door closed and the lights went off. Looking down with my night goggles I could sees a fine wire held in place just high enough to let the forest's small animals pass under it. It was about three feet in front of me. We weren't the only ones thinking about the unexpectedness of wire, I realized.

Once inside of the perimeter I encountered no further obstacles and made my way directly to the building that we thought held the alien, since only a few people appeared to have access. Looking through the window I could see a man watching one of the new holograph sets. It all looked so normal that I realized one of the best ways they had hidden this facility was to make it so ordinary it made no particular impression. I could not see any cameras, so I crept along the edge of the building. I came to a window that looked into a hall on the other side of which was a glass wall. I looked through, careful to stand far enough back so that someone looking out would not see me. The color of the wall beneath the glass, which only came half way down, was a blue green, and somehow I knew this was the Blue Room. The realization stopped me for a moment. There was a being from another solar system just through these walls. It was staggering. As I started to move again, for just a moment through the window I thought I saw something move on the other side of the glass. I froze; suddenly within my head I heard the same cool, almost sardonic voice I had heard in my dreams, only this time I could understand it.

"Hello, Arthur."

It wasn't words exactly so much as a sense of, what can I call it, knowingness about the message. "I have no vocal cords; we do not communicate that way."

The voice was completely conversational, relaxed, interested, even urbane. I wondered what the limitations of such communications were, and as the thought formed the voice responded, "Now that I have seen you we are linked." The thought immediately emerged: how could that be possible? The answer came into my mind, "You as a living organism have a kind of individual coordinate in the information architecture of consciousness. What you might call the all that is. With your coordinates I can hold the intention to link with you. When you are aware of that you'll comprehend that all life is interconnected and interdependent. And you will quickly learn by the experience how to link with me." I stood there in the dark and all of this poured in. It was beyond weird and yet seemed completely natural.

"From now on you can communicate with me simply by holding the intention to do so. Distance is not a factor. It doesn't matter whether you are near or far."

"You mean like ESP or something?" I formed each word in my mind, and felt very awkward.

"That's a crude approximation," was the response, and with the words I got a sense of wry amusement.

"Your species as your culture has evolved has suppressed its native affinity for opening to the matrix of consciousness, and when it does happen you call such people geniuses, or prophets, or witches. But you can be trained. Some of your species already knows this, that's why meditation is part of the program in both dojos and monasteries. Here's the key, Arthur. It is the essence of your beingness, the totality of who you are that is unique, and it serves as a kind of beacon. Now that I have seen it I can find you, and if your mind is open to me you will be able to perceive me. Remember, distance doesn't matter, because the linkage is not in spacetime. It is a matter of consciousness. Now, go back to Rachel. You don't have to be this exposed."

"How do you know about Rachel?"

"She is in your thoughts. It's more than that, but that will do for the moment. I'll pick you up again in about an hour." My sense of being linked reduced, but I could also feel it did not entirely go away. By now the experience seemed something like a daydream, subtle and ephemeral but very real.

Carefully working my way back up to camp, I found a very anxious Rachel.

"When I heard the alarm, I had no way of knowing what had happened to you, and you didn't come back. I thought I better stay put."

"You did the right thing. Try never to lose contact with your allies." I explained what had happened. Midway through this, the voice told me to hold her. "Kiss her." In mid-sentence Rachel was surprised as I leaned forward and followed the directions. Her body melted against mine and suddenly a look of surprise came over Rachel's face.

"I hear it!"

"Yes, I saw you through Arthur's eyes so now we are also linked, Rachel," the voice said, and I could hear it too, and realized the voice could speak to us both simultaneously.

"What do we call you, what gender are you? Or does that even make any sense?" Rachel held the thought in her mind.

"You can call me Mike, a nom de guerre, as it were. I don't have a gender in the sense you mean it. I am neither a he nor a she, but both, and yes, it takes two of us to procreate."

"How are you communicating with us?" she asked.

The answer was not at all what I expected. "Your species hasn't worked out yet that consciousness is causal and fundamental. Your Max Planck, the father of Quantum Mechanics, said it clearly in 1931. Einstein agreed, so did Pauli, Schrodinger, Heisenberg and other modern greats of your physics. But materialism was still too strong. Maybe because on my planet we evolved as a species that had a mouth opening but no vocal cords, learning to open to the part of consciousness that is not physiologically based was a survival skill. It shaped our world view from the beginning."

"What do you look like?"

"Bi-pedal humanoids are a basic model in the universe, only the details vary," was the amused response.

"How can you speak English so well?" I formed the intention of the question in my mind.

"I have fluency because I've spent almost 100 years watching your media, from the first radio to television, to holograms. For the last 12 years in the Blue Room, I have had full access to your net. But more than that we aren't really communicating in words."

He was right. The experience was more than just absorbing comprehension; it also came with nuances of emotion, context, things words can only suggest.

"What are you?" Rachel and I formed the question at the same time.

"You might think of me as a cultural anthropologist, although I am not as culture-centric as your lot because I know there are hundreds of thousands of species and cultures throughout the galaxy." The implications of this comment hardly registered at the time. Now I think about it regularly.

"I do very much what your cultural anthropologists do when they study a primitive, as they see it, indigenous tribal group." I could see by the change in her expression that Rachel also heard Mike's laughter. "It's so cultural-centric. Being an outsider I guess it is easier for me to see there are a lot of ways to be a human being. You can be sophisticated in different things. Anyway I did what you would call a dissertation on the cultures of post-electronic earth."

I could not quite process any of this, nor how calm Mike seemed. I was at such a heightened state of adrenaline I was in an altered state, a feeling I remembered from combat. Mike seemed in no hurry, and asked me how we had tracked him down. The ordinariness of the question helped me center, and in a kind of blast of data I shared it with him. This exchange happened in a timeless time, so I am not exactly sure how long it took. This way of communicating was so very strange to me then. I realized I couldn't hide anything, because it wasn't just what I said, it was the whole background of my feelings and memories that went with my "words."

Mike took it all in then said, "Arthur, I first picked you up when your attention focused on the idea I might exist. But I could only get to you in your dreams when your rational mind relaxed, and because I hadn't seen you I only got the barest contact in the information matrix.

BR13814239"I need to get out of here, and with your help I can. I'll help. That's not the real problem though. The real problem is I cannot get myself to where I need to go. I can't do it without help; I look too weird. I don't have any money. Obviously I can't fly, and I don't know how to drive a car. I have been waiting years for someone to do what you have done." And then after a pause, "Will you help me?"

It was at that moment that I realized again with full awareness what we were doing, and then understood one of the considerations of communicating in this domain. As soon as the decision is reached it is known, as are all the reasons for making that choice.

"Can you commit to us that you will do no harm? That nothing human will be harmed, nor the planet?"

"Absolutely." And we were flooded with the integrity of Mike's intention.

Contact was suddenly broken, and I think both of us found the retreat of this new linkage almost as unnerving as the first connection. After five minutes Mike was back. He explained to us what we had pretty much already concluded. The facility was essentially a prison embassy where for over a decade they had both studied him and tried to communicate with him. "They have monitors in the walls that track my brain wave patterns, my body chemistry."

"Yes, we tapped into that data."

"They are obsessed with my physical data," and again we caught Mike's humor.

"The staff is scientists, some people I can only think of as diplomatic, a few guards and some support staff. Those people never come into this building and don't know I am here, although they all suspect it. They don't ask."

"How do you communicate?" I asked.

"I type on a tablet. They know I can't talk, so that's what we have worked out. It's rather like the late Stephen Hawking." Again his sly sense of humor came through.

"Do they have any idea what you are capable of?" Rachel asked.

"Not a clue. After 12 years it has all become very mannered."

"Do you tell them the truth?"

"Of course. What I tell them is entirely true. I take my diplomatic part very seriously. Also in my culture lying isn't really possible for reasons you can probably now appreciate."

"What about technologies, information about weapons?"

"I'm an anthropologist, so in my culture's terms not very technical except in the areas I need to be, just like here and, in any case, the technologies are far too advanced to be meaningful to your culture. Even my routine knowledge is vastly more sophisticated than that of the scientists who study me, and it is grounded in a very different perspective. They wouldn't understand my technology. But I don't talk about it. And while that question about weapons in your culture seems perfectly reasonable, in mine it is meaningless. Space-capable cultures all understand you have to work at a completely different level."

"So they know about your ability to communicate in this way?" Rachel asked.

"Not at all, and it has been easy to keep it a secret. The concept alone is so foreign to physicalism as to be nonsensical. If they could believe it possible at all it would only be as some feeble phenomenon that could just yield tiny results. If you think consciousness arises from matter, as they do, you are completely backwards, and cut off from anything but spacetime. Matter arises from consciousness. That fundamental truth is known by all space-capable species."

"How did you end up here?" I asked.

"I was injured in the accident. Once captured I couldn't leave, for the reasons I told you. Also there were benefits. I got greater access, I was able to research things I would not otherwise have been able to. But something urgent is happening to your planet, so I have been reaching out and waiting for someone like you two to help me get out so I could make a difference before it is too late."

As the exchange went on I had the sense that Mike had been studying his human captors and their world far more effectively than they had been studying him. He told us that he would steer me away from contact with anyone else in the compound, and would take control of the various sensors.

"Can you control the electrical systems?"

"Yes. I told you Arthur, you have to completely rethink reality. I am working in the domain of consciousness, but I can also, through quantum processes, enter into spacetime. Reality is much more a dance or a song than a machine."

"I don't understand that," I told him. "But we can't stay here much longer. People are looking for us. We have been here for several days, and every day ups the risk of discovery. If we are going to get you out it will have to be tomorrow night. We need a day to prep." I imagined as I said it, food, water, the essentials.

"I come from a planet considerably larger than yours, and like yours mostly water. That is one of the reasons I was interested in you. I don't eat flesh, and there are some of your plants I can't eat. But I can eat a much broader range than you can, and do so with pleasure. I also have a supply of supplements that I will bring with me. I know your botany much better than you do. The matrix of reality is much larger than your science yet understands. I leave you and Rachel now; I have my own preparations."

We got back to camp, and over a curry dinner that was surprisingly good we discussed our plans for the next day, testing each choice. We went to bed, made love, held each other for a long time knowing everything would change tomorrow.

CHAPTER SEVENTEEN

We were up before dawn and erased our presence as we broke camp. I realized we had to ditch some of what we had brought because we had no means but the bicycles to get Mike back to the jeep. We debated what we needed and what we could leave behind, and culled through everything and wrapped what we didn't need immediately in a poncho, took the entrenching tool, and hiked far back into the woods and buried it. Once again, as I looked down on the gear, I wondered if I would ever see it again. It seemed to me that little by little I was shedding the Arthur Davies I had been, becoming someone else. I didn't have a very clear idea though of who that was.

We worked the rest of the day on our preparations for the night, struck the tent, left the ground cloth on which we set our bags and got everything else prepped for a quick exit, then went to sleep early in the open air, awakening at one in the morning. We packed the sleeping bags and the ground cloth, got everything prepped, then smeared our already grubby faces around the eyes with the camouflage paint, put on the ski masks and pulled up the hoods of our nylon parkas. Then we sat as Mike had instructed us in a meditative state, focusing on him. I now thought of him as a him. After a few minutes his consciousness was in our heads.

"Over the years I've tracked the entire electronic system of the installation, and I will guide you in and block the sensors one by one as you go."

"Can you control it that closely?" I asked.

"I've had over a decade to work this all out while I waited for someone like you and Rachel."

"How did you know we would come?" Rachel asked.

"As I said, I didn't know specifically you, but every day for 12 years I have stopped and held the intention like a beacon that someone would. I knew it might take months or maybe decades until the link occurred, but I knew it would happen and that I had to be ready. In the meantime I studied Earth, which is what I was doing anyway. In order to answer their questions I told them they had to give me access to your digital communications web. Let's not get into that now. Stop for a minute... I need to turn off a camera so there is no apparent break." We stood still in the forest night for maybe 45 seconds, during which we heard the whooo of an owl call twice. Then, "Okay keep moving."

From where we came out of the forest we moved across the lawn, then began working our way slowly down the side of the building, with its board and batten wall on our left, pausing before turning left and moving across the face of the building.

"Stop," and again before turning the corner we did. "Okay, you can go ahead." We came around the corner and looked down to the porch and entrance to the building. We could hear the flag rope slapping against the metal pole in the slight breeze that was coming down the hill. Otherwise everything was quiet.

"How are you doing this, Mike?" I asked.

"In my culture our whole technology is based on nonlocal perturbation, as your scientists would call it now, mental intention causing changes in spacetime. It's how we control everything, so it's a design feature in our systems. The problem here for me is the crudity of your technology. It's like pushing sludge to get things to work. Your devices weren't designed for direct mental action." Then a pause and, "Go up to the front door."

As we got to the door we heard the lock click. But before opening it I gestured to Rachel, mimicked the action, and we pulled on our rubber gloves. "Very smart, Arthur," I heard in my head. "I'm glad you thought of that." As the door opened Mike said, "I'm sorry, I can't do anything about the guards and other staff."

Warily glancing right and left we entered a hall, and stepped softly into the front room of the building which looked like an old camp lodge. Our entrance, I realized, was covered by the sound of the holographic movie which the guard with his back to us was watching.

Very slowly I moved behind the man, and took from my pocket a rope body cinch that I threw over his shoulders and part way down his body before he could even react, effectively pinning his arms to his side and his body to the chair. Rachel ran forward. In her hand was a disposable diaper soaked in the ether I had stolen from the vet's office. She awkwardly held it over his face as he struggled. Then he slumped into unconsciousness. This really wasn't very satisfactory because we were unclear how long he would be out. I figured 20 minutes, and the ether meant we did not have to kill or hurt him. We kept moving down the hallway, each sound increasing the tension. With Mike's help we located the switches to move the sliding door that made up one side of the Blue Room, and as it pulled back it revealed that what I had thought was one room was actually a complex of rooms. Some of it seemed to be below ground. The first was an extremely high-tech complex, part surgery, part computer room, part laboratory. No one was around, but on the walls screens revealed some kind of readings, and electronic devices chortled to themselves.

Mike guided us to the corridor that sloped downwards into the ground. He cautioned us that there was a technician on duty, but that he could detect no particular level of stress in the man. Through all of this, Mike's "voice" had a calm and detached quality. Just as we were turning a corner he conveyed to us:

"A second technician is somewhere in the corridor. I can't tell the exact location, but inferring based on his thoughts about various pieces of equipment he is checking, he is in the side corridor about 20 feet down to the right. I know the layout. I have the camera off so you can't be seen but I can't see him either."

Mike withdrew. I'd come to recognize when his attention shifted. "That's right," he came back.

Just as we started to move we heard the man's footsteps coming down the corridor. I pivoted and pressed on the door behind us, and it gave way. Rachel followed and we stood in the dark. We went through what was some kind of insulated door; suddenly it was cold and there was a strange blue light. After the steps passed, we turned away from the door and saw tiers of what looked like glass freezers on shelves that could be raised or lowered to bring a glass box to the height of stainless steel gurneys standing in front and parallel to the glass coffins. There were 10 of them.

As we crossed the room, we could see in the nearest one lay the body of an alien bathed in a soft blue light. Rachel and I looked at each other, then back; we were stunned. We went to the next container which held a body that was quite different from the first, and we realized these were not all aliens of the same species. As we examined them, some were much larger than others and the features were different, as was their skin, although that isn't what I would call some of it. Not all of them were bipedal. Their colors were very different, as were appendages. So very different, but as Mike had said there were general similarities. Some bodies, I noticed, were in pieces, and one of the containers only seemed to contain parts of a body.

Mike got our amazement I am sure, and with something like a laugh asked, "Did you think you were alone in the universe, or that there was only one other species, mine? There are many that we know about only by their consciousness presence, their information architecture."

Then Mike shifted again in this new nonphysical dance we were experiencing.

"There has been more than one crash; I am just the only one to live." In that instance, and for the first time, I had a sense of the great chasm that lay between our view of the world and Mike's perspective.

"Quickly," Mike warned us, and we left the room moving at a run through a maze of corridors. Most of this facility I now understood was underground. As we turned another corner, Mike's warnings and a man's physical presence simultaneously intruded on my awareness. Both of us were so surprised that it took a beat for each of us to react. Training took over and I lashed out with my aluminum flashlight, crashing it across the man's jaw, and he slumped to the ground unconscious. Just as we were about to move Mike told us, "We need this man's body, or at least his hand. It is the only way into the Blue Room where I am."

Rachel grabbed onto one leg and I the other, and we dragged the man down the hall feet first to a large door in the middle of which was a small window. Next to it was a hand print outline.

"Put his hand in the print, and respond to the recorded voice by saying '726 Jupiter,' that is the code for the day." We propped the man up, followed Mike's instructions, and the door swung open.

Inside was a room that looked like a professor's study, all in blues and grays. Along one wall were three curved monitors. All three were on. Standing in front of them was what at first looked to me like a muscular 10-year-old boy with a slightly oversized completely hairless head and skin that was a kind a soft gray-green. There was something sleek about him, like a shark or a seal, and the first thought that came into my mind as I looked at him was "aerodynamic." He looked like he was built for speed. The pictures I had seen when I was doing the UFO research were like cartoons of the actuality; he was not at all what I had expected. He was dressed in a smartly cut plum pullover tunic and trim gray almost Japanese-style soft pants. On his feet were a sort of canvas espadrilles.

"Do you like it? I designed it, and told them how to make the fabric. I had a technical suit on when the crash occurred. Not something you would want to live in, and they took it away anyway."

He spoke with his back to us, then he turned to face us fully and we saw that he had only a small slit for a mouth which didn't move much; which was disconcerting as he spoke in our heads. Instead of ears he had angles formed into his skull, ridges along the side of his head to capture sound and channel it down a small hole. Mike had pronounced cheek bones, indeed his whole face had a taut angularity to it. He had only a very slight nose. His eyes were larger than human eyes, and shaped more like tear drops with the point in toward the nose, but nothing like the large doe-eyed E-Ts one saw in movies and comic books. Nor was there anything spindly about him as in most of the E-T images I had seen. He looked muscular but not overbuilt. His overall bearing was austere; he looked competent and formidable despite his size.

On each hand I saw there were only three long fingers plus an elongated thumb splayed at the end with what looked like webbing folded back against the finger length. His face was unnerving because it was so deadpan, almost devoid of expression. Without hesitation he walked over and gravely shook our hands. His mouth didn't move to shape the words appearing in our heads, and no sound occurred, as he told us "We must hurry."

Mike swept up a bunch of bottles with some kind of pills, and two small metallic cubes about the size of large dice with no distinguishing features. "The pills help my digestion," he said into our minds when I looked at the bottles. "I had to teach them how to make them for me."

Without a backward look he led us out, stopping only long enough for me to secure another of my rope cinches around the unconscious technician, tying him to a door and gagging him with gaffer's tape I had brought on my war belt.

Following a different route, we worked our way back out to the entrance. The guard in the front room was just waking up, groaning about his head, and not quite sure what had happened.

"Mike," he shouted when he saw him. He was so fixated on Mike he didn't see us, and Rachel and I slipped up behind him and did our ether routine again.

"Sorry," I said to the man, who for a second time slumped into unconsciousness.

CHAPTER EIGHTEEN

We had just reached our former campsite, put on our packs, and were going through the forest as quickly and quietly as we could when a siren erupted and the lights came on throughout the compound. We knew we had very little time to get lost in the woods, and the three of us moved as quickly as we could through the trees. As we did so, watching Mike I realized that his range of vision was greater than ours, even with the night goggles.

We got to the bicycles, quickly secured everything, and I helped Mike get seated on my pack strapped to the rear pannier. It was immediately clear to me that we had miscalculated. Going down was easier, but going up we made very slow progress, and it wasn't any easier when we got to the fire road. Balancing two people on an already loaded light trekking bike was exhausting. We got out on Highway 23, then down to Route 62. By then it was clear there was no way we were going to get to the jeep on the bicycles. It was too physically difficult and looked too weird. Mike proposed a solution. He knew from the staff and his own research into the area in which he was being held, although he had never seen it except on Google Earth, that there was a wild river, the Buffalo, nearby. We stopped and pulled behind the hulk of an abandoned roadhouse, got out the topo maps, and located it.

We talked it over without making a sound, and decided that we had to split up. It would be safer and really the only way to make it work. At the same time this made Rachel and me very uncomfortable and nervous. We looked at each other and linked in a way we never had before, fully comprehending for the first time things about ourselves we had not known though we had spent every minute of this entire experience so far within reach of one another. And in that look we acknowledged how important that had been.

"Oh that is quite wonderful," Mike said. "I have never experienced that before. When you two look at each other it is like warming my hands in front of a heat source."

It made us both blush. "We're going to have to set up some limitations, Mike. Can we do that?"

"It is very strange for us, Mike, to live quite this exposed," Rachel added softly.

"Have you noticed that I withdraw, and yet I'm still there?" Mike answered. "I will teach you how to do that."

Just then, up the road back towards the facility, the SUV went past us at speed. We heard it before we saw it, and continued to watch after it had passed the building and was pulling ahead. It put me on edge, and I realized there was something I wasn't hearing. Sirens.

"You are maybe the biggest secret in the government, Mike. They can't call out the police, that will bring the media, and they don't want anybody to know you exist let alone are missing. In a sense the government has hidden you in a miasma of scorn and ridicule. They can't suddenly reverse that."

"I hadn't thought of it that way," Rachel said. "But that doesn't mean they will give up."

"No. I'm sure they haven't given up. We are probably being depicted as 'persons of interest' for some other thing entirely, with no details. That's why we have to stay on guard. They are going to be both covert in purpose and out front in execution, although still quiet. They'll use law enforcement agencies to do the on-site work, but it isn't going to be squads of police with riot gear on. It'll be someone brushing by us with an umbrella, sticking a syringe in Mike, and walking on," I said, mimicking the act.

We stared at the map for a moment, then Rachel said, "Okay. I will go get the jeep. You and Mike rent the canoe. I don't know anything about canoeing anyway."

"You're right. That way the chance of someone seeing him will be much less, and we can get most of the way there."

"Where do I meet you?" Rachel asked, and at the time I don't think either of us realized that we weren't actually speaking.

"Look here on the map," she said. "It's only about 20 miles more to Ponca. When we get there I'll ditch my bike; sorry about that," she said with a rueful shrug. "You can rent a canoe, and I will meet you at Grinder's Ferry. You can turn in the canoe there, and a campsite is nearby, close to Interstate 65. I think that would be a good rendezvous point."

"Are you sure, Rachel?" I asked. "I can't predict when we will arrive down to the day, let alone the hour. It will be at least three days, I estimate, and I am certain that some kind of chase must be fully on by now."

"Yes, but will they expect a backpacker, and a man with his son on a canoe trip?"

She was right. I assumed searchers for us would presume we were in some kind of vehicle on the road. They would set up road blocks ostensibly to check for alcohol or something.

It was about eight in the morning when we passed an old clapboard country general store with a porch upon which sat a rusting metal cooler with a Nehi logo painted on its side. There was just a small display window and an old wooden screen door. At the building's side was another old-fashioned phone booth.

I motioned for Rachel to pull over, and we stopped at the edge of the parking area. "I feel like we should check in with John and Topher to see what things look like from their end," I explained, when Rachel gave me a quizzical look.

"You can never be sure, particularly in very rural areas, whether the old hard-wired system works or is still maintained," she said.

"True, but with the store here I think it probably works."

The store was open. "Stay here," I told them and went in. There was only one other person in the store, a woman behind the counter, and I could see she was just getting set up for the day.

We exchanged pleasantries while I looked around. I bought a child's baseball cap with a razorback logo on the cap, child-sized hoodie with "Arkansas Wilderness" stitched on the chest, a pair of sunglasses and some adhesive tape, and took it all up to the counter.

"For my son," I said to the woman when I got to the counter. She smiled at me and I paid, asking her "for two dollars in quarters." "You'll probably need more than that," and she handed me four dollars in coins saying, "The phone works, we just replaced the handset."

I thanked her and went back to Rachel and Mike and gave them everything. Then went back to telephone booth, used one of the quarters and dialed the number John had given me.

A robovoice asked me for the 12-figure code. I punched it in and as I waited looked over and saw Mike put the glasses on. Because he had no real ears Rachel taped them to his head. Then she tied the bandana covering his neck. He put the hoodie on. I looked at him from maybe 20 feet away and, at a casual glance, with his gray pants, plum-colored hoodie with the bill of the cap sticking out, and the glasses and bandana covering most of his face, he looked like a 10 or 11-year-old boy. It wouldn't hold up to any close observation, but casually at a distance, if they didn't see his hands, I thought it would work.

Just then the robovoice came back on, "What's going on?" and I knew it was John.

"I was going to ask you that."

"I am going to dial someone in; give me a second," the strange voice said. After a pause, I heard another robovoice pitched just a little different and heard Topher say, "Hello."

I debriefed for them the headlines of what we had been doing, then asked, "What's happening at your end?"

John's robovoice responded first, "They have your digital pictures up, so you can assume facial recognition software is in play."

"I think we are okay on that count, as long as we wear the sunglasses and stay out of chain stores that are linked into the net," I responded, and started to say I would send new .jpgs when I thought better of it. "We've made some other changes as well," I said, but didn't specify what they were.

"You are listed as 'persons of interest' to be detained. It's gone out all over the country."

"It's what I thought would happen."

Then Topher's robovoice, "It's very weird. On the surface everything is unperturbed. You've taken leave and are off-trail backpacking. That's what the office knows. But underneath that is a total shitstorm. I have been questioned twice, know I'm monitored. Pardoe himself had me over for a bowl of chili. Pretty good, actually. I told all of them the truth, 'I didn't know.' Are you all right?"

"At this moment, yes. A minute from now I couldn't say. It's very weird. It's like non-violent combat."

They wished me well, I promised to stay in contact, and we rang off. It was all pretty much as I had thought.

I went over to the bikes, ready to leave, and Rachel said, "Wait a minute," and went across to the store. She came back in a minute with some white cotton painter's gloves and box of tampons. She shoved a tampon into the other fingers, and Mike put his three fingered hands into the gloves.

"He doesn't look any weirder than a lot of kids," Rachel said, and I agreed. Through the whole costuming process we could both sense Mike's amusement. Just as we were leaving a biker gang came into the lot. They looked at us but were uninterested, and we pushed off without a problem and continued down to Ponca, stopping about an eighth of a mile before the turn-off.

CHAPTER NINETEEN

"Okay. This is where I leave you," Rachel said.

We waited until there were no cars to be seen, lifted the bikes over the guard rail and pushed them through the woods back into the trees quite a way. We disassembled both of them, wrapped them in two of the ponchos and buried them. Those Koga-Miyata had cost me $1800 each and I hated to lose them, but there was no other option I could see. I noted the location though, and blazed the most prominent tree. I had noted the mile marker on the road and could get back to the bikes. But I wondered if I ever would.

As we were doing a final packing, Mike picked up one of the backpacks with one hand, and I suddenly realized that he was much stronger than he looked.

As soon as I thought it, he said, "My planet is larger than Earth, with much stronger gravity. My muscles developed in that world."

As we were removing any sign we had been there, I think for the first time we openly acknowledged what we had not really yet discussed. Where were we going? Again Mike provided the answer.

"I need to get to Florida, and from there to the Grand Bahamas Banks," he told us. The request seemed bizarre, but in that moment it gave us a focus to work on, and we left any questions for later.

"You'll need money," I told Rachel as she was gathering her kit together, and reached in my pack and took out four of the $20 stacks of bills and handed them to her. She put one in her pocket and the rest in her pack. Rachel was ready to walk out to the road carrying her backpack. We looked at each and then embraced. It was not easy to separate.

She started down the hill, while Mike and I stayed hidden in the trees, positioning ourselves so that we could see the road but not be seen. "I'll tell them I have been on the river, but my ride stood me up," she said in our minds as she got to the road. She was only there for about five minutes when a woman driving a pickup went by, stopped, and Rachel got in.

"Remember to talk, Rachel, using your mouth," Mike said as she pulled away.

After she'd gone I put on my pack and we climbed down the hill to the road, turned right, and started walking to where we could get the canoe. I reminded myself to breathe properly as we got closer, and the chance of discovery amped up my alertness by orders of magnitude.

We turned onto a gravel road that arced in a long sloping curve that took us down to the banks of the Buffalo River. As we came around I could see there was a green board and batten building and attached to it a long, covered but open on the sides, pipe frame shelving structure where canoes were stored. A couple in their 20s were getting into one of them at the little plank mooring that paralleled the river bank. Off to one side were two covered picnic tables with benches. Other than the couple pulling away there were three young men who looked to be in their late teens or early 20s spread out across the river bank, each wearing green shorts, white T-shirts and reflector safety vests that marked them as staff.

"Hold my hand," I said to Mike, and he reached up and did so.

"A father and a son coming to rent a canoe," I thought.

"Leave it to Beaver," Mike responded.

When we got to the flat ground of the bank we walked over, I took off my pack and Mike dropped his smaller daypack, and we set them down on the benches around the furthest most table. Unbidden, Mike got out my smartphone, even though it didn't work, and sat hunched forward as if using it. Just as he did so, one of the men came over to me.

"Jerry Byrd. You here to rent a canoe or just eat?" he asked, putting out his hand which I shook, and led him away from Mike.

"Oh, to rent," I replied, and started walking to the green building, cueing him to do so as well.

"That your son?"

"Yes, he's just turned 11. He's autistic and very sensitive to light. His mother and I thought this trip would make him more secure in himself. At least we hope it does."

He was a decent guy and immediately empathetic. "Oh, wow. Yeah. That must be tough. Does he need anything special? You're sure he can handle this? The river has some rough spots. We have several stretches of Class III," he said. Then we were at the building which had a window across the front. Jerry went in and came to the window.

"Do you know what you're doing in a canoe? I have to ask."

"Oh, yeah. I have done treks in Alaska and Canada up to Moose Factory on Hudson Bay," I said honestly.

"Oh wow, I've read about that. Did you do the Eatsatona Rapids? I hear they're awesome."

"I did. We spent the night before on the Onnaga, then got up at dawn. Six canoes spaced out. It was wild." I could see he had looked it up on the maps. For people into canoe trekking it was a dream run.

"OK. I saw your gear. You obviously know good stuff. You're going to need two paddles, two vests, and the canoe, of course." He went away from the window and came back holding two flotation vests.

"You have to wear these whenever you're on the water. You understand. It's a state law."

"I do indeed… not to worry, Jerry."

"All right," he said, and pushed a pad of paper with a form on it towards me along with a ballpoint pen.

"You have to sign a waiver that we take no responsibility for what happens to you while you are using our gear."

"I understand," I said, and signed and dated it.

"How do you want to pay for it? It's $65 a day for the canoe. Where are you thinking of getting out?"

"I'm not sure. I guess it depends on what my son can do. Why don't I pay you to Buffalo City; I know it won't be any longer than that. Can I get a refund if I get out earlier?" Looking out to where Mike sat, he said, "Sure, we can work something out. Do you need the shuttle to bring you back up?"

"No, my wife dropped us off and she'll come get us when we call her."

"No problem."

He handed me the invoice and I mimicked reaching for my wallet. "Oh my God. I left my wallet on the dashboard of my wife's car." I waited for Jerry to begin to react, then said, "But wait, I have cash."

"Cash. Wow, you hardly ever see that anymore. Ahh, let's see. He looked at the wall, read something, then looked back and told me, "You'd have to leave a $200 deposit."

"I can just do that; I got cash at the bank just in case." I gave him a rueful smile and counted out the twenties. "This is more cash than I've carried in months, but out here I wasn't sure cards would always work, because of the hacking attacks."

"They don't always." We shared a laugh and he said, "Okay. Let's get the paddles and the canoe. Does your son want to come over to pick his paddle?"

I shook my head, saying, it's awkward for him with strangers," and he let pass.

We were walking down to the canoe shed, when a state trooper drove down the hill. The trooper got out and looked around, then got back into his car and picked up the comm mike to make a report, I guessed.

Keeping the trooper in my line of sight, I helped Jerry get a canoe off the rack and put it in the water. We went back; he unlocked a door and inside were paddles.

"How old did you say?"

"Just 11."

"This ought to be about right," he said, as he passed the paddle back to me.

"You're right, that should be fine," I agreed.

"You're about what, 6'2"? Try this."

I took the paddle, and as I reached for it the trooper got out of his car again and started to walk towards us. As he did so one of the other staff guys went up to him and drew him over to a line of porta-potties, where he started to explain something.

I put the paddles in the canoe which Jerry had tied up with a bow line, and went up to get Mike. I made a show of putting on his pack, and my own, and we started walking back. Jerry started to come over to us when a laughing car of teen-agers came down the hill with music blaring.

"Oh, the rafters," Jerry said, adding, "Can you handle things from here?"

"No problem," I replied, and he went off as the kids spilled out of the car. The third staff man went as well just as another car of teens drove in.

For a moment Mike and I were alone. I climbed in, as did he. He untied the bowline, and we pushed off. Just as we did so the trooper turned away from the porta-potties and started coming towards us. I don't know whether he wanted us, or was just walking that way, but I was very glad to be on the river and away.

CHAPTER TWENTY

For the first half hour we just fell into the pattern of paddling, me in the stern and Mike as bowman. I quickly realized again that he was much stronger than his size would indicate. As I thought this and watched him, he came into my mind. "When I first got here I kept bouncing into the air," and I could see his memory for just an instant. "I also have in your terms heightened endurance."

At that moment the absurdness of my experience overwhelmed me. I was canoeing down the Buffalo River with a being from another planet. It made me laugh and Mike joined in.

"Why are you here?" We had touched on it a little, but I wanted a clearer understanding and now seemed the time to ask.

"My family have been studying your planet for over 500 years," he said, and I could feel him reaching for a comparison. "We're like your Leakey family. My grandfather monitored your Constitutional Congress in 1787. I got involved at the end of 1917. Yet this is as strange to me as it is to you." And I could feel a flood of sensations and emotions. "I have never had a personal relationship like this, and never expected to be going down a wild river in Arkansas, in the United States, on Earth, with a human."

"My God. How old are you?"

"In your terms just entering middle-age, about 150 Earth years."

"You live 300 years?" I asked, not fully comprehending what that meant.

"Or a bit more, that's the average. A number of us make it to 400."

"So what are we doing, Mike?" I asked in my mind, and comprehended objectively for the first time that I was finding this form of communication natural, increasingly easy, and bedazzlingly nuanced.

Mike turned to look at me and we stopped paddling for a moment. "Yes, no matter what else happens, Arthur, work with me. Work with

Rachel, and others. This is the gift I am giving you, for the gift you are giving me."

Then turning forward he began to paddle again, continuing in my mind, "We are getting me down to Riding Rocks, a limestone ridge of small islands on the Grand Bahamas Banks, or as close as possible."

"What's there?"

"Nothing is there yet, but let's go into that later. It's very important that we improve our connection for you to understand, and the same is true with Rachel. Just ask me questions and focus on me."

"What is your real name?"

"There is no answer in sounds. My species, not having vocal cords, experiences the auditory part of our world entirely passively. For a human my name would be an emotion." And as he spoke I felt a sense of brave resolve.

We floated on a little further, then entered a part of the river with a large granite bluff along the right side. As we did this I was suddenly flooded with a new level of feeling that caused my body to visibly quiver; a kind of frisson went through me. I had never felt anything like it. My mind filled with a melodious sequence of mental tones, and an entirely new level of communication hidden within me opened up. Looking forward everything seemed normal. Mike in a hoodie sat in the bow as we paddled in the easy unison you get when two people make a good crew. Steady but not strained; we were letting the river do most of the work for us.

Seen from behind Mike looked like what we had hoped he would, a sturdy 11-year-old boy, so visually everything was very ordinary. At the same time I was in a mental space unlike anything I had ever experienced; no drug, and I had tried most of them, had ever taken me here. I had no trouble moving in the physical world even as I continued to be open to this oneness. I steered with an occasional J-stroke and kept us on a straight course. On our left across from the bluff was Arkansas forest. Over my shoulder the afternoon sun sank below the cliffs on the right. A young red-shouldered hawk came from behind us diagonally across the water. In a picture it would have looked completely idyllic, but inside of me nothing was the same.

"What just happened, Mike?"

He pulled his paddle up, turned and took off his sunglasses, and looked at me. There was a brief moment where my perception of reality shifted again, and then I saw myself: an image filtered now through Mike's perception. It was wildly disorienting. Sight was strongly increased; details I would not normally have seen became clear, but the color values seemed to have shifted into the blue range. Hearing was much the same, but without some of the resonance. Smell, much the same. But what was radically different was the extension of senses I had never noticed before. With this shift of awareness I could see an additional pulsing network of what I perceived as life-light linking every consciousness, from plants to the dragonflies that skated over the water like the helicopters I remembered from Iraq and Afghanistan.

If Mike focused on a light strand he could bring it into a level of awareness and that, in turn, opened to other sub-structures. It was like having the internet in your head as a hologram. This net was just on the edge of visibility. If Mike gave it no attention it almost vanished. When he did focus his attention, the strand he focused on arched out to something else, and I felt there was no limit to the depth of detail to which I could go. For the first time I really understood what fractals are about. Beyond even this there was a kind of holographic spectrum of thoughts and feelings. Through Mike I floated, independent of my body, looking down on it in the canoe. Feelings washed over me like colored winds. Then I was back.

"I have been reducing it to words," Mike said, "because your language and usual thought processes would be completely disoriented, as you just experienced if I communicated entirely as my civilization does. Words are easier and clearer for you. The rest I throttle back." And as he said it I had no sense at all of condescension, merely an unemotional scientist's acknowledgment of a fact. "But it can be learned, Arthur. Humans possess the capacity. You've just experienced it. This is what great spiritual teachers experience. Physicists, poets, and painters, all the people you think of as being outstandingly creative have some measure of this experience driven and framed by whatever their intention was: to see their idea of divinity, a fundamental principle, to create transforming music. Many of them tell you about their experiences. Very few listen."

"Who are you?"

"I told you, I came here as part of a research team. My first visit started in late 1917; the Spanish flu epidemic had begun, and I was here to do the field research on your medical response for what you would think of as my doctoral dissertation." Then in mental tones modulated to mimic the stuffiest human academic, "The Earth: An Early Pre-nuclear Carbon Based Meta-culture on a Humanoid Dominant Planet and a Case Study of the First Use of Planet-wide Technological Medicine in an Epidemic."

Then more seriously, "I can't really convey to you yet the experience of a large cohort of consciousnesses leaving corporeality, leaving their bodies."

"What about that epidemic caught your attention?" I asked.

"We are particularly interested in humanoid species for obvious reasons," Mike said, turning and running his hand down his body. "Your technologies are operated without understanding the importance of wellbeing, not only for your own species but for the other beings with whom you share the planet, and you are creating the climate change that is throwing your world into crisis. This is one of the big changes. To survive, you must make wellbeing, from the individual, to the family, the community, nation, and your planet and all who live on it, your first priority. We have watched this process a number of times."

"What happens?"

"It only resolves itself successfully about 65 percent of the time. I am here to watch you go through it. The next 20 years will set the course. But again, let's put that off a bit."

"Where do you come from?"

"From a planet in the Horse Nebula. You don't see it yet but you will, I would estimate, in another two to three years. The timing depends on how a line of research that's begun at the University of Amsterdam is supported, and when the Chinese learn of it."

Once again I found myself seeing the Earth through Mike's dispassionate perceptions. "And you know how the story comes out," I said.

"No. I know the options and how each is likely to resolve, based on what has happened elsewhere. It is up to you humans to decide which course to take."

We went around a curve in the river, and there was a small gravel shelf where we could camp and still be secluded. I steered the canoe to the bank and we focused on setting up camp. When the tent was up and everything was laid out, Mike took the dish towel out of the pack and said, "I'm going to go get my dinner; I saw some very nice things. While I'm looking why don't you meditate and focus on Rachel. I think she would like to hear from you, and you'll find after this afternoon's experiences that you can make a deeper connection."

I rubbed on some herbal mosquito repellent and sat in the twilight, and for a moment I was very sad. I could see my cottage on the canal. I could see myself on the Hill briefing a group of Senators. It made me convulsively sob, but it passed, and in the quiet I focused on Rachel. Almost immediately she was in my head. She seemed to be with a group of people, but seemed safe. I didn't get any sense of fear, just a little edginess. I couldn't connect with her as I had with Mike, but at least I could feel she was okay and could relax about her. Just at the end, I felt her reach back.

"Arthur?"

"Yes, it's me. I'm so glad we can connect. We have to do this regularly. Both ways. Mike has shown me... I can't explain it. But we can get to a point where I can share it." I held this in my mind, not knowing how much she had gotten, but the connection was suddenly broken as her attention shifted to something in her environment requiring immediate attention.

Looking down at the water I began to replay what I had experienced, trying to make sense of it. The main thing I understood was that consciousness was both spaceless and vaster than I had ever imagined. It was breathtaking, literally. I was so focused that I suddenly became aware I wasn't breathing and took in a deep breath, letting my abdomen go out and relax.

As if on cue, Mike came out of the woods and into the clearing, and that brought me back. He had the dish towel filled with various greens.

"I felt I connected with Rachel. I even had a sense of where she was, and she was okay. It wasn't like you and me but it made me feel better."

"Now that you and Rachel have made this connection you will never be out of touch, and the connection will get stronger with use. The ability to open to this domain is inherent to all living beings, because consciousness is fundamental and everything is in the matrix. But since your species has not selected for it in more than 2,000 years it must be cultivated."

As I was heating up the water to pour into a freeze-dried chicken cacciatore envelope, Mike was sorting out his greens. Some of the plants I knew: sassafras, wild greens, dandelions and some others. Some I knew to avoid. Some I had no idea what they were. And there were also some fungi. He separated them out and set a small selection aside for me, saying in my mind, "This will make a nice salad."

He took off his hoodie, pulled up his sleeves and chopped everything on the little cutting board that was also the lid of the spice box, and quickly had a kind of rough puree. As he worked I could really look at him. I knew already he was much stronger than he appeared. His three fingers and thumb were longer and splayed on the ends and much more agile than mine. I realized he was actually very handsome, and that he had a personal sense of style, something I had never thought about concerning aliens.

He took one of the bowls, put the puree in it, and poured a little oil, vinegar and Braggs over it. Then he took one of what I had thought were drug capsules and pulled it open letting the contents spill out over the food. "I need some help processing some of your compounds," he said as he came over and sat down next to me.

I took my greens, gave them a little dressing, and we both began to eat. For a moment we sat in companionable silence, then Mike said, "You have so many edible plants," and I could see in my mind's eye the beauty he saw. I thought of myself as a more than competent woodsman, but I understood then my knowledge was minute compared to his.

"How advanced is your civilization?"

"That's not an easy question to answer, because our cultures are based on different premises. As a result our technologies are based on a different science; or perhaps more accurately partly the same science, but viewed from a different perspective. However, we had a phase similar to yours, which happily we survived, so I would estimate we are about 10,000 years further along."

"So it would be like me going back to the Mesolithic, the middle of the stone age."

"That's where it gets complicated. Your species was once very much in touch with this aspect of your consciousness, as all hunter-gatherer cultures are because to survive they have to be much more integrated into the life matrix of their planet. Actually your ancestors were quite sophisticated; it was just another way of being human."

Mike poured us each a glass of sun brewed tea, and went on, "In your 16th century the Roman Church, mostly in response to the Protestant Reformation, claimed anything to do with consciousness, what they called 'spirit,' was the Church's domain. Through the Council of Trent and the Inquisition, they violently persecuted anyone whose views diverged from this orthodoxy. Your scientists of that time simply saw consciousness as a life-threatening taboo and stopped talking about it or researching it. For more than 10 generations getting involved with areas the Church claimed as its own could get you tortured, or even burnt alive. Scientists consoled themselves with the spacetime domain they were allowed to research, and it was so productive that very soon interest in consciousness per se withered; a taboo formed and produced materialism."

As I thought about what he was saying I realized Mike was right. There was nothing in science as a process that precluded consciousness.

The dichotomy was an anthropological and cultural affectation that had become so deeply embedded in Western culture that it was assumed that materialism was scientific, and anything to do with non-physiological consciousness was not.

"You made a deal in which religion took matters of consciousness, and your science matters of spacetime. That's where you went wrong and it warped your entire science. You lost perspective on the role of consciousness."

I had sat through a dozen science courses, but I had never heard that taught, nor had I ever thought about it that way. If I hadn't just had those experiences with Mike I doubt I would have believed it as an argument. But I had to. It was too much to take aboard all at once though, so I changed the subject.

"Are there a lot of you around Earth?"

"No just a small community of researchers. Can you remember back when the Arctic still had ice, and governments maintained research stations there?"

"Sure… I think they closed the last ice station when I was 25 or so."

"Well, that's kind of like what I was doing. Interstellar travel isn't like your movies, or establishing your base on Mars. Even with hyper drives, and worm holes, it takes years; you have to get to a worm hole. And moving physical objects in spacetime is costly. There are many tens of billions of planets in the universe. Only a small percentage of them have some kind of life on them, but even that numbers into the billions. Even we don't know how many, and there are hundreds of millions of planets that have civilizations as your culture would define that. And tens of millions that are space-capable."

"Are there empires, that sort of thing? Galactic Wars?" I said, and felt his amusement.

"No. All cultures capable of interstellar travel understand that consciousness is causal and fundamental. You can't enter deep space without that worldview, because only that paradigm allows the necessary technologies to develop. That means those civilizations that do reach that point also recognize the continuity of consciousness. From that perspective killing in wars is understood to be counterproductive. All you do is complicate things and drag out time lines. You learned a kind of crude version of it beginning in the 1950s with your Cold War, when Mutually Assured Destruction, MAD, was the dominant geopolitical strategy."

He paused for a moment, and I got a swirl of images and the emotion of the 1950s culture, and for the first time saw what human society looked like from the outside: stupidly bloody and violent.

"And you can't have empires with the distances involved, the time and the expense. During your colonial period your human societies could barely handle subservient colonies an eight-week sea voyage away. How could one planet or even a group of planets affect any meaningful control over another light-years away? Empires are your cultural myth. Think networks instead, all geared to one thing: creating greater harmony and wellbeing."

"Why?"

"Because all life is interdependent and interconnected, as you have now experienced. What those of us who are interstellar want is social wellbeing. No one individual, or even one civilization, can visit all the planets or even a meaningful proportion of them. You must think on a completely different scale and from a very different perspective." And for a moment I was so moved by the image of the universe Mike shared that tears filled my eyes.

"When a planet reaches a certain technological level there is a tip point. If the dominant species figures out that continued survival requires recognizing the role of consciousness because survival requires working with the planet's meta-systems, not across them or against them, they survive. If they don't, they don't. You haven't done that yet. Humans still have a dominionist worldview; they think they have dominion over the earth. That is what created the climate change that now threatens your existence."

Then after a moment of silence, "Civilizations snuff out, Arthur. Species go extinct. It's a frequent occurrence. The planet survives of course, and after a while another cognitive species arises and begins the long trek. My planet, and my institution as you would see it, have been studying the process for 7,000 years on a number of planets similar to your own. Yours is just one of them. I am an Earth specialist, as one of your cultural anthropologists might specialize in a particular Amazonian tribe. We compare our work, and there is a very clear pattern as to how this process of advancement happens."

"Are you in contact with one another?" I had to ask.

"Yes, we share with other civilizations and they with us. In that way, we get even higher orders of insight. There are civilizations as far ahead of mine, as mine is of yours."

"Why Earth?"

"Because your planet is mostly water, as is mine, and you have a bipedal dominant species, and because you are very close to the tipping point."

I was stunned. I understood really for the first time that I was talking to a scientist. An individual who was doing research, studying my culture, studying my planet, and he knew far more about all of it than I or any human did. It was a very bizarre feeling, a humbling feeling, and not very comfortable.

"At the rate you are undergoing change and the direction of that change, you have about a 35 to 40 percent chance at this point that you will have a civilization breakdown and revert to hunter gatherer status within three centuries with a precipitous, violent, and ugly downward spiral getting there. We also think that if that happens, you have a 67 percent chance of going extinct. That's an extraordinary thing to be able to study."

As Mike spoke in my mind, at that moment I just didn't know what to do with this information. I knew instinctively he was right. As we ate I suddenly began to see a pattern I had been living. On the Hill I spent almost half my time focused on climate change, sea rise, and the massive dislocations it was causing, particularly its effects on the military. Most military bases, obviously naval bases, are on or close to coasts. We had already spent $235 billion rebuilding the Hampton Roads on the

Chesapeake Bay. Florida below Ft. Myers was going quickly, and a massive migration out of Florida was underway. The best estimates were that New Orleans and much of the Gulf Coast would be gone within two decades. The Jefferson Memorial was already an island. Looking at it through Mike's eyes, and suddenly I was doing that, I understood we were clearly not succeeding.

"No, no you are not." And I was flooded with Mike's compassion, but also his objectivity and disinterested perspective. We were a species he was studying.

We went over and sat along the riverbank. We could hear the soft bubbling flow of the water as the insect chorus ebbed and surged. As we looked at the water a snake left the bank and began swimming across the river in the moonlight. Its twisting body created ripples that broke up the reflection of the moonlight as it moved. On the other bank across the water the tree line stood in silent silhouette, and above it, in the clear night, the sweep of stars.

"Is your planet like this? I know you have water, and I know you have vegetation, but anything like this?"

"In many ways yes. We have rivers, but it is not like here. This is a wild river specifically set aside to remind you what your planet was. But you live mostly in urban technological cities. For me, allowing for differences in vegetation, this is like my neighborhood." I felt his nostalgia but it was mixed with my growing sense that he was right: we must change. It was now the only thing I wanted to work on.

I looked at my watch: it was 10 o'clock. "I think we should turn in; we need to get an early start."

"You go on, Arthur. I have been studying Earth for many years, but I have never been able to sit on a riverbank and watch the moonlight. And I don't sleep very much anyway. You may find me in what you would call a deep meditative state. I am very happy here, the happiest I have been in 12 years. I'll be fine."

That night for the first time in several weeks I slept really deeply and well, and awoke at 6, hearing the splash of Mike swimming, and felt his contentedness. I got out of the tent, walked over and took a leak, turning around just in time to see Mike dive from a large boulder at the edge of the shelf. After several minutes I became alarmed. Even allowing for differences in physiology I didn't see how he could hold his breath that long. Then he was in my mind, "I'm fine."

I got out a packet of granola and some coffee and started heating water. I was through the granola and was washing up 30 minutes later when Mike surfaced holding a number of things I could not identify. He started the stove, added some water and heated the mix up. Then ate it.

"How do you do that?"

Mike brushed the side of his neck and pulled back what I had thought was just a contour, revealing a slitted opening. "I have a kind of gill. We live a good part of our lives in the water. Our waters are very pure. We've been working for thousands of years to strengthen the balance of our ecosystems. My house," and I could see a kind of organic structure in my mind, "is on the shores of a lake and half its rooms are underwater. House isn't quite right though, but close."

We were just casting off, when a low-flying helicopter came down the river. Were they looking for us? Suddenly all my paranoia was back. Mike reached up his gloved hand and waved. Just what you would expect from a kid, I thought, which is what the canoe rental company would have reported. The helo rose further up into the air and veered off, leaving me relieved but once again on edge.

Two canoes of Boy Scouts went quickly past us at mid-day, paddling competitively, and the couple that had gone ahead of us must have still been ahead, so that except for those few moments we saw no one that day or the next morning. By then Mike and I had settled into a camp routine, and went along comfortably together. About 2 o'clock that afternoon we began to hear the rush of a rapids. According to what I had been told it was Class III, so it required serious attention.

"Are you up for this, Mike?"

"I think so. My job is to keep us going in the direction you aim us, and fend off rocks, right?" I could feel his interest and excitement as he said this in my mind.

The rapids came into view and the water speeded up. I could see there was a nasty turn midway through, large boulders on either side. Then we were in and I steered us over so that we could go down the center of the V of wildly rushing water. As I did that I saw that a tree had fallen out from the bank and a large branch at about face level lay across our path. By then the water had us and I had to concentrate on holding our course. I looked up just in time to see that the bare branches of the limb were lined with snakes basking in the Sun. Just before Mike in the bow went under the branch, we both thought, "Duck!"

As we went under, a four-foot snake fell off the branch onto the packs in the middle of the canoe before sliding off to the bottom. I knew instantly it was a water moccasin. There was no time to deal with it as we fought to stay upright and off the rocks, the water roaring in our ears, paddling and pushing as we shot through. By the time we were in still waters the snake had disappeared from my view, and I steered us over towards the shore and a quiet eddy so we could find it. As we moved into the calm byway I saw movement, "It's headed towards you, Mike. Be careful, this is a poisonous snake, and a big one," I cautioned.

The agitated snake rose to strike and Mike, faster than I would have thought possible, snatched the snake in mid-strike and held it up in front of his face, looking it in the eye. He focused on the snake, and after a moment its body quit writhing and relaxed. Very gently he leaned over and put it back in the water. It was still for a moment then swam away.

"It was very frightened," Mike said in my head.

"I had no idea you could move that fast."

"I'm nothing special. My muscles have a different structure than yours. I trained differently than you, and live in my body differently than you do, again because I start with consciousness not matter."

We moved out into the river and began paddling again for a while in silence.

"Is it lonely?"

"Lonely?"

"You're here all alone. You're out of contact with your world. You say you're middle aged. Is someone coming to get you?

"No. No one is coming, but I'm not out of touch."

"How is that possible?"

"Because in the domain of consciousness…"

"I still don't understand what that means."

"The dominant view in your science is that consciousness arises from matter, and is entirely physiologically based. When the body dies consciousness expires."

"Yes, I know that."

"It's not correct. As I keep telling you, matter arises from consciousness. Consciousness exists before you incarnate, and continues after you are corporeally dead. Episodically the non-physiological aspect of your consciousness chooses to manifest another personality, and incarnate. Not the same person, but the same information architecture, if that's clear."

"You mean the religious belief about reincarnation."

"There's nothing inherently religious about reincarnation. That's just the way humans deal with it. It's a process, and it goes on all over the universe because consciousness is fundamental and timeless however it chooses to be expressed."

"But how does that have anything to do with your communicating with your own people?"

"My planet is many years away in spacetime. But in terms of information and emotion that is not a limitation. Distance and time are part of an information package but do not define limitations. I am in contact. They can't do anything to help me physically, and since there is no precedent I don't think they really understand what I am going through. They can give me information, though, and that is very helpful." He paused then for a minute before resuming.

"I will never see them again. Like you I will die on Earth. It consumes too many resources to rescue me, and I knew the risk, which actually is very small. In 7,000 years we've only had a handful of crashes, and none like this. You have other visitors than my people of course, although the total number is still quite small. But several civilizations study earth. You don't know about them because we are all very discrete.

We don't want to be a factor. We try not to influence your choices, but to study them. However, we do favor life and wellbeing."

As Mike explained this I once again saw in my memory the Blue Room facility and the bodies Rachel and I had seen there, and it dawned on me that the best protection Mike's project had was the fact that the tabloids have made aliens into an urban myth. Such stories aren't about truth, they are about belief. Many knew Mike's story; fewer, but still many, believe it at some level. It titillates without requiring any action. From Mike's perspective this had a cloaking effect. The myth camouflaged the reality. Made it non-serious.

"Yes. You have it exactly, Arthur. Would you mind pulling over. As you would say I want to take a leak."

"It's almost five, why don't we just stop," I thought, as I steered us to the shore.

That was our last night on the river. In the morning we got to Buffalo City, where there were huge granite cliffs overlooking the river, and on the right we could see there was a camp located there. As we paddled towards it I recognized Rachel because, as we had agreed, she had a familiar scarf tied around her canvas sun hat. She had parked the jeep way off to one side, and we drove the canoe onto a shelf of gravel and sand near where she was parked. She came down immediately, and took Mike by the hand and led him up to the jeep. I unloaded everything and paddled around to the canoe rental place, and tied up.

"Good trip?" I heard as I was leaning over, reaching into the canoe to get the paddle. I looked around and there was a blond-headed boy about 18 in shorts, a T-shirt, and the standard safety vest.

"Wonderful."

"Says here there were two of you, a boy," he said, as he looked into the canoe and then took the paddles I was holding.

I said as casually as I could, although I was having trouble modulating my voice not having used it for several days, "Yes, my son. He's with my wife now." And I gestured over to where Mike and Rachel were just finishing loading the jeep. The boy waved, and Mike and Rachel waved back.

"He enjoy it?" he asked, looking across at Mike in his hoodie as he got into the jeep.

"I think it will be a lifetime memory."

"Cool."

A moment later Rachel pulled up, got out, came over, and gave me a kiss. "Ready?"

"Yep. Thanks, for everything," I said as I shook the boy's hand. We walked over to the jeep and got in, with Rachel driving. "You know, we're just beginning." Rachel said the first four words aloud, and then we were back in contact.

CHAPTER TWENTY ONE

As we lapsed into mind speech, I asked Rachel what had been happening for her. She told us a nut farmer and her mother provided half the trip, and a woman bank officer the second, dropping her off at a bus stop.

"I was being very careful. Taking the trip in stages. When I got on the first bus I asked the driver for the crossroads where I knew from the map I could catch a bus into Little Rock, but I got off before that, waited for the bus to leave, then hitchhiked. I was very paranoid. I wondered if they somehow knew about the jeep. I got out several blocks from the lot where we had left the jeep and walked down side streets until I got to a place where I could see if anyone was watching the lot. I saw a police car with two men in it parked near the entrance. It was unmarked; I only identified it by the red LED strip pointing backwards in the rear window. The car did not move and I felt conspicuous standing on the sidewalk staring. So I walked down the street to a coffee shop. An hour, a piece of pound cake, and three cups of coffee later, I had gone through the Little Rock paper and the car still had not moved, and I was convinced it was waiting for us.

"Thirty minutes later, with the paper long read and the waitress becoming curious, it was still there, and I realized I would have to move or start attracting attention. I got up to pay and had just walked out the door, when police cars poured into the street and the detectives got out of the stake out car. They walked towards me, and I could feel myself fainting. They went past me and into an alleyway. Ten minutes later they came out leading a group of hand-cuffed men. I had to run back to the restaurant ladies room, where I was sick over and over.

"I cleaned myself up, picked up my pack, and went out again, still feeling weak. Then I became paranoid. If I walked over to the garage and got the jeep now, after sitting in the coffee shop for so long, I thought it would look very suspicious. On the other hand I began thinking about CCRT cameras, and thought if I didn't move I would stand out and be easy to identify. I also began to worry that if we were stopped we would not have licenses, and realized I had to get online.

"So I walked down the street, unsure of what to do or where to go. There was a church with a sign for a youth hostel. I adjusted my pack and walked in. A young man in his late teens was behind the desk, dressed in black leather and nose and ear studs, long black hair, a leather cap. His young smile contradicted the heavy metal image. It was nineteen dollars a night, and I could eat at the church; no drugs, no alcohol, no tobacco, and 'they don't like us sleeping together,' he told me, looking at my breasts the whole time."

"At dinner I met another woman, and she had a computer. I asked her if I could check my email, and using the pathway he'd taught us, got hold of John. I had taken a picture of you after we had taken the SIM cards out of our phones, and I took a selfie. I sent them to John and asked him for checkable licenses. I know you were leery of that, but I could see after what had happened that if we were stopped we would need them."

"It makes me very uneasy to travel under a false name, but you're right. Getting Mike where he needs to go is the main deal. We have to do it," I told her.

"The next morning, I told them I was going into town to see my cousin, left my pack and said I would be back for it late, and went off to get the jeep."

As she was telling us this in a flow of images, emotions and analysis, we drove through a light industrial area into the heart of Little Rock and then to the hostel that was in a building next to a 19th century redbrick church. By their shared architecture the two were obviously connected. Rachel parked the jeep, went in, and a few minutes later came out with her pack and an express mail envelope.

She put her gear in the back and we changed places. As I was driving back out of the city she tore open the envelope. Inside were two Oregon citizen cards: one with my picture as I looked now, in the name of Roger Keith, the other for Rachel in the name of Deborah Keith. Both showing we were authorized to drive non-commercially. I put it in my wallet, still unsure the card would stand up to examination when its chip was examined, if I had to show it.

Rachel, reading my thoughts, said in my mind, "They will stand scrutiny. John says you now have a whole history that can be checked," and she handed me two pages with my new name at the top. "John said to memorize it and burn it. He and Topher put it together."

There were two pages for her as well. Then she shook the envelope and out fell a registration card for the jeep. "How did he know?" I asked.

"I wrote down the VIN number and the license plate when we left the car, to make sure we got the same one back."

"Smart girl; that's why I married you," I said, and we laughed, but underneath all three of us felt the reality behind my words. There was a kind of contented hum in our connection, a shared emotion that made me feel happy. I welcomed this commitment. I knew Rachel in ways I knew no other human being; and she knew me in the same degree. Going through this experience had bonded us; we were life partners.

We carefully weighed whether it was safer to take freeways or blue highways, and settled on continuing on small roads. We crossed the Arkansas River on the Main Street Bridge and drove through neighborhoods paralleling Interstate 30, eventually winding our way out into a pine woods on County 367.

Keeping away from built up areas and always staying on blue highways we were less likely to encounter anyone, and there was in fact very little traffic. Few people, unless they live there, realize that 200 miles inland from a coast or 20 miles from an urban node like Little Rock, the U.S. is mostly empty now.

As we drove my sense of connectedness to both Rachel and Mike increased. It drifted out of words into, I'm not sure what to call it, knowingness. Rachel and I understood that Mike wanted to get to a place called Riding Rocks, an atoll in the Caribbean, and he had a sense of urgency about it.

"Why?" I held the thought in my mind.

His answer came back clothed in compassion, and yet with that same professional disinterest.

"As I told you, the breakdown that climate change is causing has a high potential of throwing human societies into chaos leading to mass death, social breakdown, and probably nuclear war over who will dominate the collapse. By our calculations, even if you survive as a diminished species there is a 52 percent chance another order, the cetaceans, will become dominant within the next ten thousand years."

I was staggered that anyone thought in those terms, and I could tell so was Rachel. That was followed by another darker emotion, and I could feel Rachel reaching the same understanding. This really was a world changing secret. Quinton was right. If we could get Mike on the web, humanity would experience an epiphany. Linked as we were we realized that we might not come out of this alive. There would be enormous forces that wouldn't want this epiphany to happen. As I thought this, Mike objected.

"That's not the way to do it. That would just cause chaos. If you want to change a society or a civilization the way you do it is non-violently, and the way to do that is to change yourself."

"How am I going to change myself; what needs to change?"

"You already have changed; observe how we are communicating. You and Rachel learned to do this. It is a teachable skill. I told you, this is the gift I am giving you in return for the gift you are giving me."

We were in a kind of bubble as we drove on those little roads across Arkansas and Alabama. Because we were always on county roads, it was easy to stay in state parks. And all of this was done in a cocoon of consciousness in which the three of us were linked, gradually giving us not just an individual memory, but a collective one that was both a part of and apart from us.

Our abilities expanded rapidly. Once you get started and you interact that way all the time, it's very natural. Also there were just three of us, with Mike to guide and explain. Rachel and I just let ourselves open to a soft cushion of consciousness. It was like stepping through a door that had always been there, but had been unrecognized.

The miles moved by, and somewhere in Alabama it seemed natural for Mike to drive. He loved it, but the structure of the jeep was all wrong for his body, even when he was sitting on a sleeping bag. His control of any kind of system just seemed to be innate and once again I saw that his physical strength was far greater than his size would indicate. We also learned he had a special kind of reserve. We parked on a mountain vista point, and I didn't set the brake correctly. It gave way. The jeep began to roll. Before I could even react Mike was in motion. By running faster than the jeep was rolling he was able to catch the door frame and pull it to a stop. Mike was so quick and fluid; it was like watching a big cat bring down a gazelle.

"It is just that I can command all my physical power. You can do it," he said, to our disbelief. "The ability is there. It happens on drugs like PCP sometimes, but there is no control with that; or sometimes people train for it with martial arts, meditation. There are many doorways." There was something in the way he said things. Dispassionate. Matter of fact. We learned his form of communication allowed for tact but not deceit. Emphasis was in the feeling tones, not adjectives.

We were in Georgia. I was driving, and we had almost relaxed to the point of comfort, when Mike suddenly warned us of an intent to dominate us. A moment later, the siren of a highway patrol trooper began. There were clearly three of us in the car, and no time to hide Mike. It was hot, and the jeep with its canvas top didn't have air conditioning. Mike wasn't wearing his hoodie.

The trooper spoke into his PA system telling us to pull over. We did so, and he got out and stood protected by his door, pointing a shotgun at us, and telling us over the PA, "Driver put your hands on the steering wheel, and the woman and the boy put your hands on your heads."

"He does not know who we are," Mike said. Then after a moment, "But he has been told to stop us and report." As Mike said it I could see in the side mirror the officer walking toward us. When he was outside our canvas door he said, "Please open the door," and I did.

"Let me see your license and registration, please."

"I have to take my hand off the steering wheel to reach in my pants."

"Go ahead."

To get my wallet I had to turn slightly, creating just a bit more room. Mike simply grabbed the man, pulled him into the cab, and with his other hand grabbed him by the neck, holding him in place. As he did this, the trooper turned his head and for the first time looked at Mike and really saw him. We could see and feel him go into reality vertigo. He suddenly slumped as if struck on the head, and his upper body came to rest limply in my lap. His Smokey the Bear trooper hat was pushed onto his back.

Through all of this, we could hear the radio as it squawked throughout asking the trooper for his GPS coordinate. Rachel and Mike got out of the jeep, went around and pulled the trooper back, laying him on the ground.

Mike took the tablet out of his hands and looked at it, then held it up so we could all see it. There was our license number and a video of the jeep. "He hasn't transmitted yet." Mike looked at the tablet and I realized he was changing it. He manipulated it in some way I didn't understand, even as he shared it. The screen went dark, then rebooted. When it returned it showed a blank case report form.

"How long will he be out?" I asked as I got out of the driver's seat.

"About an hour," Mike responded.

"What did you do?"

"I changed his brain patterns, basically the same process as healing prayer. There is no damage. You had a researcher back in the 1960s, Carroll Nash at Pittsburgh, whose studies showed consciousness could manipulate the wellbeing of organisms positively or negatively depending on their intention. Nobody paid much attention," Mike added, and I could sense a giant "Duhh..." in his emotional tone. "But there is even more to it than that. I'll show you in a minute. I have to do something first."

He knelt over the trooper for some time, maybe ten minutes, then stood up, "He was much too tense, had a liver problem, and was diabetic, all of which I fixed," and for a moment I could see what Mike saw: the man as a series of networks, making up a meta-network, an architecture of information. The experience was unbelievably intense.

"What am looking at?" I asked.

"The human brain has about 80 billion neurons; about 800 million are firing at any one time. That's the flashes of light you see in his neuroanatomy. If you go further in, well it's not really further, but your languages are all based on a spacetime view of the world. Deeper, no that's a space word as well. Anyway you get the point." And he saw that I did, and so did Rachel.

"If you focus your intention further, you will see the information base upon which all matter is built. I changed the pattern, and I also changed his DNA so he won't pass his genetic-based problems on, and they won't recur. This is where medicine goes, Arthur," he said, and looked up at us. And I realized what he was saying. What he was really saying.

Then I was back to thinking about what we needed to do. "How much will he remember, Mike?" I asked.

"He will remember stopping but not why."

"Then let's take him back to his car."

So we picked him up and carried him back. We laid him on his back in front of his car, as if he had fallen. I went around and opened the hood, and as I looked at the engine Mike came around, made a quick movement amongst the wires. There was a flash and the smell of burning insulation. "He will not start this engine. It will look like he stopped to check it, shocked himself, and it caused him to pass out."

"But he already called it in," Rachel said. "It won't make sense."

"Ninety-nine percent of it does; that's enough in this situation. It will be one of those odd stories but no more if we do this right. I have been watching humans for many decades, the last 12 stuck in one place but with a depth of access I could otherwise never have achieved, as I told you. I could see anything; that was the deal. I am sure they tracked me, but it didn't matter. They did not see your world the way I do. Their analysis was always false because of that. I cannot tell you how grateful I am to have survived the crash, to have been in that Blue Room as they called it, that they had built for me. And now to be here. It's exciting."

He was right. In the middle of what he was saying, when I disassociated and moved into what I had begun to think of as our common consciousness space, I could see it. Mike wiped the tablet down, wrapped it in a piece of paper, took it over, unwrapped it, and put the trooper's hand around in several ways.

Rachel came over, watched for a moment and said, "We all agree this is just going to buy us some time."

"Yes, that's exactly the way to see it," Mike said. "All he is going to know is that he got out of his car. So they can't be even moderately sure it's us. All they know is that he is somewhere on the mountain, and he's not responding to calls. They will send someone out, several someones, I think."

"But, something we did has allowed them to capture us," Rachel insisted. "Facial recognition probably."

We looked at each other, and I suddenly saw us as others would. Our body language would look impersonal, suggesting indifference, or dislike. The weird thing is that when you are in someone's consciousness and they are in yours, you don't actually look at each other as much. You don't need to. You can keep on doing something because you get the full communication in your mind and experience it in your senses, it's much more comprehensive and nuanced than relying on body language. But when I looked over at Rachel when Mike made her laugh, her delight was mirrored in her face. Okay, happy loners taking a trip together. Either way, weird, and I could feel the others agree.

"But this means we have to change our game again,' I said, and we all agreed.

"No illusions about the imminence of pursuit," Rachel said; and we had none.

CHAPTER TWENTY TWO

We didn't think our pursuers would think of trekking, so we drove another 30 miles then turned up a fire road, went 10 miles back, and made camp for the night, camouflaging the jeep and sleeping under trees on the tarps. I was pretty sure we could evade visual, although not infrared if a helo got close and was looking, but it was a risk we had to take.

We sat in the dark, magically comfortable, even with all the stress. We could hear the sounds of the night, and if we concentrated we could bring the small life forces that made those sounds into focus as well. I understood why Mike's people, open to consciousness in this way, had created an architecture technologically sophisticated but still in touch with the rhythms and forces of nature.

After a while, though, we had to get back to it. "Think about this," I said. "After watching Congress members for more than a decade," and we shared that gestalt as I said it, "I think we are correct in thinking that whoever is seeking us has the power to use government agencies without disclosing to them their real purpose. It's a cabal within government. But they can't involve too many people because if they were to catch Mike, it would be hard to keep it a secret. So they are looking, but there are limitations."

"Yes," Mike echoed, and Rachel agreed.

"We have to surrender the jeep. I don't see any other way. We have to get off the road, or travel it in a different way," Rachel said. And she was right. I was suddenly very tense and could feel Rachel felt the same. But to my surprise Mike was not.

"Wait," he said. "I'll show you in the morning. But you need to go to sleep." That's what we did, and slept well.

We awoke at dawn, made a good breakfast, and worked our way back out to the county road but stayed out of sight back in the woods.

"This morning I'm going to show you something else," Mike said. "Let's just sit here," and we did. "Now move into intentioned focused awareness with me." It was as if we went up into the air a couple hundred feet.

"We're looking for a consciousness open to opening."

"What does that mean?" I asked.

"You'll see," Mike responded. "Just imagine you are looking down on the road, as it comes off the mountain.

After a moment, helped by Mike, Rachel and I began to feel just on the edge of awareness people driving down the switchbacks of the mountain road. I couldn't tell what they were driving, or how far away they were, but Mike could so we all got it. Traffic wasn't heavy, which helped, giving us time to bring the link into focus.

"What are we looking for?" Rachel asked.

"A spark. You'll see."

After about an hour, I felt it; there was a kind of spark to a consciousness coming towards us, and we all knew this was the one. We drove the jeep out onto the verge. A few minutes later one of the new electric long hauls came lumbering down the road. Mike just stood there by the hood of the jeep unconcerned. We waved and the truck pulled over on to the turnout and stopped. The driver got out, a big-bellied burly man with a leather vest over a white T-shirt. He saw Rachel and me and then Mike stepped around the jeep.

The driver's attention was immediately completely focused. You could see in his face everything else fade away. Then suddenly I was aware of his consciousness, and the pulse of his attention.

"Well shit! Are you from outer space? Are you an alien? OhmyGod!"

I was completely unprepared for his reaction. Fear. Hostility. I was prepared for those, but not immediate curiosity and interest.

We could feel Mike reach into his mind as he had reached into ours, and watched it happen. "Yes, I am, and we need your help." The driver began to smile. "No shit. You really are from another planet?"

"I am, and I will tell you all about it, but my friends and I need to move quickly. Will you help us?" Mike spoke to him and the man's emotional tone responded just as I had done, and he said, "Roger that." I focused on him and immediately knew he was a vet like me. Then he suddenly realized that actually nothing had been said vocally.

He spoke aloud, then paused and thought it in his head. "This is just... you know I listen to audios when I drive. I have read dozens of books on UFOs. I saw one... one night, outside of Chattanooga. I was at the truck stop; a bunch of us saw it." As the memory formed we went into it with him, helping him let his consciousness open. It began with him understanding that we were there. That we were linked.

We stood there on the side of the road, three humans and a 150-year-old gray-green being from the Horse Nebula.

"My name's Charley, and I think we ought to get moving. There's sure to be some traffic behind me."

He reached in the truck's cab and brought out his tablet linked to his GPS, and we all looked at it. There was a quarry about five miles further down the mountain.

"We have to get rid of the jeep. I'll drive it down to the quarry lake, and we'll sink it there." I envisioned the steps in my mind, and much quicker than I had, Charley opened to our net of consciousness.

We began transferring our gear into a storage locker under the truck, and Mike and Rachel climbed into the truck's back compartment where they could see, but not be seen. I looked in. It was a kind of mini-RV with a bunk, television, small fridge, a combination microwave convection oven as well as a separate small toilet/shower. To my eyes it was state of the art. But I realized to Mike's eye it must have seemed very primitive. There was a mirror over the bunk. Charley saw me notice it, smiled again, and looked at Rachel.

"Charley," Rachel said, "I'm flattered," and we all laughed.

We drove down to the quarry, and while driving learned from Charley that he was 44 and from Blairsville, Georgia, where he still lived. He went into the army after high school, became a Ranger, and did two tours. Came out and used his educational benefits to go to community college to get an Associate Degree in EV transportation.

As he shared this his memories evoked my own, and the two of us understood we had shared combat in some of the same places. That moved us up into a level of trust that shared experience engenders. As that happened, Mike and Rachel joined in, and we all knew that in Charley we had a partner.

We came to the quarry. Its sides were so steep that the deep green conifers growing in the meager soil of the wall niches reached out two feet, then made an elbow turn and hugged the granite walls as they grew upwards. There was a turnout created by people stopping to look out across the lake. I got the jeep behind the rail guard just as the turnout started. It was very precarious for about 50 feet, but then it widened out considerably until I could turn the jeep and point it at the lake. There was even a little room to back up, and I hoped it was enough for what I had in mind.

I set the brake but left the motor running. Even though I didn't think anyone would ever find the jeep, at least not in a time frame that mattered to us, I took off the license and VIN plate. Then I went back and found two sturdy sticks. While I was doing this Charley pulled his rig into the turnout, which left no room for anyone else. He let his truck idle almost silently. This had the effect of blocking anyone from seeing what I was doing with the jeep.

I took one of the sticks and wedged it to hold the accelerator down and keep the engine revved. I took my shoelace, tied it around the other stick, and wedged it to hold down the clutch. I moved the stick and upped the revs, put the jeep in gear, released the brake, got out and pulled the string.

It popped the clutch and the jeep jumped forward, gathered speed and ran off the cliff, going out about 20 feet. For a moment, just like the old Wiley Coyote and Road Runner cartoons, it hung in the air. Then, nose first, fell into the water and sank without a trace. I could look almost straight down and waited several minutes, but nothing showed.

I went back to the truck, and we drove off. As we came off the mountain to rendezvous with the highway, several state troopers, two in marked cars, one unmarked, came off the other side maybe 300 yards away, and raced up the mountain.

As we drove, Mike worked with Charley, as he had worked with us, to open his consciousness, and asked us to join in.

"Do you see what I am doing? Do you see how as Charley reaches out with his intention, that I link to it and support it? This is how you open people to consciousness. Do you see it as well Charley? This is as much for you as for Rachel and Arthur," Mike told us.

"You know I never doubted your existence. I never believed that aliens hurt people, otherwise they would have taken over the world," Charley said in his mind, then added, "This is very cool." Then "I've seen documentaries saying they did some kind of experiment on some women." This came with several graphic images about this process that made Rachel wince. "Do you do that?" he asked Mike.

"No," Mike responded. "I don't need to take physical biological samples. The informational structure gives me that. We're not the ones doing physical sampling. That's not my civilization. They don't hurt people by the way. What they're trying to do is understand your genetics and manipulate it to keep you from killing yourselves" he said, and stopped there; but we all knew there was much more.

By then we were on a four-lane state highway, and after a while Charley said, "I was only on the mountain to make a delivery at that last town. I have to get on the interstate in the electric lane to recharge my batteries, and it's almost twice as fast. Where do you need to go?"

"We need to get to a boat dock where we can charter a boat to get to some islands on the other side of the Gulf Stream in the Bahamas."

"You need a boat?" Charley's amused surprise swept over us.

"Yes, one big enough to get across the Stream and to be able to stay on station for several days. Mike has something he has to do," I said. We drove in silence for a while, and then pulled into the electric lane where Charley locked in the auto-pilot. Now we were one truck amongst hundreds, each carefully spaced and moving at about 110 miles per hour, a train of independent boxcars. As we drove, Charley's batteries recharged wirelessly from the road itself so that they would be full when he went off the photovoltaic roadway. He logged his route, then turned around and told us there was some cheese, a salami, and most of a salad in the little refrigerator. Rachel got food out, as well as a very good non-alcoholic beer and some sparkling water. She put it all on the little table.

We snacked and focused on eating for a moment, sharing how each of us reacted to a particular food. But then it just came down to silence. It was in that silence of the road, linked in consciousness now including Charley, that we had a kind of collective epiphany. Mike said "Not everyone may agree with what I am doing but I think it is the right thing, and I am the one here on the ground," and we realized he was speaking more to others than to us. In that instant we saw the network of conscious civilizations that were Mike's reality.

A buzzer broke the moment and Charley looked at his controls. "It's two hours and 15 minutes to the next node."

"Do you have any regrets?" Charley asked, looking at Mike.

"We crashed and I was captured," Mike answered. "It happened before I was able to see the nuclear reactor sites and experiments that were a special area of interest on this trip. How you deal with nuclear is one of the doors a civilization that develops the technology has to go through. You're at a kind of tipping point." Then, with a mental shrug, he added, "As I've told Arthur and Rachel, getting captured made it possible for me to study things at a level of detail that would not ordinarily have been possible. It's not easy to study a civilization without impacting it, or impacting it only in controlled ways. You have a similar principle in your anthropology."

We could feel Mike's silent laugh. "My captors showed me anything I wanted because they assumed I would never leave, and were hoping by my comments, or answers to direct questions, that they would obtain technological gain. They wanted me to understand your civilization, in hopes that I would recommend to them things to do, or share technology. But they had no concept of this. Had no real idea what I was doing, or why."

He paused and let us process what he was saying. Then he said "I did contribute carefully controlled bits. I made contributions in solar and potable water, for instance. As you would say, I put my thumb on the scale. That's what we do. If the overall trend is life affirming we support it with a kind of social acupuncture. But we do it in such a way that our involvement is unknown or, in my case, only known to a very few. We make as little impact on a culture as possible. We don't want to distort. If you distort the construct you change probabilities. That's the consideration that has to be kept in mind. Is my thumb too heavy?" Listening to Mike, and not only hearing the mindspeech but also experiencing a flood of sensations as we saw the world a little bit the way he did, I wondered if any humans except the three of us had ever felt this way: not being the dominant species.

I turned my passenger side chair around, completing the transformation of the space into a tiny living room. Mike asked Rachel, who was closest to the little kitchenette, "Could you make me a cocktail, please?" She had watched Mike make it, giving her a running commentary.

"Yes, it makes learning very different," Mike explained, catching my thought.

"How many languages do you speak?" Rachel asked.

"I speak 37 human languages."

"And your accent changes, but you use very little slang."

"You're becoming southern," I added.

"We are moving further south; Charley made me realize that. It makes people more comfortable if you create the linkage in a shared accent, even mentally," Mike said. "Slang is too labile, too complex for me to keep up with it."

"How did you learn all those languages?" Rachel asked, as she pulled out of the knapsack greens Mike had picked earlier. She added some water, a little Braggs, opened one of his capsules and sprinkled it in. She closed the container and put it on the shaft next to the oven. It whirled for moment. She took it off, handed it to him, observing, "That's the last of it. We'll have to stop someplace."

Mike opened the container and drank, simultaneously saying in our minds, in answer to Rachel's question, "I learned them in language school. Once you open to this part of yourself you learn things differently, at a different rate, and you have different resources to draw on. You'll see. Also I have been monitoring Earth for a long time in your terms."

Mike took another drink, and what he told us next is why you are reading this.

"Your civilization is poised to either enter the conscious universe, or destroy itself. How you deal with climate change and what is coming will determine it, as will nuclear war. There are several paths to destruction, only one to flourish. Your dominant cultures are unconscious. You must become conscious, as we are now. You, this group, are only at the threshold of the matrix of consciousness. As you use this part of yourself, you will open to other potentialities."

But there was something else, and Rachel turned to Mike and said, "We're like a tribe of natives for you, aren't we?"

"Yes. Yes, you are," Mike responded, with no attempt to soften his answer. But at the same time the knowingness came wrapped in a compassion that arose from a depth and breadth of knowledge that was ineffable. It was the truth; he was 10,000 years ahead of us.

"But, here's the point, Rachel. Do you think the indigenous peoples of your planet now or in antiquity are a lesser order of beings because they lack your particular technology?" He turned and looked at Rachel. "Are they less likable, or less important as human beings for this lack?"

Mike's outsider view confronted us with our stereotypes.

"I don't think so," Mike answered his own question. "I have been studying human cultures longer than any of you have been alive, and I've had full access to what my colleagues and family learned and experienced." For just a moment I saw the arc of humanity from its distant past.

"While I sat in my very comfortable suite," Mike told us, "I didn't just study your databases. I talked with aboriginal shamans and others around the world. There are already individuals who have developed the ability to communicate in this way, at least to some degree. What is mistaken for primitivism by one culture is usually a different way of being. Earth's hominoids still express themselves in many ways."

For a while we just sat and thought about that, sharing memories and images. Then something on the dash beeped, and Charley turned around and fully focused on driving.

"Junction coming up," and I recognized his southern drawl.

When we got to the node, we transferred to a spur of the interstate and locked in again. We kind of collectively comprehended that we were dealing with a being from a society so advanced we often missed the nuances of what he was saying. We could experience something like his memories of his house, but much of what he said came from a perspective we could hardly understand. Part of it was that he thought in a time frame difficult for a human to conceptualize.

Our verbal silence was broken by Charley, who got on his phone and called a friend.

At the next rest stop Charley drove in going nearly to the end on the trucking side. There were very few other long hauls, and he pulled in in such a way that no one could see the woods behind his length.

He said in mindspeech he thought it was safe to pitch the tent so we did, then cooked a dinner in his microwave convection oven. After dinner Rachel, Mike, and I went out to the tent, and Charley got into his bunk.

The next morning we stopped for breakfast at a diner Charley knew. Then back on the road driving a few miles further on, where he pulled his truck to the curb in the outskirts of Dania, Florida, a small town surrounded by Ft. Lauderdale. After Mike got his hoodie, bandana and gloves outfit on, we climbed down from the cab. Mike and Charley shared a moment of final contact. Now, almost effortlessly, we were able to retreat and give them privacy.

Charley came to where Rachel and I were standing. "Here's the number of my buddy. He's also a vet… the third Iraq. His name is James Peterson. He's got a car dealership, and a horseshoe pitching pit, or some other kind of damn fool business, a little ways out of town. I talked to him; he'll do what you need. And Mike: Will you tune him in too, please?"

"Of course. And Charley you know how to do it now, so you will be able to stay in touch. Remember distance doesn't matter; just hold the intention as I showed you... and when you see someone and it feels right, show them too."

"Thumb on the scale, right?"

"Right."

Then Charley put out his right hand. Mike took off his glove, extended his hand, and Charley enfolded Mike's three-fingered version in his own. He stepped back and looked at us, got into his truck, pulled his horn, and drove a mile down the road where we could see him drive up the ramp and back into the interstate traffic. With Mike following like a kid playing, Rachel and I, mom and dad, walked over to the Vagabond Motel.

"I wish I'd brought my own sheets," Rachel said, in mindspeech, and the image was not a pretty one.

"Remember to verbalize," I reminded both of us.

We went into the tiny office where a middle-aged Indian woman looked us up and down with disapproval as we stood there in filthy jeans and work shirts, but currency kept the process moving.

After long hot showers and a discussion over whether I should keep my beard, which in the end Rachel tidied up a bit, we sat down around the room and watched CNN to see what was happening in a world I, at least, felt disconnected from. We sat for an hour, but there was not a word about us, so we all relaxed a bit. As we watched, Quinton's words about putting Mike on television came into my mind and I put it to Mike.

"Mike, suppose we got you on television? That would have enormous impact, and might protect you. Us as well come to that."

"No, Arthur," Mike said with finality. "It would change the whole course of human civilization in ways no one could predict, and many of the unintended consequences could be very negative. It's too big. Too sudden. No, and please don't ask me again."

We sat in mental silence for a while, each of us in our own internal space.

"He's right," Rachel said after a while, leaning over and putting her hand atop mine to both make her point and to show me support.

"I can't even imagine what would happen if Mike suddenly appeared on CNN, no matter what his message was. It would blow the world up emotionally."

I saw their point; they were right. We worked through it collectively in our minds. I could see it would undercut what Mike was trying to do.

"But, Arthur, I have been thinking along those lines as well," Mike said. "I want you to take three pictures of me. Enough to make a case and stir interest that over time will grow into the mainstream. Enough to make a difference, but not enough to make a scene. Put up two of the pictures. And when the time is right I want you to upload the log you have been keeping so carefully along with the final picture on the net. I have been watching the process for years. It will go viral, and accomplish what you have in mind, but in a slower, less traumatic, less blatant way."

Rachel and I agreed, then Mike said "But that's only a piece of it. You and Rachel, and now Charley, are the seeds. Awakening people to this aspect of themselves will put them in direct touch with the matrix of life. Just as happened with you… spread it," he said.

"How will we know who to pick? Now we are just doing it to get you to where you need to go."

"Can you both remember how we waited with the jeep for the right person to come down the road?" and as he said this we did. "When you see that you'll know. Also remember, you cannot lie; deceit is not possible in this realm because your motives are available. Power comes in the form of collective deference to those who foster wellbeing."

"How many people will it take?" Rachel asked.

"Ten percent. When you have 10 percent the entirety of humanity will change in consciousness. I am doing two things now. I am placing my bet that humanity will survive. But I am also transferring information to the Cetacea. If you survive you will have a wonderful partnership with them. If you don't, the Cetacea will become the dominant species.

As we all sat on the bed, Mike told us in that dispassionate objective way of his, that about 50,000 years ago another civilization had changed our DNA in such a way that it rewired our brains.

"It made complex speech possible, and hominoids went from being a large mammal widely scattered but with a low population, to a force that changed the world. I am laying the groundwork for the Cetacea for the same reasons."

I didn't know what to say to that, and neither did Rachel. Then something shifted; there in that funky motel Rachel, Mike and I worked out what we were going to do next.

CHAPTER TWENTY THREE

It was just as Charley had said; Peterson agreed to pick us up in the morning. Rachel and I had argued with Mike that revealing his presence might not be a good idea, but he was adamant. "Don't you see, I am linking you together. You can contact Charley as easily as Rachel. It's a matter of holding intention. I don't know why this is happening and why this particular group of humans are the ones that are linking. I just know that I should expedite it," Mike explained to us, and the imagery of the linkage brought Charley back into the conversation.

"Wow, this is cool," he said, and then bowed out.

It was also in the motel that for the first time Mike made us understand that we had to hurry.

"My reason for coming here is to make contact with a genetic line of dolphins we have been working with for the last 3,000 years. We manipulated their genes to facilitate cognition."

"Why are you doing this?" Rachel asked.

"There are two major long-term scenarios for humans."

"Only two?" I held the question in my mind with great intensity.

"Basically, yes. We've touched on this before. Human civilization will either awaken to the fundamental nature of consciousness, comprehend that humans are part of a matrix of consciousness which includes all living organisms, and that all life is interdependent and interconnected. You will really comprehend as a culture that consciousness can affect matter. It starts with understanding that matter arises from consciousness, not consciousness from matter. If that is the scenario that plays out you will see your way through climate change and thrive, and advance quite quickly. There will be a burst of creativity like your Renaissance, and maybe even more apt, the Axial Age 8th to 2nd century BCE."

I had never heard of it, and neither had Rachel, and once again we realized that humans were something Mike studied, as his father and grandfather before him had studied human civilization, all its cultures and sciences, across thousands of years. When I thought that, I felt for just a moment the intensity of Mike's commitment. Of course he knew more about human history than we did. His view was longer, his study more objective and intense, his source incomprehensible from our world view, and he wasn't caught up in the immediacy of living it, with all the emotions that entailed.

"In that historically small time period," Mike said, looking at us intensely, "most of humanity's great pre-Christian religious movements and philosophical lines developed:
Plato
Parsva
Mahavira
Siddhartha Gautama
Confucius
Zarathustra
Lao Tzu
Homer
Socrates
Parmenides
Heraclitus
Thucydides
Archimedes
Elijah
Isaiah
Jeremiah
Deutero-Isaiah Judaism

Pythagoras
Heraclitus
Parmenides
Anaxagoras

"Human consciousness changed in a short space of time, and you are poised for it to happen again. I hope that's what happens. On that path your relationship with Cetacea will move into a very different plane. A partnership that you can't even imagine now."

As Mike spoke his thoughts evoked in me my memories of twice diving with a wild pod of dolphins that had come up to me. Rachel joined in with her own images of diving and encountering a dolphin pod. Those images, plus the idea of partnering, blended into my memories of Mike's house.

"Humans will do it differently than us," he said. "We have gills. But yes, you have the idea. The world looks very different, doesn't it, when you are in communication with other life forms."

"And what's the other scenario?" Rachel asked.

"Just what I told you. Your civilization will wither; you will go through a very dystopian period and revert to a much smaller population clustered in viable areas living a different version of the hunter-gatherer model. It's not clear to us whether you will ever climb out, because after about 10,000 years the Cetacea will emerge as the planetary leaders. What we have been doing benefits the Cetacea either way, although we think the better outcome is that you partner. Not just dolphins by the way. Whales. All the Cetacea."

"Why do you have to get to this particular pod?" Rachel asked.

"This is a subgroup, descendants of the pod we contacted. I am going to make what you could think of as a course correction. That's not all though; if things have worked as planned there will also be a super pod of humpback whales assembling. Another team back then did the same DNA mutation with several whale species."

"Humpback whales don't assemble in super pods, or any kind of pod. They're solitary," I said.

"We'll see," Mike responded.

"Do the Humpbacks and dolphins communicate?" Rachel asked.

"Yes. That's one of the reasons I want to be there. It's the same thing that was done with you, although, as I said, not by my people," he added almost as an aside.

"What do you mean?" both Rachel and I asked in surprise at once.

"How do you think Homo Sapiens became the dominant hominoid?" Mike asked. "About 35,000 years ago another group assessed the chances of the Neanderthal, the Devonians, and felt your lot had the best chance. That's what those cases about people being taken into craft are about. Garbled to be sure, but basically accurate. We make small changes and monitor how things are going. As I told you we aren't the only civilization at work here. There is a council that oversees the work."

I could hardly process what Mike was saying, even though I knew it was with good intentions. But the idea that I was part of a species that had been selected and manipulated by another was a weirdness too far. Rachel and I just looked at each other as it sank in.

"If it's any consolation, it was done to my species as well."

"Do you really mean there are species of beings going around the universe manipulating things in a life affirming way?"

"Yes. It's part of what the conscious planets do if they are space capable. Not all choose to be."

"It reminds me of gardening," said Rachel.

"It is, rather," Mike responded. "It replaces war. It requires the same big toys, the adventure, only it fosters wellbeing not death and destruction. All conscious cultures want more people to awaken. I'm sure you can already feel that."

And he was right. I did, and so did Rachel and Charley.

For the first time I detected a slight personal tone; Mike wanted us to work it out. He was putting his thumb on the scale in a much bigger and subtler way than I had appreciated.

I called Peterson and introduced myself as Roger Keith. He did not question me, saying only Charley had asked him to help where he could. We made an appointment for two hours later, and he showed up at our door to the minute. He was even bigger than Charley, and not fat at all. A bear of a man, dressed in farmer's denim overalls, a T-shirt with the arms cut off, and a baseball cap reading "Jarvis Steaks. We'll slip you the best meat in the South."

He came into our room and we spontaneously reached out to make contact. At that point Mike was sitting on the bed with his legs tucked under him and his hoodie up, a kid watching television, and Peterson paid very little attention to him initially. But suddenly we could feel the connection.

"Whoa, what's going on here?" There was more emotion than cognition, and it was intense. Mike turned to Peterson and pulled off his hood.

"You're an alien…"

"He is," Rachel told him verbally.

"I don't understand what's going on here," Peterson said, and we could all sense his agitation.

"If you'll trust me for a minute we can make this all clearer."

"You damn well better."

"Sit in the chair there," I told him, and he went and sat down.

"This is going to seem very strange, I know, but give me 20 minutes and it will all become clearer."

"Ya got 20 minutes."

"Put your feet on the floor, now take a deep breath and let it out… now take another, and close your eyes, now a third. Okay. I want to you hold the intention that you can connect with Charley. See him in your mind as if he were standing in front of you." And so began what was becoming a standardized ritual. It took a minute for Peterson to relax, but with all of us reaching out to him it helped, and I could see how it speeded up the process.

"Charley… is that you Charley?"

"It's me."

"Where are you?"

"I'm linked in on the 75 and programmed for Atlanta to pick up a load. I wish I could be with you, and I am I guess. This is amazing stuff

Peterson, just relax; they'll guide the way. Oh, the little guy is Mike," Charley said.

"Mike…Mike. Whoever heard of an alien named Mike?"

"It's just the name I use with humans because my name is more an emotion than a word," and once again I felt that sense of brave resolve I had felt before when Mike shared his real name.

"It gets much richer the more you do it, Peterson. You aren't going to believe what's possible," Charley said, then, "Gotta go… I'm coming to the node where I offline…." And with that he was gone.

For the next half hour we guided Peterson through the steps to strengthen the connection, and he became more enthusiastic as he opened to it.

"Now that we have a connection we can keep it going even if we are moving, and we need to get going," I said in mindspeech.

We gathered up our things, put them into Peterson's converted milk truck, and Mike and I climbed in the sliding door.

Rachel went to the passenger side, and Peterson, moving with unusual grace for a man so massive, got there first and opened the door for her.

As we were driving down the road, he said, "I can't wait to hear this story. It's gotta be a doozy."

"Let's have some lunch," I said, "but first Rachel has to get some things. Is there a health food store around here?"

"Yeah, about a mile from here," he replied, like all of us when we first started, part verbally and partly in mindspeech.

"Let's go there first."

Peterson waited patiently while Rachel was in the store in a small strip mall. She came out with a bag full of the amino acid and supplement liquids, and the greens which constitute Mike's diet, while he quietly sat in the back of the truck.

We drove on a ways and stopped at a fish joint on the bayou. It didn't look like much, but Peterson said it had great food, and the best alligator fritters in the county. I wouldn't know, I wouldn't eat one and neither would Rachel.

We sat at a green outdoor picnic table with a red and white striped umbrella a little distance away from the restaurant, near the bayou bank. I went in with Peterson and ordered his alligator fritters, as well as a dozen oysters, a paper cup's worth of lemon slices, hot sauces, two grilled snapper sandwiches, cole slaw, a big thick wedge of grilled fries, and a pitcher of cold beer. We waited while the food was prepared; I paid in cash, which didn't seem odd in that setting, and we took it back outdoors. With Mike at the far end of the bench with his hoodie, just a kid having lunch, we laid everything out, speaking verbally, which was suddenly an incredibly restricted way to communicate. As I spoke, I could feel Rachel reach out to Peterson. Mike joined in. But we still had to have parts of the conversation verbally. We were asking a lot of Peterson to open to the connection this quickly. He was trying as hard as he could.

"The key is to hold intentioned focus," Rachel said. "It will become easier and easier as we do it. Just relax, there is much more than words."

'Got it," Peterson replied.

"Mike needs to get to a place on the Bahamas Banks called Riding Rocks."

"I know where that is," Peterson answered, adding "But there's nothing there except a single tree."

"It's not the land I'm interested in," Mike told him.

Peterson took that aboard for a moment as I poured another beer into Rachel's glass. Our eyes locked and we fully acknowledged how much we had changed, how far we were from the world of the "Hill," bureaucrats with careers moving smartly up the Federal escalator. It made us laugh.

"What's so funny?" Peterson asked.

We told him a highly edited quick version of our story, watching his demeanor change as we did so. "Great story," and his interest and good humor about it radiated out to all of us.

Then he pulled his phone from the pocket of his bib overalls.

"Skunk, you're not going to believe this. Call Leon: ask him if he'll make a night crossing of the stream. I think the whole trip will take maybe four days."

With a look at me, "There'll be pay. Ask Erica if she'll come. This has nothing to do with drugs. It's a much better story. Charley sent these people to me. You remember him, the machine gunner at Gizab? ... yeah, that's the guy... and Day Chopan too, that's right."

While he was still talking I dug out one of the pre-paids and called the number John gave us. It rang and his computer voice came on,

"My goodness what are you doing calling me from Slovenia," he said, and I almost corrected him when I realized the call had somehow been routed there and back again. "How's the weather?"

"Passable," I responded.

"Let me tap someone in," and after a moment Topher was on.

"Even on the surface it's beginning to crack. You're over time now. No clear story line. Same with Rachel. Actually in her case there is genuine concern something untoward has happened to her. It is getting very sticky. I have been interviewed four times now. I would say there's no coming back," Topher said in the strange robovoice.

"We suspected as much; it's okay, we weren't planning to return," I responded. Then, thinking of Quinton and Paul, "Could you please let those we mentioned last time know we're all right? Say I will contact them shortly."

"No problem, we'll handle it," Topher said.

John came on, saying "The good news is there's no agreement what you look like now. I think the paperwork is still safe. The bad news is just what Topher said."

"I don't want to ask any questions, so I don't know anything," Topher said, and John agreed. "We'll let some people know. Try to stay out of trouble, and I would hurry things along as much as I could." And they broke the connection.

I took the battery out of the phone, then the SIM card which I broke in two. I broke the phone itself into pieces, walked along by the bayou looking down into the water like a tourist, and threw in the pieces one by one.

When we finished lunch it was mid-afternoon, and we got back on the road headed to what Peterson described as "the docks." Each turn seemed to put us on a smaller road, and in the end we were driving down a gravel road, past the back of a customs storage shed and a microwave tower. There was a guard at a gate house, a sour-faced man with a dog. I was getting worried, but as we pulled up he recognized Peterson's truck, gave a crooked smile, and waved us on.

CHAPTER TWENTY FOUR

The entry road opened onto a wide revetment that sloped down to cement docks. Extraordinary yachts, the largest I had ever seen, were moored along the wharf edge. Sleek, white and black, looking like elegant space craft, they filled each mooring space. A large barn-like structure fronted by a walking crane was off to one side; inside another 100-foot yacht was under construction.

On the right there was another long concrete dock, and we drove to that one. At the end was a completely different kind of ship. Smartly painted blue and white but working class in origin and purpose. On her stern were two large L-shaped tubes, raised and secured to a catwalk frame.

"A low-rise utility vessel from outta the oil patch. We bought her in the Gulf in Texas... Aransas Pass," Peterson said.

"What do you do with her?"

"Find things," he said with a laugh. "We all like to dive, and with Vigilant we can do it very comfortably and even get paid. We do contract research, oceanography and archaeology, and on our own we find things."

"Treasure?"

"Once. Nothing really major, but very nice it was. It paid off the loan on Vigilant."

As we stood by Peterson's truck, an ancient station wagon with an incongruously purring engine pulled up and a wiry dirty blond long-haired man with a spade beard got out. He was wearing a black T-shirt that hung over his jeans on which was stenciled a naked woman with dive gear and the words in a circle around her: "If you're Gonna Dive With Me Dive Deep." He opened the wagon's back and pulled out a dive bag which he put over his shoulder. Peterson introduced him as "Skunk."

Just as Peterson was finishing that introduction, a Harley pulled up with a passenger on the back. "This is Leon; he's a vet too, but Navy.

He's the ship's master," Peterson said, starting to do it in mindspeech then remembering and verbalizing as the man took off his helmet. Leon was taciturn and hard eyed. "What are we doing?" he asked, with an accent that placed him as being from Maine or Vermont. And behind him on his bike was Erica, a blonde in her 30s, lean as a greyhound with a permanent tan.

We spent a minute unpacking gear, then Peterson said "Let's get aboard." He turned and led everyone up the gangway. It was all so hurried, I don't think Mike in his hoodies, sunglasses, and gloves had registered yet as anything more than a boy.

We went halfway across the open rear deck, which I guessed was about 24 feet across. It was about 65 or 70 feet back to the stern. There was the catwalk across the deck about 15 feet up, to which were linked the two massive bent steel tubes.

Leon saw me looking at them and explained, "We lower them into the sea so prop wash can be directed downward to clear sand away. That lets the archaeologists come in from the side as well as from the seafloor down."

I realized it must be a massive job, and Peterson said in mindspeech. "Trust me, it is."

We turned left and through the ship's steel door into the main salon. In contrast to the exterior, a very handsome wood-paneled space about 16 feet wide and 20 feet long, very traditional and nautical. What you would expect to see on one of the better yachts.

Peterson, noticing me take in the surroundings, said "When we got her from the oil patch everything was utilitarian. We gutted all that and put in our own interior."

On the starboard side was a green U-shaped banquette around a table of softly buffed cypress with a handsome brushed steel pedestal securing it to the floor. The last five feet of that bulkhead was a walk-in cooler, and on the port side there was a well-equipped galley with a long island.

Everyone slid into the banquette with Mike going last, sitting next to Rachel. Peterson and I were the only ones standing.

"Okay. I think everyone has met," then gesturing at me. "Do you want to tell us what's going on?"

They all looked at me, and I was back in Afghanistan, briefing my guys before we went out. And I must have looked different, because Rachel said in my mind, "Arthur, I had no idea. Go for it."

For a moment I just stood there. Then I thought, what do they need from us to get underway quickly? And I felt Mike's appreciation.

"The whole story is too long for now. But it will be told, and told to you in a way unlike anything you have ever experienced. For now let's start with this." I paused for a beat, then began. "Through a very strange set of circumstances we are here to do something extraordinary. And we need your help."

I looked at Mike, and he slid out and came over to stand next to me. "Here's why we're here," and I gestured to Mike, who took off his hoodie, sunglasses, and gloves.

"SweetJesus," Erica said, "it's an alien…"

"An extraterrestrial…" Skunk corrected.

"Where does he come from?" Leon asked.

"The Western Quadrant of the Horse Nebula, near the fisherman," I responded. "Mike can't speak. He has no vocal chords. But he can communicate in another way, and I will teach it to you, as he taught it to me. But for now let's get launched."

I could tell I was on a knife edge; it could fall either way. They freaked out and this whole thing fell apart. Or I connected on our shared combat experience, and they went into action. I looked at Peterson, telling him in mindspeech, "I need your help."

"And where are we headed?" Leon asked.

"Riding Rocks on the Banks," Peterson answered.

"It will take some time for you to fully get this," he said, "and it is wilder than anything you can imagine, but he's right, we need to get underway," he told them. They accepted that.

"Thank you," I said to Peterson in mindspeech, and Rachel and Mike came in to say the same.

Everyone knew the drill and went into it. We were shown where we would bunk, a little stateroom with wood framed tiered bunks with green curtains pulled across.

Rachel put our gear away in the locker, except one bag that I took. Mike climbed to the top bunk on the other side.

I went up to the bridge where Leon had pulled up the chart on the nav table surface. He, Skunk, and Peterson were looking at it. When Leon saw me, he said, "We're going to go out to the International Light, then turn east and cross the stream. Looking at the weather data, it could get quite intense. Then down to Cat Cay where we'll drop anchor and clear customs in the morning."

He looked at me, and added, "We're going to have to stop at the fuel docks and take on a full load. We can water there too. I assume you have money?"

I opened the bag and showed him the stacks of 20s.

"Excellent. But we can't pay in currency. People would talk about it for weeks. Vigilant has a card; we'll use that, and you can give us the currency. I'll take care of it."

"Leave Rachel and me $1000 and take the rest," I told him, and handed him the bag.

"No, I don't think we can do that, Lieutenant… or was it Captain?"

"Lieutenant; at the end, Captain. And you?"

"Commander."

"Navy guys at 0 to 5 usually stay in," I commented tentatively.

"Yeah, I know. I was up for Captain, but I left as soon as I had 20. It just got to be too much. You know what I mean? I just didn't want to order my men to kill any more people in these endless wars."

"Me too. I got out and went to Washington. I'm a Senior Analyst for a Senate Committee."

"And you're going to tell us the story?"

"We all will," Rachel said, coming up the stairs from the main deck.

It was already dark when the ship was finally ready to go. We were all gathered in the salon, and I felt I owed them a warning.

"There is some danger. Mike has been a captive for 12 years; there are people who want him back."

"Probably the same fuckers who wanted me to go to Patika," Skunk said. It broke the tension and we all laughed. Then Peterson gestured to a wooden locker at the far end of the compartment. "We're armed."

"Okay." Leon said. "Let's get her out to sea." Skunk turned to the ladder that led to the engine room.

I got Mike's query and asked for him, "Can Mike go with you? He's never seen a hybrid diesel close up." Skunk looked at Mike then Peterson, who nodded.

"Want to see our Detroit diesel hybrids do you? Okay, come along."

I walked up to the bridge after Leon and Rachel. On the deck, Peterson and Erica began casting off lines.

"Roger, would you go up in the bow and take in the lines?" Leon asked, and I went down and walked forward. As soon as I got there, Erica on the dock untied the line. "Bow away," she called. As I pulled in and coiled the line I heard, "Stern away," and we were free. Those on the dock jumped back aboard and the ship, freed from her moorings, moved down the waterway with the lights of the dock shimmering on the sea's surface.

"It will be 30 minutes to the pilot's light, where we'll meet the pilot and he'll come aboard; it's the law for a ship this size. He'll stay with us to the international light. It'll cost $250 and go on Vigilant's bill." Leon said it without even turning, his eyes ahead.

"The whole crossing to Cat Cay will take 8 to 9 hours if we have any kind of sea," he added.

When we got to the pilot light a smaller pilot boat was already there, and the pilot, who was an old friend of Leon's, went up to the bridge. Peterson took my arm and we went down the stairs, through the salon and onto the back deck stopping next to what he explained was the dive locker, a 10-foot shipping container with a platform over it, on top of which two small boats were tied down.

"We are known but even so, we can only stay for four days in Bahamian waters without attracting attention," Peterson explained. "The crossing will take ten hours. Customs opens at 9 in the morning. How close is this attention you are being paid likely to be?"

"Honestly, I don't know. Even worse, I have no idea exactly who is after us. So I don't know who to look for."

"I'm a big believer in prep, Roger…" "

"Me too," I replied.

"I suspected as much."

"So let's spend some time thinking about what that might mean."

"Agreed."

We went back up to the bridge, aft of which was the ship's office, where Leon joined us while the pilot had the helm, and hammered out what we would try to do over the next four days. The pilot called out and we went back to the bridge just as we were coming up to the international buoy. The pilot surrendered the helm, quickly said goodbye, went down to the rear deck, and jumped across to the pilot boat that had come along side. Leon took up the helm and we entered international waters, hitting the Gulf Stream 30 minutes later. It was exhilarating. Rachel and Mike, who had stayed out of sight while the pilot was aboard, came up from the stateroom and walked up to the bow.

Peterson and I linked in when we heard Rachel ask, "I want to go back to that statement you made about manipulating human DNA. I can't get that out of my mind."

I stood next to Leon in silence looking at the sea as I listened in my head to Mike's answer.

"We already knew from monitoring human communications as well as Earth's biosphere and our study of humans over thousands of years, what the general course of the planet's development was… There had been a tremendous debate on that subject, by the way… and we worked out a method that had the absolute minimum impact on the individuals, and your societies."

"Mike, do you have any idea how weird it is to have your planet and your species discussed as a case study?" Rachel asked.

"Probably not," was his reply.

Leon, who heard none of this, turned to me and said out loud, "Have you ever crossed the Stream?"

"No." I had to remember to say it out loud, while still trying to monitor the inner conversation. It was not easy.

"It can get hairy this time of year," Leon said, then lapsed back into silence, as we stood in the bridge, with just the red lights from the gauges lessening the darkness.

I sank back into the conversation as Mike said, 'There is a treaty about Earth. Unfortunately, not everyone interprets it the same way. Another problem."

"There isn't agreement?"

"There are those who think we shouldn't intervene at all," Mike responded, and I think I realized for the first time that like me in my old life, Mike was a staff scientist doing a job. And like me he now found himself in a situation for which there was no protocol.

I let this insight enter our common space, and Mike immediately responded. "Yes, we are winging it, Arthur. As long as we pick the path that fosters the most wellbeing, we won't go wrong. Remember that."

Suddenly the ship lurched, and Rachel fell into Mike's arms. It was the first time she had had a contact like that, and I could feel it as she did, even though I was on the bridge.

There was a perceptible difference in the sea, and Leon turned to me saying, "We're in the Stream now."

I looked down and saw Skunk come forward to tell Mike and Rachel the same thing, which I heard echoed in my mind.

"Midships will be best," Skunk said. "Hope ya don't get seasick, but ya will," he laughed as he walked back down to the stern.

His prediction was only partially accurate. I became sick, Rachel endured. Mike paid no attention, and we could tell he was wonderfully entertained by the pitching ship's motion. "My ears lack sensitivity in some ways. We don't speak like you do, so hearing plays a different role in my world. Also we spend a good part of our lives in water or on it. We chose instead an acute sense of consciousness linkage."

He spoke of himself in the same dispassionate objective way he discussed humans. Impersonal but compassionate. Then he told me something that really changed my thinking.

"You will discover as you explore this aspect of your consciousness that there is a continuity of consciousness. It is outside of time and space, and so far as my people can tell, eternal. In human religious terms I think you would call it the soul. It existed before you were born, and will exist after your body dies. Episodically, for reasons we do not fully comprehend, it creates another personality and incarnates again. You are one of them," he said into my mind, and I confess into my heart.

"Is that true for you too?" Peterson asked.

"Yes. Consciousness is eternal," Mike responded.

CHAPTER TWENTY FIVE

Mike remained fascinated by both the ocean and its effect on people. "It's so much different than just the visual presentation. This is extraordinary. The waves are very different from my world; I never expected this." But he never shared what the difference was.

We stood there for a while looking out across the sea. As Erica came out and walked over to us, I could already see that she, Leon, and the others found it odd that when Rachel, Mike, and I were alone together, we didn't speak much or at all.

I turned to her and said verbally, "It's extraordinary. What are they, 10 feet?"

"No... you poor boy. This is only about 6 feet. It's going to get much more interesting."

As she said this my nausea came back and I had no choice but to lean over and vomit, and felt Mike stagger slightly in his mind from the emotional blast of my discomfort. There was no point in being embarrassed, so I just wiped my mouth and took a swig of water from the water bottle Erica handed me. She went on talking as if nothing had happened. "Did you know Benjamin Franklin was the first person to report the Stream scientifically? On one of his crossings he took temperature readings."

"What do you do?" I asked her.

"I'm an environmental oceanographer. I work for the state," she replied. Then asked, "Does Mike understand what we are saying?"

"Oh, yes. He understands 37 or 38 languages; I can't remember."

"But there's more to it, isn't there?"

"Yes, and as soon as we stop doing this and can have some undisturbed time, I promise you it will all be made very real."

"You've got my attention," she said. "I'm going to go in and put some food together. Everybody will be hungry and it's best to eat something now. Leon thinks it's going to get rough tonight. What does Mike eat?"

"Rachel can show you. Mostly a kind of green drink," I replied.

After that nobody really asked questions, just handled the boat. We didn't really eat as one group. Erica, with some help from Rachel, put out a crudité of vegetables, apples, and a good selection of stilton, aged cheddar, and brie. Also some smoked white fish to put on a cracker. Things you could hold in your hand. Mike got one of his drinks, which he casually held as if he were standing on a terrace and not a pitching boat.

An hour later the wind had picked up and so had the sea. The moon was up. It was very dramatic as the ship rolled from side to side at the same time that it pitched up and down. Half an hour after that, a rain squall came through and pelted the ship. The waves got even higher.

"We got some serious shit coming down here," Skunk said with a wild laugh, as he ran out of the salon and past me under the canopy attached to the aft end of the super structure. Barefoot, and in torn jeans, with his long hair plastered down his back, Skunk looked like a serious stoner on an acid trip out in a rain storm. But his movements were sure and precise. He checked lashings holding down pieces of equipment, and once I saw what he was about I ran out to join him and was soon drenched in rain. Peterson came out hitching his overalls after taking off his T-shirt. As he went into the dive locker to check everything I could see there was a long workbench filled with all the tools a marine salvage operation might need. All meticulously cleaned and arranged. "This is Erica's world, and she likes things neat," Peterson said from inside the dive shop.

Suddenly something tore loose in the galley and crashed. "We need help," Erica shouted at me from the door, pulling a sweat shirt over the tiniest bikini I had ever seen. "Help Rachel and me pick up these canned goods. One of the damned larder latches broke." Then, "Thanks Peterson, how does it look? I was coming out when the latch gave out. We've got cans and packages flying everywhere."

"No problems, babe."

For the next hour it was a wild ride. Then we were out of it and the seas calmed, the rain let up a bit. After another hour Leon's spotlight lit up and swept out catching a finger of land sticking out into the sea.

"That's the end of Cat Cay's north island," Erica told us.

Rachel and I walked up to the bow and stood there with her body tucked into my arms for warmth and closeness. Vigilant looked like she was headed directly towards the rocks as the ship's spotlight played across them. The rain began to pick up again; in the distance we could just see the answering point of light of the Bahamian Defense Forces beacon warning us off the point.

"Ya got to cut it a mite close coming into the Cat; the channel runs right along those rocks," said Skunk coming up to stand next to us. "Mostly Republicans out here. They don't go out much in bad weather, so it don't much matter to them." Skunk gave me one of his maniacal laughs as he pulled out a vape pen and stuck it into his mouth as water ran down his body as if a bucket was being poured over his head.

I will never forget that final 15 minutes of that crossing, waves slapping madly against the rocks, the ship less than 20 feet away from their black fangs, everything sporadically caught in the light of the ship or the beacon. Midway through the passage the rain increased even more, and visibility got worse. All of it happening in the slow-motion manner of ships, so different from cars, planes or trains. Then we were through and into the harbor. Everything suddenly calmed. Sailboats rode at anchor in the lee of the rocks, bobbing up and down with their mast lights dipping and swaying in the sheets of rain.

Leon steered an open space of sea and dropped anchor. Once it was secure we all gathered in the galley for coffee, more apples, and hot oatmeal with milk and brown sugar dished up by Peterson.

As we sat around the table, Leon said, "Does Mike understand we're in a foreign country? And we need to get a sense of what's in store. But it's late, and everyone's tired. I don't think anyone will bother us tonight, so let's go to bed. Customs doesn't open until nine, so let's be ready to go by 0800."

Rachel and I woke up about 7 and weren't surprised to see Mike was already gone. We went down the corridor to the head and took quick showers and went up; everyone else was already there. This time Peterson was making pancakes, and Erica was putting out plates and little pitchers of organic maple syrup.

After we finished, Leon said, "Chapter Two," and looked at me.

"Here's what we need to do." As my thoughts formed I could feel Mike's approval. "Mike needs to get to Riding Rocks where he thinks he will rendezvous with a pod of dolphins and, if everything works as he hopes, a superpod of whales. I know humpbacks aren't supposed to form in groups, but Mike thinks they will."

"There was an incident in South Africa, several actually, back in 2017, where they formed superpods," Erica said. "But how could he possibly know when this would happen?"

They all looked at me, and Leon said, "We're going to get to that and everything else as soon as we clear customs, I assume?"

"Yes. Everything. I can't tell you how much I appreciate your patience, but you will understand," I said to them. Peterson nodded his affirmation. They trusted Peterson; he had trusted Charley. It's the thing you learn to do when your life is in someone else's hands. Having done that, everything shifted back to the operational.

"I think I may just have a mask small enough to fit him," said Erica.

"Does he know how to swim?" Skunk asked.

Mike stood up, went over to where they sat, and pulled on the side of his head to show the little slit on the side of his throat. Both Erica and Skunk were fascinated.

"And you have lungs too?" she asked, and he nodded.

"Does he have any idea how his body reacts to compression on this planet, what its rate of nitrogen processing is?"

I explained Mike's planet to them, thinking all the time how impoverished my explanation was because I could not share with them the domain of consciousness Mike had shared with me.

I turned to Leon, and asked, "How long will customs take? Will they come aboard?"

"I don't think so. They know us here. It's a small station as you can see, yet a lot of very rich people clear here. They could, though, but I will come back and let you know about that before they arrive," Leon said, and I knew by his tone to take this seriously. "You should be ready though," he added. "Also I need your identity cards. Will they withstand scrutiny…Roger?" he asked, and I knew he knew it was a phony name.

"Tell them the truth," both Mike and Rachel said into my mind.

"I was going to do this later this afternoon," I said verbally, "after we got out of here, but I think now is the time. My name in Arthur Davies. I am, or was, A Senior Analyst for the Senate Science Committee." Gesturing with my hand I said, "This is Rachel Carter, who was a Senior Researcher at the Library of Congress. We had to have different identities, and a friend arranged them. And yes, Leon, they will pass muster."

'That's what I need to know," he said, and the others nodded as we passed over our identity chits.

We walked aft, just forward of the catwalk to where a 30 ton crane was set up. I helped Skunk, and Peterson get one of the Avon hard frame inflatable boats off the platform above the dive shop and into the water.

Suddenly we heard a helicopter overhead, and Mike, who was under the canopy, darted into the salon.

Two large white Hueys, with the wide red stripe and blue insignia of the U.S. Coast Guard, swept overhead.

"Could be something. Could be nothing at all. We're in the middle of the largest drug trade route in the world, so lots of things could be going on," Leon said, but his voice was tense.

"Is it possible to skip customs?" I asked.

"Not a chance. Everything that moves out here is plotted. The Bahamian Defense Force, U.S. Customs, the Coast Guard, Homeland, the Air Force, everybody is looking through the keyhole," Leon answered. "They know all of us; we're over here regularly. We often bring guests or clients, so unless you and Rachel set off an alarm and they come out, in which case there may be facial recognition scans, we shouldn't have any problems."

The ship's small boat was lowered by crane into the water, and Leon and Skunk rode it into the Cat Cay dock about 500 yards away. A low long open blue boat Peterson called a cigarette, with a radar mounted on a kind of rollbar, passed through the channel and once out in open water accelerated with incredible speed.

"Customs. They'll do 80, 90 if it's a dead calm. Fastest things on the water, though the chop must bust your ass," Peterson observed.

I felt queasy with anxiety, and I could tell that Rachel felt the same; but Mike seemed unconcerned.

It took about 45 minutes, and then the tender left the dock and came back out to the ship. As I looked over the rail Leon called up, "No problems, we have a four-day permit."

"Something's going on though. Hard to say what, but everyone was unusually alert," Skunk observed as he climbed back aboard.

When we had lifted the little boat back up on the platform, Leon gestured to me and we walked into the salon and up to the bridge.

"It's time to get this all out. How long will you need?"

"Probably three to four hours," I responded, and he looked at me sharply. "Longer would be even better."

"Three to four hours… well then I propose we go down to Sand Cay and drop anchor there. It's calm and nobody will bother us."

"That's the plan then," I said.

CHAPTER TWENTY SIX

We drew up the anchor and headed back out the same channel we had used to come in the previous night. But now it was a different world. Both sea and sky were calm and the water was an extraordinary turquoise blue; so clear that the startlingly white sand on the Caribbean sea floor hurt your eyes. We steamed at about 12 knots heading south along the edge of the bank and three hours later we were at Sand Cay, so called, I was told, because it had the most stunningly white beaches. They certainly were the whitest I had ever seen.

"Oolite," Erica told me as we secured. "Calcium carbonate in minute rounded concretions, like white fish roe."

Rachel and Peterson had put together a lunch of chunks of fresh lobster that Leon had gotten on Cat Cay, with Louie dressing and crisp lettuce, served with cold quinoa and mint, crusty baguettes, and a very nice Sauvignon Blanc.

"You guys eat well."

"It's Peterson. In addition to being a master welder, nuclear qualified, a black belt, and a very accomplished diver, he is a stone gourmet," Skunk said, wiping his mouth.

After we cleared things away it was time. We went outside, got folding chairs from where they were secured to the side of the dive shop, and sat next to the long work table facing each other under the canopy over the deck.

When everyone was settled, I said, "I told you Mike cannot speak because he has no vocal cords, but I am sure you have all figured out that we are communicating with him."

"Pretty hard not to notice," Erica said.

"We are doing it mentally. With Mike and Rachel's help we are going to show you how to open a door in your mind," I said, and straightened up in my seat. Rachel did the same.

"Why don't we start with the story of what's going on?" Skunk said, and the others nodded in affirmation.

"Because if we do this first, the story will take on a completely different dimension, and that's important," Rachel said.

"Sit like me," I said. "Feet on the floor, sitting up. Now here is what is going to happen. We are going to do a kind of meditation, and when I tell you, I want you to reach out to the three of us, mentally. Hold the intention firmly in your mind that you are reaching out. We will do the same. This may take a while, it might even take several sessions, but it will work. I know that because Rachel and I learned to do it, and we taught Peterson's friend Charley to open and do it."

And Peterson said, "And me too," which earned him some sharp looks.

They all did as I asked. "Take a deep breath. Now let it out. Take another deep breath... let it out...take a third deep breath... and as you do let your mind clear until it is like a still pool in the forest. Now reach out with your mind to contact Mike. Imagine that you are linked."

And while they did this, Mike, Rachel, Peterson and I reached out to them by holding a clear intention that we be linked.

It took about 20 minutes, when Skunk suddenly said in our minds. "Wow. This very cool... oh my goodness, Rachel, you're just beautiful. And Mike... Arthur. Wow."

Then Erica. "OhmyGod," she said, "Oh now this is very fine." And finally Leon.

"It's like another dimension... like a submarine problem. Two different... two different realities," he said softly in our collective mind.

"Open your eyes," Mike said. "Now get up and do whatever you would normally be doing, but try to hold the connection."

And they did. For the rest of the afternoon everyone worked at something or just sat on the deck looking out to sea. Very quickly these old friends who had already known each other for years slid into the common space. Mike taught them how to partition off what they wished to keep private. But for the most part they reminisced as they worked or sat, going over shared memories, using them to polish skills.

"No, Peterson, he didn't come in through the door, he came up from the basement," Skunk said, and we were in Afghanistan in a battle, and the two memories blended perspectives.

"Is there a distance limitation?" Erica asked, and Mike told her there was none.

"Now that you are linked, you can contact one another no matter where you are physically. Try Charley," Mike told them, and they reached out.

"Charley, can you hear me" Peterson said, and suddenly Charley lit up on the net. "Whoa, so you guys are awake now. All of you?"

"All of us," they responded.

"How about underwater? Does this work underwater?" Skunk asked. "Erica let's go get dinner."

"It will make no difference," Mike replied, "but you will have to hold your focus, which may not be easy with your gear."

They went out on the back deck and into the dive shop, coming out with wet suits and diving gear.

"If you have the gear, I'd like to come," I said.

"Me too," Rachel added.

"Do you have your licenses?"

"Yes, but I'm pretty rusty; its been a few years. And I think that's true of Rachel as well."

"It is."

"Okay," Erica responded. "This is a good place to get back up to speed. It's very calm and only about 20 feet deep here, so decompression on one tank is not an issue. But you need to look at the charts and relearn the decompression tables."

She went back into the shop and handed us tight lycra swimsuits. A bikini bottom for me, with a top for Rachel. We went back down to our cabin, put them on, came back out and found Erica standing next to a scale.

"I need your weight to calculate your weight belt." We stepped on the scale and she went back into the dive locker, and handed out weight belts, then held out two blue and gray wet suits.

"I think these will fit," Erica said handing them to us. When I pulled on the suit I understood why the trunks needed to be tight and smooth.

In a few minutes more we had on all the gear and were off. Everyone except for us had a fishing spear and lobster bag. Just as we went down the dive stairs Mike slid into the water next to us, and swam off by himself moving in a dolphin-like motion. I noticed for the first time both his hands and feet were webbed. As we swam I realized that everyone was lost in the experience we were having together, and all questions about past things were forgotten for the moment.

We swam out across a sea floor as white as snow, with marine plant growth sticking up from it. It reminded me of a snow-covered Kansas wheat field in winter after the harvest. As I looked at it I could also feel Mike's joy at being in the water.

We swam over to a submerged coral reef with a coral archway. Using it as a ramp and walking up looking like bumper-to-bumper cars on a freeway, were lobsters. Not the big Maine lobsters with giant claws, but a smaller Caribbean cousin.

"I'll swim over and get enough for dinner," Skunk said into our heads, as Leon and Charley chimed in.

Erica speared a grouper, and then we spent the next 20 minutes just swimming the reef.

As I came around one end, I saw a shark.

"A black tip" said Peterson.

"He's begun to put his fins down and to move them up and down."

"He's getting upset," Erica said. "That's display behavior to tell you you're in his space."

"What do I do?" I asked.

"Just veer off," Skunk said in my head. I did and the shark turned away as well.

"I'm running low on air," Rachel said, and we all turned back to the ship and surfaced at its side and climbed up the dive steps.

As Peterson took the fish and lobster to the galley he asked Mike, "You live on a non-flesh diet. How do you feel about this?"

"I don't have any judgment, Peterson. My type of body evolved under very different circumstances, and we have been evolving for thousands of years longer than you humans. Your genetic default position disposes you to eat flesh although individuals can overcome that predisposition. In vegetarian countries like India, where flesh storage was difficult, a vegetarian culture arose that has overridden genetics, and DNA has changed to accommodate the culture. Milk intolerance is another example of what I mean," Mike said, treating Peterson's question with the same dispassionate professorial impersonality that was so disconcerting.

"Perhaps 5,000 years from now you will all be vegetarians. For tonight enjoy your lobster and fish. Remember, consciousness continues," he said to all of us as he wiped himself down with a towel, and we realized that was the point of his answer. I confess it gave me pause to watch Peterson cook the lobsters, but I helped grill the fish without a qualm. Such are humans.

As we sat around the table and ate, passing plates and wine, verbal speech dropped off and long stretches of silence emerged broken occasionally with laughter. It was a wonderful meal I will never forget.

After dinner we cleaned up everything and gathered under the canopy again. "Okay. Now it's time," I said, segueing to Mike who told the others what he had told Rachel and myself, about how he had come to be in human custody and what it was like.

Rachel and I shared our story. How we had left government, found Mike and gotten him out; how we had come to meet Charley and then Peterson, who picked up the thread and shared his experiences.

"And they woke me up earlier," Peterson said. "I thought you would be mad…"

"We wondered when you were going to tell us," Erica said with laugh.

Then Mike explained what he was doing with the dolphins and the whales, and why. With his usual impersonal precision he described what our chances were as humans. What the time frame looked like. He laid out the two paths. I could see the emotional impact this had on Leon,

Skunk and Erica, and Peterson, even though he had already been told part of it.

There were a lot of questions at first, but they died down and we just sat quietly in our silence and went with him. It was one of the most extraordinary experiences I have ever had. As I absorbed what Mike was sharing, Robert Frost's great poem *The Road Not Taken* came into my mind, and I began to share it:

Two roads diverged in a yellow wood,
And sorry I could not travel both
And be one traveler, long I stood
And looked down one as far as I could
To where it bent in the undergrowth;
Then took the other, as just as fair,
And having perhaps the better claim,
Because it was grassy and wanted wear;
Though as for that the passing there
Had worn them really about the same,
And both that morning equally lay
In leaves no step had trodden black.
Oh, I kept the first for another day!
Yet knowing how way leads on to way,
I doubted if I should ever come back.
I shall be telling this with a sigh
Somewhere ages and ages hence:
Two roads diverged in a wood, and I—
I took the one less traveled by,
And that has made all the difference.

"Yes, exactly, Arthur. You humans stand at just such a crossroads. I have already told you and Rachel this, but let me tell the others," Mike said, and we all felt his seriousness.

"The best gift I can give humanity is not pictures of me, or my appearing on video worldwide. Or any teaching. This is not about starting a religion. What needs to happen for your species to survive is for individual humans to change the nature of their beingness, their character, who they are. You all are the first. Just as you learned, so can you teach. Rachel and Arthur can show you how to evaluate whether to approach someone. You need to get 10 percent of your population to awaken. When that happens, the whole of humanity will make the change. Just as you quit smoking, or accepted gender equality. It's a change of beingness. That's your job. You seven. You're the beginning."

With that we broke up. Rachel and I took two folding chairs and went to sit in the bow again. It was magical to have that moment in the night, a sky filled with stars. Dark, but in a different way than a forest, and holding hands we went to bed.

CHAPTER TWENTY SEVEN

The next morning we had been underway for just over an hour when a low narrow limestone island came into view. It was mostly barren, but along its crest were some ground-hugging shrubs, and in a clearing at the very top, a single cedar tree carved by winds into a haunting shape.

"This is Riding Rocks; we're going to go to the lee side east of the Stream," Leon said, the first two words verbally, the rest in our minds.

Following the mark made by Mike, Leon maneuvered the ship exactly to that spot. Skunk went out to set the anchor. Mike came out and I took the first picture of him, just sea in the background. Then a few minutes later when I could again get a blank background, I took the second, and then the third.

"Remember, put them out separately, the last one with the manuscript," Mike reminded me.

It was a beautiful Caribbean day. We didn't know when the pod would come by, or even if it would, so we decided to go diving. I think we were all excited to keep the link open and dive again, because diving while linked together in consciousness was an exquisite experience.

We all surrendered to the beauty of the reef. It was quite shallow, 20 feet maybe, and the afternoon light came through in clear shafts. Once again I could feel Mike's pleasure in the dive. I also realized that Erica was always aware of him, looking out for him.

"How many people come from another planet," I thought, "and get to go reef diving in the Caribbean?"

"I can safely say that I am the first person of my kind in all of history to have the privilege of diving in this way with humans." It was an odd yet startling little statistic.

"I would say the same," I told him. And Leon and Skunk who had tuned in agreed.

Normally when diving you are quite cut off. But now it was an altered state of consciousness. I came upon a young octopus that rose and swam off. As it did I reached out and just for a moment brushed its consciousness. A frisson went through me. The others could sense what I felt, and I was conscious of them reaching out, until suddenly we were all in a matrix of life, in all its forms. It was profoundly humbling. As I swam along the reef, if I looked at a crab or fish, its life force was perceptible, and I absorbed the differences in consciousness, how some had more complexity than others. A branch of the reef went off to one side and I followed that; as I looked down I realized I was swimming over a giant ray.

As I focused on it, I connected with it, and it rose up under me. Instinctively I gripped the leading edge of its wings, and with a flip of the tips we were off, much faster than I could ever have swum. The ray turned to the right and came back the same way, then shivered slightly. I released my hands and it was off.

When we were back on deck Rachel said to me, "I don't even have words to describe this experience," and neither did any of the rest of us. We were in the matrix, submerged in it. We had dinner, and once again Rachel and I went up into the bow and sat in quiet, immersed in the web of life. Then still in that state, went back to our state room and met Mike going out. "I'm going to sleep on the deck" he said, and was gone.

We climbed into bed together, with just one soft light in the bulkhead shining through the green curtain, and made slow love, moving to the rhythms of the pulsing life in the sea around us.

The next day we saw no one, neither human nor cetacean, made two dives, and explored the matrix of the ocean world, each in our individual way. It really was another planet linked but distinct; the matrix was very different.

To a certain level you could sort of tune in to what someone else was doing. But just to a certain level. I learned this looking up at Erica, who was up on the catwalk staring out at the sea. I could feel her assessing what she was experiencing in the context of her science specialty. Leon was lost in weather. Peterson stood most of the time at the work table holding pieces of metal. Skunk reached out to birds, and at one point he shared the world as it looks to a gull.

That evening, driven by an instinct I did not fully understand, I took the little microdrives and transferred my diary/log to all eight of them, and added one of the pictures. I gave a microdrive to each of them and an extra to Skunk, who told me he would hide it in the boat, "Where no one will find it, I guarantee. At least this much of your record will be preserved."

The third day, we had just finished breakfast when a pod of about 16 dolphins suddenly swam up and formed around the ship. Mike ran back inside and came out a minute later with the silver metal cubes he had taken when we freed him. It had been so long since I had seen them, I had forgotten them.

As we were standing at the head of the dive steps on the ship's side, ready to go into the water, I asked him "What are the cubes for?"
"Think of them as amplifiers; they make it easier for me to manipulate timespace." And with that he stepped off the dive step and was amidst the dolphins, leaving us all standing, looking out to sea as the dolphins frolicked leaping into the air to breathe, then submerging to move in what I now understood to be a kind of dance.

All of this was interrupted when suddenly screaming just a few feet above the bridge an F-22 fighter came streaking over our heads; we could feel the pressure waves and the sound stopped all conversation.

"We're about to have visitors," Leon said in our minds. "Get ready."

A helicopter came out of a cloud and hovered overhead. We heard on both the helicopter's public address speaker and from the radio in the dive shop, "Research Vessel Vigilant, heave to and prepare to be boarded." We could see a crewman dressed in combat green with a yellow vest and an aviator's helmet, polaroid visor snapped down, microphone in his hand. And next to him a crewman with a 50-caliber machine gun pointing down at us. It was designed to be intimidating, and it was.

Because of the noise the pod quickly moved out of the area, and in that moment Mike was forgotten.

Leon went back inside and up to the bridge. A minute later, we could hear him on the radio, "Coast Guard helicopter, Coast Guard helicopter, this is Research Vessel Vigilant."

"Switch to channel nine, Research Vessel Vigilant."

"Copy that. I am switching to channel nine, Coast Guard helicopter."

"Heave to and prepare to be boarded."

"What do we do now?" I asked, both tense and relieved that Mike was not on the boat.

"We do what he tells us," Skunk said.

Suddenly around the island came two of the low blue cigarette boats we had seen at Cat Cay. In the distance we could see the gray form of a Bahamian Defense Forces corvette coming towards us. They were all obviously in communication, and as the larger Bahamian craft stopped, standing off from us about 150 feet, we heard, "Research Vessel Vigilant, we are sending over a boarding party."

Leon came back out, and we waited as the cigarettes bobbed in the waves 100 yards off from the larger vessel. In each there were four men with machine guns. The boarding party, though, came from the Bahamian vessel which stood astern of Vigilant, a small rubber boat with four armed sailors and a young officer.

"Remember to talk verbally," I said as they came towards us, "but stay in contact."

They threw out a line that Skunk secured around a cleat and they came aboard.

"Who is the ship's master?" the officer asked.

"Me," Leon said, and put out his hand, which surprised the young officer I think, but he reflexively shook it.

"May I go into the ship's office?" he asked.

"Of course," Leon answered.

"Is everyone aboard?" the young officer asked, and my stomach did a little clench.

"Yes. Everyone is aboard," Leon answered.

In my head Leon asked again, "Will your papers stand up?"

"I think so," I replied.

"I would like to search your ship, Captain. Do you have any objection to that?"

"None whatsoever. On your own, or would you like one of the crew to go with you?"

"By ourselves. If we need anything we will come back to you."

"Why don't you take off your wetsuits," the officer added. "This will take some time."

Leon stripped his off and went up to the bridge, and a moment later came out holding a heavy clear vinyl envelope with a water seal containing our papers that he handed to the officer.

As he was looking at them we took off our dive gear, which earned Erica and Rachel a look.

"Do you mind if we shower?" Rachel asked, indicating the two outdoor showers.

"I'm sorry I can't let you do that," the officer said.

Then he turned to three of his men and said, "You know your briefing. Go to it." They went into the ship, leaving us with the officer and one man. He began to go through the identity cards. He had a reader, and as he prepared to put my card in I knew it all turned on the next minutes.

"Mr. Keith," he said look at the readout. "What do you do?"

For a moment my mind froze, then Rachel said in mindspeech, "You're a consultant forester, based in Ashland, Oregon." Her memories quickened my mind, and it all came back.

"I'm a consultant forester based in Ashland, Oregon."

There was a moment until something came up on his tablet; he read it and handed my identity card to Leon.

"And you sir, "he said, looking at Skunk, taking his card and putting it into his tablet. "Otis Stinkman is it?"

"It is, but nobody uses it, including me. Would you?"

It elicited a small smile; Bahamians are naturally courteous. "No I suppose I wouldn't. What do they call you?"

"Skunk, what else?"

"And you are?"

"The engineer. And I am also one of the owners." Then gesturing to Erica, Peterson, and Leon, "They all are. We own her together."

And that is how it went for the next 30 minutes.

Finally he asked, "And what brings you together here?" he said looking at me.

For a moment I realized we hadn't discussed this, but then it was clear, "Afghanistan, Iraq, and Yemen," I said, which evoked a quizzical look.

"We're all Vets; we met overseas. They're Army, I'm Navy." Leon said. "Roger and Deborah came out to do one of our surveys and get some diving in."

The officer looked at his tablet, reading the data, then gestured for Leon to put the identity cards back in the envelope with the ship's papers. He signaled his men to get back in the boat, speaking into his shoulder mike to the helicopter and the cigarettes as he did so. The helicopter lifted off, the cigarettes pulled back, and the inflatable tender returned to the Bahamian ship. As suddenly as they had come, they were gone

"Has anyone seen Mike?" Erica questioned all of us in our minds. "Arthur, do you have any idea how long he can stay underwater?"

"I am fine, Erica, I never doubted this would happen," Mike said in our common mental space, as if he were standing on the deck.

"Listen to me now. I've had a chance to observe your cultures and your species in ways no one from my world ever has. I told you I've seen it in a way that no amount of electronic monitoring could ever match. When I came here, I only thought to fly over, monitor, land, and possibly take a few samples. I have lived through the very period I came to study. If my body has been caged, you know my mind has not. I have learned something. I've realized my people have made several important miscalculations; our plans must be changed. But I cannot give this knowledge to you. It contains technical information your societies are not yet ready to attain. Getting it too soon would disrupt humanity so much it could go into a crisis. And, to be honest, giving it to you would weaken your character."

We stood on the rear deck in verbal silence as Mike told us all this, and then Erica shouted both verbally and in our minds, "Look! The whales!"

Further out beyond the limestone bank where the water depth went from 20 feet to 1700 feet, I could see the humpback whales. First a few, then dozens, then what looked like more than a hundred. Rising and falling, blowing water spouts. It was electrifying.

"The dolphins. They're joining them," Peterson said, his voice filled with the excitement we all felt.

"Can we get in the water, Mike?" I asked.

"I think so," Mike responded, and as quickly as we could, we were in our gear and into the Avon inflatable headed out to where the whales were in the deep water off the bank.

We threw the tender's anchor over where the water was still shallow, and swam west to where the depth dropped off.

As we looked on in awe, the whales and dolphins rose and fell, and in their midst was Mike.

"I am sharing with the whales and dolphins everything I have learned, everything I have stored in the cubes. It's going to take some time. The Cetacea have been in their body forms for 30 million years and are very social beings," and as he said that we could all feel him swimming gracefully along. Through him we contacted the dolphins and the whales, consciousnesses so strange, and yet so welcoming and playful, that for a moment I was lost in it. I think we all were.

"Like my species, although for different reasons, Cetacea have opened up to that part of the mind that is consciousness of the matrix, and they can communicate in this way. I have no vocal cords; they have a body that will not permit technology to assist them in communicating. For different reasons we have arrived at a similar place. The cube will tell me, and I will tell them, my entire report. They have extraordinary memories, having no way to record things exterior to themselves. They will turn my report into a song and it will wait. In the process the whales and the dolphins will complete the linkage they began several centuries ago, and locked in in 2017, Erica. That's why the superpod formed off the coast of South Africa that year." Then, in answer to our unspoken question. "Not me. But another part of our team, on another trip."

After a pause, "I will not be coming back. My years have been a gift that I never hoped to gain, and I will cherish always knowing you. And at least for a while we will be in contact, if you need me. But I could never be free here and I will not be rescued. My species is long-lived and free-ranging. I don't want more decades locked up. Now I want to explore the 70 percent of your planet that is underwater."

For a moment Mike was gone and we just looked at one another, thoughts swirling at what we had been told.

Then he was back, "You have helped your planet and your species in ways I do not have the time or the right to explain. You are now in contact, linked in consciousness, and beginning to explore the matrix of life. Stay at it and stay together, no matter where you are or what you are doing. In your terms you are an Order now and, as I told you, where appropriate awaken others. When you get to 10 percent of the population, your whole species will awaken and a new chapter of human history will begin. You will join a wider universe than you can possibly imagine."

We reached out as a group, and as a group both the dolphins and the whales reached out to us. We lived in such different realities that all we could really do was share images and sensations. To them, with their sonar, we looked like someone viewed through a sonogram. They saw into us. I had never understood that.

Our air began to run out, and we climbed back into the Avon. Once in, we looked south. The dolphins leapt into the air, once, twice, three times, then the whales breached together, and then more quickly than any human could move, they were gone, out into the open sea.

We got back to Vigilant, took off our gear, cleaned it and ourselves. All of us had tears running down our faces, and we spontaneously came together in a collective hug. We got the chairs out and sat down. No one was hungry, no one had much to say. But we were in the matrix, just absorbing what had just happened.

CHAPTER TWENTY EIGHT

That night at dinner and all through the next day we talked about what Mike had said to us, trying to work out the next move. We decided to work very discretely waking people up. It seemed the right strategy, and as we shared what we knew it became clear to all of us that this was the way to go.

"You say Gandhi was the only man to win independence for his country without a war, right, Arthur?" Peterson asked.

"Yes," I responded.

"He got the idea from Henry David Thoreau."

"Walden Pond?" Erica asked.

"The same. In 1888 Gandhi, a British-trained Indian lawyer, was sent to South Africa. He bought a first class ticket, but they told him he could only ride in 3rd glass with other people of color. He refused and they threw him in jail. Somehow he got hold of a copy of Thoreau's *Civil Disobedience*, and it changed his life. That was how he led Britain to choose to leave India."

"Dr. King," Rachel picked up the thread. "He read about Gandhi, and that led him to Thoreau; and it changed his life as well. My mother heard him on the 28th of August 1963 when he gave the "I Have a Dream" speech at the Lincoln Memorial. It changed her life. She talked about it until she died."

"If it worked for Thoreau, Gandhi, and King, I don't think we can improve on it," said Skunk, and we all agreed.

I explained what Mike had said about the three pictures and the log itself that I had given them.

"Mike thinks it will become an urban myth hiding a truth, just as his capture had been an internet myth and yet true. He said he followed what was in the media very closely, and saw how the process played out. I think he's right. It will provide a background."

"We know it's true," Erica said. "We're living it, and as people wake up they will have access to it as well."

"Which will make it even stronger," Leon responded.

"Mindspeech transparently reveals motive and emotion," Rachel said. "There can be no lying."

"I've noticed that," Skunk said, and we laughed.

We heard nothing from Mike, but the dolphins came to visit late in the afternoon, and we had a final dive with them and connected in a much deeper way. We got their sense of welcome and expressed it back, but their reality is sound based, so it was hard to be specific. It was like Mike's name. As we swam with them we realized this pod was another expression of what Mike and the other space cultures were doing with us.

When our air ran out we got back aboard, took up the anchor and went up to Cat Cay where we moored for the night, planning to clear customs in the morning.

We were awakened by a U.S. Coast Guard cutter that had come into the harbor and was hailing us.

CHAPTER TWENTY NINE

They came over that morning in the tender: an officer, several enlisted men, and a man in civilian clothes.

Once aboard the officer said, "Mr. and Mrs. Keith, we need to take a picture of you. Could you please come out on the deck?" It was not really a question.

"Take off your sunglasses, please," and in that moment I knew we were caught.

He took the pictures and uploaded them. We stood there silently on the deck.

"They're going to find you," Leon said in our minds.

"Yes, they are I think, and they are going to take us off," I responded.

"We will listen to what you tell them, make it as close to the truth as possible, and we will support you. I'm sure they are going to question us as well. But there is really no evidence."

"We're a group of vets who knew each other from fighting in some AOs," he said, giving me a look to say he knew I knew what action in operational areas meant. "We got together after a long time out of contact, and we invited you out on Vigilant. There's nothing to contradict that." It took about 10 minutes. He looked at his tablet and said, "Dr. Davies, Dr. Carter, you will come with me please."

"Are we under arrest?"

"No but you are government employees whose personal involvement in something is in the national interest," the young officer said, and we could feel his confusion and unclarity on how to treat us.

"Where are we going?" Rachel asked.

"My orders are to take you across to the cutter, where the helo can land" he said. "Or we could put you in a sling and hoist you aboard."

"Let's go over to the cutter," I said.

"That would be my choice," he responded.

Then he turned to Leon, and put his hand to his ear. "Captain, I am requested to tell you that you should return to your regular mooring in Dania, where you will be met."

"We can get our gear?" I asked.

"Yes."

We went back, quickly packed, and came back into the salon.

"Okay," Leon said, and Erica, Skunk, Peterson, and Leon gathered round. We shook hands and hugged. We said very little verbally but we knew something was expected, and said expected things to one another.

"You'll let us know where you are?" Erica said.

"As soon as we know," Rachel replied.

We got aboard the tender, went across to the cutter as the helo landed, and were immediately hustled up to the flight deck and flown to Patrick Air Force Base at Satellite Beach, right on the water.

A jet was waiting and we were flown back to Andrews Air Force Base, where they keep Air Force One. From there we were driven out to an estate somewhere outside of Winchester, Virginia. It was evening when we got to an antebellum mansion down a long lane with white fencing on either side. It was too dark to see what was in the fields.

We had stayed in touch with the others regularly, but we didn't really know much more than we had early that morning. They had cleared customs after we were taken off, and by the time we got to Virginia, they were coming to the international light.

As soon as we got out of the car and up to the house the door opened, and it was clear we were in one of the safe houses the government maintains. It was elegantly but impersonally decorated.

Two men were in the foyer to meet us: military haircuts, one blond, one black-haired, buffed out, impersonal and very polite. Both dressed in a kind of house livery, tight white cotton jackets, dark trousers and well-shined shoes. One took our small bags; most of our gear was still in Peterson's truck. The other said, "Have you eaten? We could prepare a supper."

"That would be lovely," Rachel answered, and I could see she had to pause to think to verbalize, although I don't think they noticed. I think they saw us as very quiet and self-contained, and I didn't think that was a bad thing.

They seated us around a lovely 18th century table that could have seated 12, and might well have been made by Thomas Chippendale himself. The house was a mix of very colonial era antiques and over-stuffed chairs and couches in fresh modern floral slipcovers. Clearly it was a place for discrete high-level meetings.

The blond man served us and offered up an excellent gazpacho soup followed by an asian shrimp salad, with jumbo shrimp, snow peas, Napa cabbage, a ginger-soy dressing, and a very credible chardonnay. It was all intensely civilized in that impersonal style you see at the top of the government.

We were entirely alone, except for the man who served. He said nothing, and we said hardly a word verbally. I could hear the ticking of the beautiful old Georgian tall clock in the hall.

"I am sure the entire place is bugged," I told Rachel in mindspeech.

"I agree. So why are we here?"

"What do you think?" I asked.

"I think we need to keep up a level of speaking," she said in my mind, then verbally, "Very nice food, and just right for what I needed, after this long day."

"Yes, and the wine's very nice," I said verbally, adding, "Let's pack it in after dinner."

Then in my head, "Whoever is doing this is doing it very intentionally. We're not here by accident. "I expected to go to Guantanamo to be honest," Rachel confessed. I could feel her fear, and looked up into her eyes.

"Me too. I didn't want to say it."

"So why are they being nice to us?"

After dinner we told the man we were tired and wanted to go to bed. He led us up the stairs to a wide hall with a really fine highboy in the middle of one wall, and two doors on each side to adjoining bedrooms.

Our gear was already laid out. We looked at each other; Rachel got her stuff and brought it into the room I was in.

Verbally, "I'm going to get ready," as she went into the bathroom.

In my mind, "Do you think they have bugged the bedrooms… and the bathroom?"

"I assume so."

"Well I'm wearing your T-shirt then, and we're not making love. I didn't sign up for porn."

After she came out I went in. When I came out wearing my shorts, she was already in the king-sized four poster, where I joined her.

She handed me a book and took up her own, and we sat there in bed verbally silent.

"I assume whomever is coming will be here tomorrow after breakfast," she said in mindspeech.

"I agree. And I think it is going to be somebody I know. There can't be many people in this loop, or it would have leaked. To me the question is: what do we tell whomever it is?"

"I think we should do what Mike has done," Rachel told me. "Don't say anything about awakening. They don't expect it; it doesn't fit their worldview. Don't bring it up."

"I agree. But what do we say?"

"Do you remember what Mike said when he knocked that trooper out?"

"Ninety percent. If it is logically overwhelming will be accepted."

"That's what I think we should do. I think we should tell the truth with just 10 percent of edits."

"You're right. But everybody has to be on board." We put out a linkage call and one by one Charley and the others checked in. We brought them quickly up to date on what had happened since our last connection, and they did the same.

"Rachel and I think we should tell the truth, each in our own way, adding our own details. Just leaving out awakening."

"We agree," Leon replied. "We reached the same decision down here. We've been told to make ourselves available to be interviewed all day tomorrow," and as he said this I turned the pages of the book without really seeing them, lost in the imagery and information of their experiences.

"You all should listen to us tomorrow, and we will tune in to you," Rachel said. "We'll put out a call. We think we're also going to get interrogated tomorrow."

We broke contact, and I said verbally to Rachel, "That's it I'm going to sleep."

"Me too."

We put down our books, tossed one of the pillows on the floor, kissed, turned out our lights and slid under the covers as spoons. Under the covers I slid my hands up to cover her breast.

"Not a chance, White boy," then she pushed her body back against me and snuggled in my arms. We rolled apart a few minutes later, and were asleep.

It went just as we thought it would. We got up, went downstairs, and were served a very nice breakfast of French toast by the black-haired man, then were asked to go into a conservatory that extended off the back of the house. We had only been there a few minutes when we heard cars come down the lane and stop. We were sitting in two chairs next to a little antique stone waterfall fountain, when Senator Pardoe came into the conservatory. He came down to us, followed by the blond man holding a silver tray with a silver service including a teapot, a coffeepot, and three cups.

We went through the formality of the service, then the man went away, leaving the tray. Pardoe turned to us. "I'm sure you're comfortable. I always am when I come here," he said stirring his coffee. "A bit formal for me, but this is Virginia," he added, as he took a drink and put down his cup.

"Shall we get right to the bull's nuts?" he said, and I could feel Rachel putting out the call and everyone coming in.

"Absolutely," I said aloud.

"You know, some wanted you to go to Guantanamo," Pardoe said looking hard at us, to let us know there were other ways this could go. "Would have been a very different experience."

"It would," I said.

"But I think something else is going on, and my view prevailed," he said, picking up his cup. "So here we are."

"Where I come from, Senator, we say 'Getting down to the licklog.' And so let me do that. We're going to tell you the truth. You can ask us anything you like, and we'll tell you, and we'll even tell you how to check we are telling the truth."

He looked at me, and I could see him working his calculations.

"You know you've broken dozens of laws. I mean, maybe they're right and I should just have you arrested."

"Then you'd have to have a trial."

"We could have a secret trial or just drop you in Gitmo and leave you there."

"Ah, but we've thought of that, and have made arrangements should we disappear. It will get out and so will documentation. It will be viral in 24 hours, you know that. So can we cut the BS, senator, and get down to it. We learned a great deal from Mike, and we're willing to share. We want to share it with you. So you made the right choice. Let's get on with it. But now that you bring this up, I am afraid you have introduced a snake into the garden. We're going to need formal documentation not only for ourselves, but for some other people as well, declaring us innocent of all crimes."

Pardoe looked at us, and for just an instant his horse face held an expression of brutally cold calculation. He pulled out his phone, spoke into it, and a moment later a man in a suit carrying an attaché case came to where we were. Pardoe took the case, opened it, took out legal papers and handed a set to each of us.

"You've already thought of this?"

"Of course I have, Arthur. You've worked for me... how many years? I'm sure we have come to the same conclusions."

"Why did you try to have us killed? That van almost hit us back in the beginning."

"You were becoming a nuisance," Pardoe responded without emotion, then added, "I'm sorry about your cottage. We couldn't take any chances; we didn't know what you knew or were trying to do."

"You tried to kill us," I said again.

"That was before you met Mike, and spent time with him… and… became valuable."

It was the naked face of realpolitik, and it was chilling.

"Now can we get on with this?" Pardoe asked. "Do I have your cooperation?"

We asked Pardoe for a pen, read and signed the documents, and handed them back. He signed as well.

"Rachel and I will tell you what Mike told us, particularly about the future. That's what you want, isn't it?"

"What's our assurance that you will not harm us after we've told you what we know?" Rachel asked.

"He's still out there somewhere isn't he?"

"Yes, he is. But we have no idea where, if that's what you're asking."

"Can he stay in the sea?" Pardoe asked. "The doctors were never agreed about that, although they thought he had some kind of gill."

"He can, and he does," I answered.

"But if he comes back you're who he'll look for. Don't you agree?"

"Probably.'

"That's your insurance policy, and I think he'll come back."

"Not likely, and certainly not to him," and Mike was in our heads. "I'm fine." We were flooded with images of a reef with fish swimming by. Then he was gone.

"We'll talk more about this later," Pardoe said, and got up and poured himself another coffee. "There's no upside to punishing you or making you miserable. I want information, and I want you to give it to me freely and honestly."

As he spoke to me I could feel Leon, Erica, Skunk, Peterson, and Charley in the room with us.

"I already told you we would do that, so you have a deal, because the truth we know is exactly what we want to tell you."

"I may ask you to do so with a lie detector?"

"You don't get it," I said, and Rachel nodded as I spoke. "Mike left us with a sense of urgency it is hard for me to convey. I think the reason he wanted to get out was to see first-hand what was going on with climate change. And that's not all. He warned us about the survival of our species. He's 10,000 years ahead of us. Mike is a kind of cultural anthropologist for his people. But I suppose you know all this."

"Actually I didn't. Mike was very very controlled about what he said, and there is only so much you can get across. How did you communicate with him by the way?"

"With tablets," Rachel said. "And hand gestures. We got very good at a certain level of communication."

"I understand."

Pardoe stood up and said to us, "I'd like to start tomorrow; if that's agreeable. Another group will be debriefing your friends in Florida."

I felt the amusement the others all had on hearing that.

CHAPTER THIRTY

The next morning, a crew of professional interrogators arrived. They set up in the library with its custom walnut paneling and library shelves. They had us sit one at a time at an elegant English library table, where we were hooked up to several sensor systems. There was an array of flowers in a crystal vase on the table, and a handsome Heriz Persian rug on the floor. It was all very incongruous.

There were three of them. One ran the video, one handled the sensors, and the third asked the questions. We sat in that quiet lovely house, in that lovely room, and told them the story of the potential end of human civilization, while in our consciousnesses everyone listened in. That worked out particularly well, because we were told in a semi-threatening way that it had been decided this same crew would then go down to Florida and interrogate the others.

It was obvious to all of us what their plan was. Armed with what Rachel and I had said, they would compare that with what they were told in Florida. For the next three weeks, starting just after breakfast every day, first one and then the other of us would be interrogated. They asked very specific questions, and would go back to something at odd moments, over and over, and from their asking we learned what they thought they knew, and how they were putting the story together. We were surprised at what they did and did not know. And since we heard each other's testimony, we made sure it all fit together, with just the little differences you'd expect.

They knew nothing of the canoe trip. It had never occurred to them. We could tell they were fascinated with the idea that we actually took Mike out in public and no one noticed.

We told them about the bike journey and where the bikes could be found. I had no doubt they were there within days. We told them about how we met Charley, just a little differently, and Peterson and the rest. We told them most of all about what Mike had told us about the chances of humanity surviving, and why he believed what he did. We could see it shocked them, though they tried to hide it. They went back over it again and again for more details, and we knew that no matter what else happened, somewhere along the line at least one of them would tell someone, a wife, a partner, a priest. How do you keep quiet your species is doomed unless you change, and there is very little time to do that?

Completely unexpectedly Mike came into our minds a few times, suggesting things one or the other of us might say to further emphasize the urgency he communicated, and we suspected he was monitoring the whole thing. We just couldn't sense him, and of course they had no idea that was going on.

We left out only a few things, like the state trooper and the involvement of Quinton, Paul, John and Topher. Otherwise we were as accurate as we could be, and even suggested where they could get confirmation.

We told the truth about almost everything. We made up a few things, like the tablet communications, saying that we erased it because we knew we were being pursued, and mimed out carefully how we had talked with Mike, so that all those in communion with us understood how to do it. They asked how we thought Mike communicated with his fellows, and Rachel said, "I don't know, maybe telepathy," which got a laugh. When I suggested perhaps it was some sonic thing above human hearing, and asked if they had ever measured for that, the interrogators, not surprisingly, didn't know. But they made a note of it. Of course all the sessions were videoed with multiple VHD cameras. We assumed all of it would be minutely gone over by neuroscientists, facial analysis people, voice analysis, the whole nine yards.

The person who questioned us was older than me, perhaps in his 40s. He was an attractive and personable man. Not at all like an inquisitor priest. It was clear his strategy was to make a human connection. As we went along I could feel his anxiety about what we were saying, although he said nothing, and his expression was always one of pleasant interest and curiosity.

We were not only telling the truth, but telling it as it was being heard in mindspeech by everyone else who would be questioned. We were doing exactly what we had told Pardoe we would do. It allowed us to be very relaxed in the interviews, and they soon got that, although they completely misread the reason we were so relaxed. As a result all the psychophysical monitoring they were doing confirmed what their experienced eyes were telling them. It was all true. To further reinforce that conclusion, when we were alone together most of what we talked about verbally concerned what could be done to get people to understand why the issue was so urgent.

What they didn't ask about and we didn't volunteer, was our awakening. We said nothing about nonlocal consciousness or mindspeech. That decision, keeping that secret, brought home to me that we really were like an order, a secret cohort, and that in addition to the work on the environment, our mission was to awaken the 10 percent necessary to cause humanity to change consciousness in a fundamental way.

To our interrogators, that all of us who were male were vets, which had been purely coincidental, seemed an important factor, particularly because our service overlapped. It made perfect sense to them as to how we might have connected. Their questions revealed they saw our coincidental connection as a framework in which to hang the entire narrative. We could feel it happening, and their questions made it clear how their thinking evolved. In the middle of all this I began to feel the man that ran the video might be a spark, but I never had the leisure to focus on him in that way.

Pardoe sat in on several of the sessions that dealt with climate change, but said nothing and asked nothing, leaving before the session ended, so we had no personal contact.

About 4 p.m. each day the sessions would end, and they would pack up their gear and leave. I don't know where they stayed, but there were several guest cottages, and I once saw the kitchen golf cart go off with a meal. But after four, except for the silent men who managed the front of the house and a couple glimpses of kitchen staff, we were alone.

We wanted to go outside, and asked the blonde man, whose name turned out to be Eric, about doing that. He said he would check, and the next day told us that as long as we wore ankle bracelets were free to walk the property. We assumed there was an electronic perimeter of some kind. But in fact we just wanted to be alone outdoors in the lovely weather.

We got in the habit of walking out along the farm's lanes on what must have been a 300 or 400-acre property. On either side there were pastures. They kept horses and ran a registered Angus herd of about 50 head. To the neighbors I guessed it was a rich estate, and they might or might not know who owned it. We were sure we were always under surveillance, but it didn't matter. Except for our conversations about how we could convince them we were telling the truth and the urgency we felt, which was all true, our real communications were in mindspeech. We verbalized just enough not to be suspicious. I am sure they saw me propose to Rachel, and saw her accept. We'd like to have that video.

But finally, as anything like this does, it wound down. On the last day, Pardoe came out again, and as before we met in the conservatory.

"I want to congratulate you Arthur, and you too Dr. Carter, Rachel if I may. I am informed your story checks out in every detail. I assume the same will be true with the others."

"You'll have to ask them, Senator," Rachel said. "We have had no phone or internet since you took us off Vigilant. But I am sure they are very honest people and will do the same."

"Now what?" I asked.

"Well, you're certainly not going to be the Deputy Assistant Secretary of Defense."

"I don't want to be."

"I don't think you're going to be able to stay in government either, although I will want to be able to call on you both as consultants occasionally."

"I don't want to be in government any longer, and it would depend what you wanted of me."

"Us," Rachel added.

"What *do* you want, Arthur?" Pardoe asked.

"Rachel and I are going to get married." I looked at her, and she smiled back at me. "We're going to work on the environment as Mike urged us to do. You know we believe everything he told us about what's coming. We're going to ask the others to join in." As I said this I could feel the affirmation of everyone.

"We might be able to work out some government funding," Pardoe began, but I interrupted him saying, "I think funding at the level I have in mind can be gotten. I've met a lot of people in that world over the years I've been doing work for the committee. Thanks, though, maybe in the future. Right now I think we can do it on our own."

"Well, we will oversee you. I'm sure you understand."

"You mean putting a red flag on our personal information out of all the data you collect everyday about every person in the country?"

"Yes, and some satellite work, as indicated," Pardoe said it as casually as he might have said to someone on his staff that his battery pack needed a rework. "There might be a drop in from time to time, and I hope you will cooperate. Just to make sure you are not in contact with Mike and not telling us. I'm sure you understand Arthur, that the fact we did not put you and Rachel and the others in Guantanamo, and have been..." he picked at his jacket pulling off a piece of fluff, "very civil, I think you would admit, does not mean that you got away with it."

There it was. Reality with the amiable mask ripped off and the monster beneath revealed. But neither Rachel nor I reacted as he expected.

"You know what. Senator, you're going to do what you do. We don't care; it doesn't matter. We're going to do just what I said. At heart you're still a carbon man, I think. Your hideaway office certainly looks like that, and so does your voting. Rachel and I have a very different view and a great sense of urgency, as we've already told you. So do whatever you think you have to do."

Although he hid it well, that was not what Pardoe expected.

"We're going to work at a more personal scale. Local groups, that sort of thing. I'm through with government in that way. I'm off the Hill, and so is Rachel." She looked at Pardoe, and he got it.

"Can I give you a lift?" he said getting up. He drove us back to Rachel's flat and left us.

The next morning I took an Uber and got the Tesla out of storage. For the next week, Rachel sorted out her life. I bought new clothes and salvaged my office on the Hill of the things I cared about. I didn't need suits anymore, but I had one made anyway. We signed a lot of paperwork, leaving government, and said goodbye to some friends.

I called Maggie twice but she didn't return my calls.

I did a video call with Jack Kazanjian, the Chief of Staff, and told him, "I have resigned. I think you have probably heard this from Senator Pardoe. I have decided not to take the position, and in fact to leave government."

He tried to make it look like a surprise for a moment, but then gave up. He knew that I knew for him it was no surprise. But he did surprise me about one thing.

"Well, we'll have to give you a party. Seriously, Arthur, I want to do that, and I know a lot of other people will feel the same. What are you going to do?"

"I'm not sure yet, but it will have something to do with the environment and climate change. I've thought a lot about this, Jack, and I think this is where I have to put my focus."

"Well, let me know if I can help. Now, how about next Wednesday? I'll arrange it with the chairman."

"That would be great, Jack," I said. "Thank you."

On Wednesday I went up to the Hill an hour before the party to see Topher alone. I told him I was at Rachel's and asked him to dinner the next night, and he agreed.

I took Rachel to the party, and that drew a lot of attention. When I said we were going to be married I think everyone was stunned. They thought of me in terms of Maggie. As we circulated through the room we both looked into the eyes of everyone, tried to sense them, and in doing that realized we were looking for candidates for the 10 percent.

"That man," Rachel said, making a slight movement with her head in his direction.

"That's Bob Jordan, and you're right. Bob's a martial arts guy and a meditator. He's working... was working, with me on sea rise. He's passionate about it."

"Look at that woman, the one in the green suit."

"That's Ginette Merriman. She's an attorney for the committee. I've gone hiking with her. Go over and talk to her, see what you think."

Sam Green, the junior senator from Washington, came over and as we shook hands, I knew he was one of us.

"I wish you well, Arthur. I've heard what you plan to do and if you need help, or I can do anything for you, let me know. Okay? You have more supporters here than you may know. I think what you are doing is right action. I wanted you to know that," he said, and gave me a hug.

Senator Pardoe gave a little talk, other senators chipped in, and then they turned the mike over to me. I gave a little goodbye talk, and told everyone what I had decided and why. It became a story of a change of consciousness, of falling in love while trekking. Everybody was very nice, a lot were enthusiastic, and no doubt more than a few thought I was crazy.

The next night Topher was prompt to the minute, and filled with questions. Rachel cooked a fine trout dinner with an endive, pear, and toasted walnut salad. As the evening rolled out we gave him an abbreviated version of the story.

By 10 o'clock we were coming to the end.

"Listen Topher, I've got a friend, and I really want him to meet you. I'm going to call him tomorrow and see if we can come down. He lives out towards Berkeley Springs. If we do go, Rachel and I would really like you to come with us. We'd leave Saturday morning and come back Monday evening since Monday's a holiday. I'd like to talk with you about what we are going to do. How about it?" I asked.

"That would be great," he answered. "Yeah I'd love to come," then reached across for a piece of bread and whispered in my ear, "You think this whole dinner is being bugged and videoed. Right?"

"Yes, it's great to see you. We've told you about us. Tell us about you. What's happening with the horses?

And so the evening spiraled to an end.

The next morning I called Quinton, and asked him if we could come down and bring Topher. He got it immediately.

"Of course. I'll let Paul know."

I told him we would leave Saturday morning early.

Friday night we went to the Kennedy Center to see La Boheme. Coming out after the performance, as we stood on the plaza in front of the theater, I saw Maggie with some people, accompanied by a man I didn't know. She didn't see me, and I was surprised that I felt no sense of jealousy. I thought it would be intrusive to go over, and decided lunch would be right.

The next morning I called again, and this time Maggie took the call. As she appeared on my screen, I was about to ask her to lunch, but it didn't go that way.

"Maggie…"

"Arthur, I'm sorry but it's over. You've gone so far off the reservation, I can't go with you. I hope it's important to you. What are you doing anyway? No, don't tell me. I have been questioned twice about our relationship and what I knew of your plans. That's a career killer, Arthur, and as much as I have loved you, and I did love you, I just can't go there. Won't."

I was completely unprepared for this, but after a moment I said, "You're right, Maggie, I just called to say goodbye. I wanted to do it at lunch…"

"No, we're doing it now, Arthur."

"I don't want to come back. At least not staff on the Hill. You were right. My life has gone in a completely different direction. When you think you can hear it, I will be glad to tell you." I meant it, and realized we were having the most candid and honest conversation we had ever had.

"I loved you, Maggie. For the Arthur Davies on the Hill I could not have asked for a better partner. I cannot express to you how much you helped me."

"I would say the same."

"Then can we be friends? I will still be coming to Washington a few times a year. I would like to at least stay in touch."

"We are friends, Arthur; stay in touch… I wish you well. I assume Rachel is with you?" she asked, and I sensed in her voice that like me she had moved past resentment or jealousy.

"She is, and I am well-partnered for what I am about to do, and I wish the same for you."

Maggie smiled a genuine smile, and I smiled back. It ended the way we both wanted.

We were up early the next day, picked up Topher at his flat on Washington Circle, and the three of us drove down in my car. Fall was in air and the trees were alight with color. The traffic was heavy with leaf peepers out to see the autumn foliage until we turned off to the long unpaved school bus road that led to the lane that took us to Quinton's and Paul's. The Tesla didn't care for it at all.

When we arrived Paul was in the garden, wearing blue Chinese farmer's pants and a cotton quilted jacket, and he came up to the house to greet us with a basket full of tomatoes and garlic. Quinton came out, and we introduced him to Topher; he looked at us and said, "I can see it's going to be a long story. You better come in."

We all went into the kitchen, and Paul began to prepare a late lunch of some cold chicken and a caprese salad, using the just picked tomatoes, accompanied by a cold Sauvignon Blanc from their cellar that was exceptional. It all seemed very ordinary and pleasant, except for the conversation in which we laid out for Paul and Quinton the headlines of what had happened to us since we had last seen one another, and said that after lunch we'd take it to another level.

After we cleaned up from lunch, we went into the living room and arranged ourselves in the comfortable leather chairs and sofa. Sunlight streamed through the large windows, and the room was alive with the accents the light created as it was reflected off the antique silver spaced around the room.

"Now I need for you to get comfortable. Rachel and I are going to show you something that is going to change your lives."

"That certainly sounds portentous," Quinton said, as he leaned back in his chair.

"He's not exaggerating," Rachel replied, and Paul and Quinton exchanged a look.

"Put your feet on the floor, take a deep breath, let it out. Now another, and let it out. Now a third. Close your eyes. I want you to reach out to Rachel and me in your mind. Don't strain, but do put your full attention to this. Imagine you are in contact with us."

We sat in a silence that stretched out to 20 minutes as Rachel and I reached out to contact them. Suddenly, Paul said, his face showing his astonishment, "Rachel you're in my head!"

"And mine."

"And mine," Topher added.

Thus began a process that was now becoming familiar to us. After an hour we stopped, and Rachel and I addressed the questions that poured out of them, part verbally, part now in mindspeech.

After another hour Quinton said, "I need to take a break and process this. I can see all kinds of implications arising from this kind of connection," and he got up and walked out of the room.

Paul said, "Me too." He got up, went into the kitchen and came back with his basket, walking out of the house through the French doors onto the terrace and to the garden beds beyond.

"Does distance matter?" he asked in his mind. I told him, "No, space and time are not meaningless, but they mean something quite different in the domain we're now in."

Topher remained, looking at us. Beginning verbally, and then lapsing into to mindspeech, he observed, "This really changes everything doesn't it?"

'Yes. Yes it does," I answered. We all got up and walked out of the living room, left the house and the three of us went down a path into the woods where we stood motionless and silent. Rachel and I showed Topher how to see the matrix and make connections. After a few minutes a baby rabbit appeared under a dogwood tree.

"You can make contact, reach out," Rachel said.

"This is amazing."

The rabbit looked up at him, nose twitching, and we all stood in that silent posture for a moment before the rabbit went back to eating, ignoring us.

"It's not words, it's intentions, isn't it?" Topher asked.

"Yes," Rachel responded. "It's not just about intellect, words; it's about intention and emotion as well."

"I've talked to a rabbit, who could imagine?" Topher shook his head. "I'll be able to contact horses... right?"

"Oh dear," I said to Rachel in mindspeech. "What have we done?"

We gathered again for dinner when Paul reached out to us in mindspeech and told us it was ready. He had prepared an angel hair pasta with shrimp, fresh basil and more tomatoes, and a salad of greens he had just picked.

As we ate, Rachel and I opened ourselves so that the three of them could get the full complexity of what had happened over the past few months.

"You can't lie, can you?" Quinton asked.

"No. Your motives and feelings about what you are saying are transparent to those to whom you are communicating," I explained. "More than that, it is modulated in a way we don't quite understand, but has something to do with intention and integrity. It works best when you don't have hidden agendas."

"But there is more than that," Rachel added. "Emotion plays a role as well. We're not that much further down the path than you are. There is lots we don't yet understand, things that Mike used to do to make things work. He healed the trooper of diabetes and some kind of liver problem, and changed his DNA so he wouldn't pass it on. It was his way of paying back, I think, for rendering the man unconscious. Hard to explain," she said, and they felt and had access to our memories of the experience as she narrated it.

After dinner we reached out to the others in Florida and Charley, who was somewhere on the road in Louisiana. We introduced them to Quinton, Paul, and Topher. With the shared intention to be in contact, the process of their opening progressed more quickly, and by the time we were ready for bed, the three new members of our circle were now awakened to this manner of contact.

"But communication is only part of it," Rachel said. "There is so much more."

Over the next two days we explored the matrix of life, and showed them how they could access information from the consciousness domain. Topher and Quinton particularly were enchanted with the information access, and Paul was wonderstruck at the matrix.

He spent long hours in the garden, saying, "I can see how the plants interact with one another. I see what they need. The worms… I have a whole new understanding of what their needs are. You can even contact the bacteria."

By the third day we were in full communication, even though we were scattered over the property.

"You have a plan Arthur, what's going on?" Quinton asked at one point. We settled into a discussion of something I had been thinking about since our last conversation with Pardoe. As we did that we drew together and all ended up on the terrace.

"As I told you, my days in government are over. Rachel's as well."

"Mine too," Topher added. "I have no interest in going back, although I guess I will have to for a while."

"I think we should all assume that we are under surveillance, that anything we say on a phone or send in an email will be monitored. But I see that as a plus, not a negative."

"How so?" Quinton asked.

"Because in the local world of space and time I think we should do exactly what I told Pardoe we would do, and what we should in fact do: work for wellbeing at every level. We all know how important that is, and now we have a chance to do it in a new way that is really important.

Let them monitor us to their heart's content. How we do the reaching out is not clear to me."

"We start a foundation, of course," Quinton responded. "I can do that with a phone call."

"Where is the funding going to come from?" Leon asked.

"Why from Paul and me, of course, at least to start."

"You have that kind of money?"

"Yes."

"But that's not what we're really doing, is it?" Peterson asked.

"At the same time we are waking people up… right?" Skunk interjected.

"Exactly," I answered. "They know nothing about this, don't even think in these terms. Mike was in his blue room for 12 years, and they never got what was important to him or how he saw the world. Beingness is the key that opens the door. We have to be genuinely and authentically who we say we are. It's just that we are more private than they realize. But how does that play out?"

"It argues for some kind of grassroots operation," Erica said, "where you can interact with people one by one."

"Vigilant can play a role. Making the connection with Cetacea was one of the main things I took away from my experience with Mike. And that pod he wanted to contact, we know where they hang out now. We can take people out on the boat, focus on the ocean, and turn them on," Skunk said, and we could feel his enthusiasm and planning.

"Imagine what we could do if we concentrated on the oceanographic scientists, environmentalists. The 10 percent rule applies to any size cohort," Erica said.

"There's a huge multiplier effect," Leon added.

"Also on Vigilant they can only monitor us visually. They can't plant listening devices because that would require transmission which we could catch." We could see in our mind's eye what Leon had in mind.

"This whole thing would do better if it were not based in the U.S.," Erica noted, and Rachel and I agreed. "I got that very clearly when they came down and interviewed us. I don't want to make an issue, but I don't think you two should be overly available. You know what I mean? I'm going to keep my job at least for a while. I'm deep into a project to try to preserve something of Fort Lauderdale. But I am allowed to be a consultant for a foundation, I'm sure."

We spent the rest of the evening hammering out what each of us could do and shaping it into a plan. In honor of Mike we would call it the Nebula Foundation, and use the Horsehead Hubble deep space image in our logo. It would be an international grassroots organization, helping local efforts with climate change. It would also awaken more people as quickly as possible.

Quinton and Paul owned an old sugar plantation on St. Lucia, outside of the capital city Castries. Quinton proposed that as the headquarters, and they said they also owned another small island at the top of Vancouver Island in the Inland Passage, "which could be used in the summer for some kind of camp."

"Perfect," Rachel said. "In both of those places we can stay in touch with the dolphins and whales, which I think ought to be another part of what we do, both explicitly and quietly."

"Yes," I agreed. "I think it's very important we not lose sight of that aspect, nor make it secondary. Mike was very clear about that, and I can see why he's right. We have almost killed the oceans in some places, and are going to need help bringing the seas back."

After mostly listening to the rest of us for a long while, Quinton asked for a break, and he and Paul went off. They came back after about half an hour, and Quinton said, "We will endow Nebula so that it can operate independently, although I think we should also seek other funding as well, including scientific governmental funding. Having money will make people take Nebula seriously; linking into other significant funding will give it international gravitas, and there are tax laws to consider."

"Pardoe told me that U.S. government funding might be available."

"Do you really have that kind of money, Quinton?" Topher asked. "This is going to be millions of dollars to do the three things we say we want to do. You and Paul live so simply, and off the grid."

"Paul and I live as we do because that is how we choose to live. For much of my life I was a banker."

"And I was a trader," Paul added.

"We were very good at what we did and made money, individually and collectively. Quite a lot of it, and it keeps growing. We have a staff of people in New York who handle it very discretely. The pleasure of making a lot of money is that you can support things you care about. We have infrastructure in place to do all of this. As we have listened to you, we think $12.5 million should do it. And we think Arthur should be the Executive Director, with Rachel as Deputy."

Everyone agreed. If Erica stayed with the state government it would give us access we wouldn't otherwise have into state level science in a state that was in particular crisis because of climate change. Charley wanted to keep doing what he was doing, while still being involved, and that, we decided would open a whole other vector into the larger culture. We needed 10 percent. It slowly emerged that the way to go about this was not to be random in awakening, but to prioritize and target cohorts. Just as Erica had proposed with ocean scientists, so Charley could do within the EV long haul community.

"Suppose we had 10 percent of America's transportation system," Charley said. "That's what I'm thinking."

By the time we went to bed that night the plan had emerged, and it was decided we would all fly down to Florida and take Vigilant down to St Lucia in three weeks. Quinton called someone and booked a plane. Through all of this there was no contact with Mike, and I began to wonder if we would ever hear from him again.

We went back to D.C. the next afternoon and set things in motion. At the beginning of the second week, I went up to the Capitol and met with Pardoe again in his hideaway office. I told him exactly what we were doing and why, leaving out the consciousness aspect. I told him Topher was going to join us, which didn't seem to surprise him. He wasn't happy with our leaving the country, but there was nothing he could do to stop us, and I think at this point he realized that he would get more from working with us. Most of his emphasis was on keeping Mike a secret.

"I see no reason to speak his name," I told Pardoe; and it was true.

I told him what Quinton had said, and asked him about government funding, saying, "You're watching us anyway."

He wouldn't promise anything specific, but said he would talk to the Director of NOAA about a research project. It could be set up through Florida state government on a federal grant, and Erica could be the principal investigator. I read that to mean "if you behave and don't do anything I won't like, I can make it happen." Which was all we could ask for.

He didn't give me any chili that time, but it didn't matter. We were concluding a business deal, and we both understood that.

As we stood up, I said again, "We have no interest in publicity that links Nebula with space men."

He responded, "I think that's wise."

A week later Rachel closed her apartment, although she had to pay three months' rent until her lease was over, which I helped her with. We detected surveillance once or twice, or thought we had. It was irritating at a civil rights level, but functionally it meant nothing, because we were really doing what we said we would.

We met at a private airport, got aboard a Lear jet Quinton or Paul had arranged, and flew down to Orlando. Charley met us and took us out to Vigilant where the others were already gathered.

We spent the next day getting ready, and that evening a Unitarian minister Erica knew came out to the boat, and we went out to the pilot light. There, tossing gently on the sea, standing in the stern with the Caribbean sky's gold and rose colored splendor as background, he married us. We had a wonderful lobster dinner and champagne.

After dinner, Rachel and I walked up to the bow and sat by ourselves on the power winch there. As I put my arm around my wife, Mike came into our heads.

"I celebrate your joining, Rachel, Arthur, and I thank all of you for what you are doing. I am down near Antarctica, and my focus is increasingly on the world ocean. I have given you my gift. It's up to you now."

And he was gone.

When it was dark we motored back to Dania on Vigilant, each of us immersed in the matrix, and I understood that these people had become closer to me than family.

We left Dania again the following afternoon and once again made a night crossing of the Stream, only this time it was as calm as a lake. Just as before, we anchored for the night in the Cat Cay harbor, cleared customs, and made our way to Riding Rocks in hopes that Mike might show up. He didn't, but we taught Quinton, Paul, and Topher how to dive. On our second day there, the dolphins appeared, and for the first time we made a really serious attempt to try to work out how to communicate with them. At first it was as it had been before. We got a sense of their perception of us but no real cognitive information. But then, confirming what we had suspected, we really comprehended that our intentions and our emotions were the way to communicate. What in humans would have passed for spoken information was equaled by sharing sensory input. I could see Rachel as a dolphin saw her. I could perceive her visually but I could also see into her, like a sonogram.

I also perceived the Earth's geomagnetic field, and understood also that the dolphins had a kind of internal clock that coordinated with this field sensitivity and gave them... me ... the dolphin equivalent of GPS. Only it was much subtler. And my hearing was vastly greater and more complex than my own. I had virtually no sense of smell.

And I could share my human sensorial experience, although what came through and how it was perceived I never felt I knew.

For Paul, Quinton, and Topher it was all magical, and everything else tuned out. Erica had to scold them several times about decompression and the build-up of nitrogen in their blood, or they would have been in the water all the time. It was magical for all of us. The Florida guys had been diving regularly and had had multiple contacts, and they had worked out the details of how Vigilant could be used by Nebula.

Their enthusiasm was what made it all come into focus as something that was going to happen.

CHAPTER THIRTY ONE

After three days we cruised down to St Lucia and moored in the harbor for the capitol, Castries, a bustling little city with colonial architecture left over from its sugar plantation past. Twice on the way down, small naval vessels on the horizon paralleled our course for a while. I looked up as we came into the harbor and wondered if a satellite I could not see was looking down at me.

It was in Castries that Quinton really showed who he was behind the off-the-grid, khaki shorts and T-shirt persona. He put on a bespoke linen suit, custom shirt and a very elegant Hermés tie. Paul looked much the same. Rachel and I did the best we could to meet their standard, and we caught a cab into town to Micoud Street past a large park, then walked a short way to what Quinton told us was the leading law firm in the country. The buildings were just a few stories tall, and along the way were large trees with overhanging branches whose trunks were whitewashed up to about four feet. Lively crowds of several races were going in and out of the street level shops.

We went up a short flight of stairs to a foyer with a large round table upon which sat a flower-filled vase. Quinton went up to the receptionist who sat behind a desk, and moments later a middle-aged rather distinguished-looking Black man with gold rimmed glasses met us in the foyer. It was obvious by his manner that he was impressed with Quinton and Paul. He put out his hand saying, "Mr. Reynolds, Mr. Liu, how nice to see you again. What has it been, three years?"

"Probably, Mr. McDermit, a pleasure to see you as well. Let me introduce Dr. Davies, and Dr. Carter," Quinton said, gesturing to us, and we both shook hands with McDermit.

In my mind Quinton said, "They all train in the Inns of Court in London, so it's quite English and formal here. I think McDermit is a Lincoln's Inn man."

"I got your phone call but you said very little, Mr. Reynolds. How can we help you?" McDermit led us down a hall to his office, which had his Lincoln Inn sheepskin on one wall, and 18th century black and white Hogarth engravings in gold frames on the others. When we were settled and had been offered and declined tea or coffee, Quinton began. "I've set up a foundation, in both London and Delaware, that will be based here in St. Lucia, so it will need status here as well…"

"How can we help?" McDermit asked. I could feel the cash register turn on, and was surprised at Quinton's and Paul's understanding and comfort with that.

"He's not unreasonable, he's just expensive. We knew that; it doesn't matter," Quinton said in mindspeech.

"You know the old sugar plantation you helped us buy?" he said aloud.

"Of course."

"I want you to help Dr. Davies, who is the foundation's executive director, and Dr. Carter, who is his deputy, to get whatever assistance they need to set up here on St Lucia. As I said, we are going to headquarter in St. Lucia."

"Oh, that's very nice. What kind of work will the foundation do?"

"We are focusing on the environment and climate change remediation," I responded. "We'll be working at the local level internationally."

"A very worthy project. The firm shares your interest, and I'm sure we can arrange for you to meet like-minded people here. In the government, of course, and we may be able to help you with other things. Are you fully funded?" he said, his eyes moving for just a moment to Quinton and Paul, who gave nothing away but confirmed it.

"We would appreciate that, Mr. McDermit," I replied. "We'll set up an appointment next month after we have had a chance to settle in." As I said it, McDermit leaned back in his leather desk chair.

"So… what we can do immediately to help you get started?"

"I think they will require a contractor to do some modifications," Quinton answered. "Would you please arrange that with the same man we used? They're also going to need some staff. And they would like to become citizens." Quinton said. Then leaning forward slightly, "I want all this to go forward as expeditiously as possible. You will see to that personally, Mr. McDermit?"

"Of course. I… the firm… we will do whatever is needed and make sure it will all go smoothly. Since you mentioned a foundation… excuse me, how should this be billed?"

"I will cover this first bit myself. After that the foundation will cover its operation. We have endowed it quite generously with everything it needs."

"I want to be sure he understands who you are and what you represent," Quinton said in our minds. "Lawyers are the same everywhere," and we caught the humor in his attitude.

With that, Quinton stood up, turned to me, and said aloud, "Just call Mr. McDermit as needed, but," looking back at McDermit, "keep me in the loop." In our minds, "He's honest, and he understands I am paying close attention. I think that's all that is needed for now. Of course you realize he will probably also be compromised, and everything any of us say to him will be monitored."

"Yes, it's weird but I don't care. I actually see a way to turn it into a plus."

We thanked McDermit, who escorted us back out to the foyer, shook our hands again, and was very pleasant.

We went back to Vigilant and found the others ready to go. They had all listened in so there was no need to debrief them. They had arranged for a van and a driver, and when he arrived we all got into the van and drove up into the hills just a few miles to a gravel lane which led us back to a picturesque sugar plantation house from the colonial period. It had twin peaks separated by a low center section, and was fronted on one side by a covered porch that ran the length of the house.

"It was built in 1835 by the original owner," Paul told us as we got out and went into the house. It was open and airy as such houses are, not grand, but built for comfort before air conditioning. We walked through to the long porch and looked out.

There were several outbuildings, and on the left a lively stream flowed down the mountain side with the stone ruins of a watermill on the closest bank dating back to the sugar days. The house had a stunning view from the porch of the Twin Pitons, the two sharp pointed mountains that dominated St Lucia visually. The property, like everything else I had seen that Quinton and Paul owned, was elegant in design, in excellent but not flashy condition, and completely understated. The house was painted a green that complemented the tropical greenery around it, with cream trim, and dark red painted long windows with shutters turned back.

"I had the caretaker open it up," Paul said.

"Think this will work?" Quinton asked, knowing perfectly well we were all stunned.

"We bought it thinking we would come down for the winter, but except for the first year we really only come down for a few weeks. It is lovely, though, isn't it?" Paul said. "Quinton oversaw the restoration, and I choose the colors and did the landscaping. It's a 140-acre property; you'll love the trails we've put in."

We settled in. There were rooms for everyone, and one of the outbuildings would be perfect for offices. The porch was wonderful. One afternoon I was standing by myself on it. I looked up into the sky, and wondered if there was a satellite looking down. I tried to reach out to see if I could get that information, but could not hold focus long enough to find out. Being in the consciousness domain, and yet knowing you are under surveillance all the time is a very strange experience. I felt relaxed. We had nothing to hide and yet we were hiding everything. We were doing what we said we were doing quite genuinely while at the same time we were engaged in a completely different mission that nobody but us, and the sparks we awakened, knew about.

McDermit called up the next day to say it would take the rest of the week to get everything set up and citizenship established. We asked him to buy an electric van and small car.

For the next four days we explored the property while keeping a running dialogue moving like a dance between verbal and mindspeech, sometimes together, sometimes apart, talking about what we should do and how we should do it. At the same time, each of us in our own way continued to expand our abilities and become more deeply immersed in the matrix. For Rachel and myself it also gave us time to really understand that we had moved, that our lives were on a different trajectory now. We weren't running away, we were running towards. We went out once on Vigilant to go diving, and encountered and connected with a pod of dolphins who were, I think, as surprised as we were at the level of communication.

We would base out of St Lucia, which was out of the way in some ways, but had a good international airport easily available. Establishing physical surveillance would be much more difficult, and it gave us at least some sense of privacy since the house sat centered in its property. We couldn't do anything about satellites, but we thought that when it was clear we were doing what we said, the cost value ratio would tip and it would cease.

We could travel as we wished. For the time being Vigilant would stay home-ported in Dania, but would make scheduled calls here. We planned a strategy in which most of us would continue doing what we were already doing. At the same time, very proactively, we would be searching for people that had the spark that showed they were ready to awaken. Our goal was to create the 10 percent. Mike had been very clear to us that this was the only way our civilization would survive. It mostly demanded what Gandhi had demonstrated: giving up deeply held beliefs about how the world worked and choosing to support wellbeing, just as the space capable cultures did.

In the beginning we talked a lot about our fear that those who could access the domain as we did might come to see themselves as an elite. But, as we discussed this question, the answer emerged as we each shared the experiences we had had since opening. We realized they all had a common theme. When emotions like anger, violence, or a desire to dominate, to take advantage, arose in our minds, we lost contact.

"You can't fake beingness," Erica said. "You have to be privately what you are publicly. You have to walk your talk. That may be a cliché, but it's the truth."

We all realized that while it was sometimes wonderful and necessary that we gather together, we could communicate independent of distance, and as that played out, we physically spread out over the grounds. The day Erica made her observation about beingness, in fact, Rachel and I were walking along the trail that followed the mill stream. When we came to a bench we sat down and sank into the matrix.

"You're so right, Erica," Peterson said, then stopped in mid-thought, paused, then continued, "I would never want to lose this."

"Me neither," Skunk responded, "you're right Erica. You can't fake this, you can't hide your true motives... anger cuts you off... I love it."

We were just together for a while letting that sink in. Then I said, "Just as we agreed earlier, we start with the environmental movement."

"The people who already care about the environment," Rachel added.

"I agree, Nebula can fit right into that world," Erica said. "That's a community already partially awakened, I think."

"I agree there will be a higher percentage of sparks there," Leon added.

We broke contact and Rachel and I walked on a ways, and I thought further about it, and broke the silence saying, "The Foundation will fund you in whatever way is appropriate. With Erica, we'll do it with a grant. With you Charley, you can take some time off when you need it without getting gigged by a loss of income. In fact, we'll contact your company and get them involved so there's no problem."

"They'll be proud. They're good guys. I was thinking of them as potentials," Charley responded.

Gradually, as it had happened before, we drew together. When we were all on the long porch looking out across the tropical forest to the sea, I realized it was up to me to make the ask. And so when we all had drinks and were seated, I said:

"Peterson and Skunk, if you're willing I think you should go full time with Vigilant. Leon, can you be the captain full-time?" I asked them, and they agreed.

"Rachel, can you oversee data?" I asked, knowing that is what she wanted to do.

"Topher, would you be willing to go back to Washington as our Washington guy?"

"Yes. No race tracks here, and now I can talk to the horses," he answered, adding, "But you'll come up to handle Pardoe and his group?"

"Yes, and you'll come down here regularly; but more than that, when I was at my going away party I understood that I should keep all those connections. Also I saw sparks. I hadn't thought I would, but I know now how important my past life will be in reaching our goal. For me to be connected but not dependent on the government is just what's needed," and I knew that was right.

"So could you get an apartment in Georgetown, Topher? It doesn't have to be much, just a place we could stay on a visit."

The last day, Quinton and I found ourselves sitting on the bench near the water wheel. For a while we just sat in the beauty and listened to the flowing water coming off the wheel. A flight of what looked like flamboyant multi-colored parrots to me, but which Quinton called Saint Lucia Amazons, landed in the branches of the trees that hung over the stream.

"Quinton, I don't know how to thank you. You have made all of this possible. You're giving Rachel and me a new start. I never expected anything like this."

"Are you kidding? It's I who should be thanking you. I'm 64 years old. For the past five years I've been growing bored; now I've found a whole new purpose in my life. One I can do with Paul, one in which I can make a major difference, and one that is entirely life-affirming, and has already given me this domain of consciousness, the most extraordinary gift of my life. Do you know how rare that is, Arthur?" he said, putting his arm around my shoulder and giving me a hug.

"Pardoe's going to lose interest in you once he thinks he knows everything you know. It won't take him more than a year to reach that conclusion, but he will want to keep you close because he thinks Mike will contact you again. Do you think that's true?"

"Honestly, I don't know. I have no sense of contact with him now. But his abilities are so far past our own that he could be monitoring everything and we would never know. He told us his people live on average 300 years, and he was only 150, so who knows."

"That's my sense as well. I predict Pardoe will want to cover his bases, so he'll come down here a couple of times to see for himself what's going on, and see you whenever you go to D.C., which I would plan to do at least once a quarter the first year and probably beyond that. I think you should keep up your connections."

"I've come to the same conclusion," I responded. "I'm going to run an international foundation, quite apart from the consciousness aspect, just working fulltime to help humans prepare for what is happening, and to remediate what we can," I said, looking at him. A look he returned with great intensity, and then a smile.

"I'm not removing myself from the world; we are just getting into it in a new more important way."

"Exactly."

Then his mood shifted and he asked, and I felt his genuine concern, "How long do you think we really have, Arthur?"

"Ten years. Mike would never answer that question. We asked it again and again in different ways, but my sense from what he did say was humanity was at a crossroads. So Okay, we start with nine of us. Oh, by the way, when you go back would you and Topher go out to John's and take him through? So with John we're 10."

"Of course. That's Rachel's cousin of some kind, the one who has some Asperger issues, right?'

"Yes, it will be interesting to see what he's like in the nonlocal. I think the spark's there, and we certainly owe him. It wouldn't have happened without him. Just pragmatically, his world, the dark net people, could be very helpful."

"So 10."

"And if each of us can help 10 people awaken, within the year we have 100. The next year, year two, 1,000 people, then year three 10,000, year four 100,000, year five 1,000,000, year six 10,000,000, year seven 100,000,000, year eight a billion. There are eight billion people in the world today,"

"But it won't go like that Arthur, you know that. It will happen faster, and it won't be uniform, nothing about humans ever is. When we get up to say about a million, the general society will become aware of what's happening. There will be pushback, social unrest. I took Erica's point the other day about beingness, so I get this isn't going to turn into some kind of consciousness fascism, but it's still going to have to be carefully managed to get to the tip point. After that I assume everyone will awaken."

"I agree, Quinton. I hadn't thought it through like that, but you're right. It's probably going to be something less than the seven years."

"What are you going to do with your log or diary, whatever you call it?"

"What do you think I should do?"

"Wait a year, let things cool off, then put it out. Just as you said, it will enter the zeitgeist and start an urban myth, and that will help change the culture. This is about changing consciousness. You've got the three pictures, right?"

"Yes."

"Then do just what Mike suggested. Let them slip out. John and Topher can do that; use the last one with the log."

The next day McDermit came through with everything we had asked for. We arranged for the construction guy to come out, the van and the car were delivered as well as our St. Lucia citizenship papers. We were instructed where to go in a week to have passport pictures, fingerprints, and a DNA sample taken.

We drove everyone down to Castries the next morning, took the Florida people to Vigilant, and then Quinton and Paul to the airport where another private jet was waiting for them. Once again I realized how my decision to visit these two men I only really knew through a former girlfriend had turned into one the best breaks of my life.

It was strange that we were all physically moving apart, and yet were still in touch, and could remain so as we chose.

Just before Quinton got onto the plane I handed him a micro drive after writing these last sentences on my laptop: "In a year we will see what happens. Ten percent, that's our goal. We have no more than ten years, and probably less."

ACKNOWLEDGEMENTS

Books don't get written by themselves; most writers don't live in isolation. I certainly don't. First, I want to thank my wife, Ronlyn. She not only supported my writing *Awakening*, she read every word several times correcting punctuation, and telling me where something didn't work. I am deeply appreciative of her loving help.

I thank Larry Dossey, Rick Ingrasci, Chris Holder, Sidney Kirkpatrick, and Michael Hansen, who read various versions of the manuscript and gave me their feedback, and Holly Thomas for her careful final proofing.

Particularly, I thank James Francis Yax who created the cover illustration.

AUTHOR BIO

Scientist, futurist, and award-winning author Stephan A. Schwartz is the columnist for the journal Explore, and editor of the daily Schwartzreport.net. For more than 40 years he has done consciousness research, and is one of the founders of Remote Viewing, and the anthropology of consciousness. He is the 2017 recipient of the Parapsychological Association's Outstanding Con-tribution Award. Current academic and research appointments: Distinguished Consulting Faculty of Saybrook University, Fellow of the William James Center for Consciousness Studies, Sofia Univdrsity,and a Research Associate of the Cognitive Sciences Laboratory of the Laboratories for Fundamental Research. Prior academic appointments: Senior Samueli Fellow for Brain, Mind and Healing of the Samueli Institute; BIAL Fellow; founder and Research Director of the Mobius laboratory; Executive Director of the Rhine Research Center; and Senior Fellow of The Philosophical Research Society. Government appointments: Special Assistant for Research and Analysis to the Chief of Naval Operations, consultant to the Oceanographer of the Navy. Author of more than 130 technical reports and papers, 20 academic book chapters, and four trade books: The Secret Vaults of Time, The Alexandria Project, Mind Rover, Opening to the Infinite, and The 8 Laws of Change, winner of the 2016 Nautilus Book Award for Social Change. He is also the producer and writer of documentaries, series, and primetime network specials.

CPSIA information can be obtained
at www.ICGtesting.com
Printed in the USA
BVHW071406170123
656441BV00002B/213